"This is craziness, Ben. I don't know what's happening. Look at me. At us."

Kate massaged her arms.

Straightening, he made no attempt to camouflage his desire. "I have looked at you, Kate," he said, running a finger over her puffy lips. "Am looking. Get used to the fact. I like what I see."

With that he sauntered off, and she was left to deal with cleaning the kitchen when she was all thumbs, trying to reconcile herself to the fact that she'd fallen under the spell of a cowboy.

It wouldn't work.

Why not? the nagging voice in her head wanted to know.

Because she'd promised never to love a cowboy again.

Dear Reader,

This story came about after I chanced to meet a man in Tucson. He wore knee-high boots, a flat-crowned hat and an interesting bolo tie. I asked if he was a vaquero, because there's a ranch down south that hires Argentinian cowboys. He said no, that he was a buckaroo from southern Idaho, in town for a mustang auction.

I'm sure he saw how interested I was, so he went on to explain more about ION country—where Idaho, Oregon and Nevada meet. He said it was one of the few places left where ranchers still run cattle on leased land and buckaroos live three-fourths of the year with those cattle. He said I should visit when they had their Rope and Ride, because it wasn't a run-of-the-mill rodeo. Prizes were handmade items the buckaroos use in daily life. He did lament that theirs was a dying way of ranching, because they had to fend off people who'd petitioned the state government to take the land for recreational use. And that group had banded with strict preservationists. He said the mining companies had gone, and it was only a matter of time until ranchers would be forced out, too.

That's really all it takes for the writer in me to be intrigued enough to visit the place and weave a story. Ben Trueblood and Kate Steele are the fictional couple I elected to put in this very real corner of the world. I hope the ranchers win their battle. In my book, that would be Ben. I hope you want him to win, too.

Roz Denny Fox

P.S. I like hearing from readers—P.O. Box 17480-101, Tucson, AZ 85731 or e-mail rdfox@worldnet.att.net.

REAL COWBOYS
Roz Denny Fox

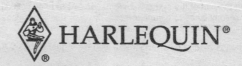

TORONTO • NEW YORK • LONDON
AMSTERDAM • PARIS • SYDNEY • HAMBURG
STOCKHOLM • ATHENS • TOKYO • MILAN • MADRID
PRAGUE • WARSAW • BUDAPEST • AUCKLAND

ISBN-13: 978-0-373-71412-4
ISBN-10:   0-373-71412-2

REAL COWBOYS

Printed in U.S.A.

ABOUT THE AUTHOR

Roz made her first sale to Harlequin Romance in 1989 and sold six Harlequin Romance titles, writing as Roz Denny. After transferring to the Harlequin Superromance line, she began writing as Roz Denny Fox. In addition to the many stories she's written for Harlequin Superromance, she's also written two Harlequin American Romance books and two Signature books. Her novel for Harlequin's new series, Everlasting Love, will be coming out in August 2007.

Roz has been a RITA® Award finalist and has placed in a number of other contests; her books have also appeared on the Waldenbooks bestseller list. She's happy to have received her twenty-five-book pin with Harlequin, and would one day love to get the pin for fifty books.

Roz currently resides in Tucson, Arizona, with her husband, Denny. They have two daughters.

Books by Roz Denny Fox

HARLEQUIN SUPERROMANCE

HARLEQUIN AMERICAN ROMANCE

HARLEQUIN SIGNATURE

CHAPTER ONE

Needed ASAP Certified K-8 Teacher
Near Owyhee, Idaho, One-room school
Grades 1-8 Approximately 20 pupils
Benefits include a two-bedroom cabin
Fax résumé to Marge Goetz,
School Board President 208 555-8809
Will do a telephone interview

KATE STEELE SMOOTHED the creased job circular and reread the ad for the umpteenth time. The promise of housing was a bonus. She checked her cover letter one last time before stealthily rolling her wheelchair into her father-in-law's ranch office and firing it off on the fax. Impatiently, she waited for confirmation of receipt. When it slid into the tray, she folded it with the other papers and tucked them behind her in case she ran into her mother-in-law in the hall.

Kate's watch said 9:00 a.m., which meant the Steeles' Fort Worth ranch had been in full swing for three hours. It would be eight in Idaho. Kate hoped Marge Goetz worked eight to five.

A preliminary search on her laptop hadn't found

any mention of the town of Owyhee, but a county by the same name bordered Idaho, Oregon and Nevada. Agriculture was listed as the county's main industry since the mines had played out. Farm country sounded wonderful. Kate had been born and raised in Kansas. At least it would get Danny away from his grandparents' ranch, which perpetuated his obsession with calf roping and rodeos.

Rolling along the hall, Kate told herself not to pin her hopes on this job. Why would Marge Goetz have to look as far as Texas to find a teacher? The hiring committee probably wouldn't be keen on the fact she was a widowed mom with an almost eleven-year-old son. Plus she hadn't taught in a while. She wondered if that was why she'd lost out on five positions in the Dallas-Fort Worth area. It was late in the year to find a teaching job, but that didn't stop Kate from crossing her fingers.

By four o'clock that afternoon, Marge Goetz had called and offered Kate the job. Once Kate hung up, she pinched herself to be sure she wasn't dreaming.

But the thrill didn't last long. At supper, Kate had to break the news to Royce and Melanie Steele…and Danny.

Melanie, Kate's mother-in-law, almost dropped the bowl of green beans she was passing to her husband. "*Idaho?* Kate…dear…you can't be serious. I said I would ask Rich North, principal at Tumbleweed, if he'd let you sub. It's just I've been busy lately."

"I appreciate that, but I really wanted a permanent job."

"Nonsense, you're not ready to be in a classroom full days."

"Dr. Pearsall thinks I am." Kate glanced at her son to reassure him. Danny had tended to worry about her since the car accident. "I'm fine," she insisted.

Melanie set the beans down and rushed from the room. Royce, a taciturn rancher, followed his wife. Kate wondered sometimes if he'd be happier if she just stayed in her wheelchair in the background. He'd disapproved when she'd ordered a pickup with hand controls and an automatic lift to load and unload her wheelchair. Royce said Colton's life-insurance settlement should go toward Danny's future. Kate didn't point out to her father-in-law that if she hadn't culled money from her meager food budget to pay the premiums, her rodeo-chasing husband wouldn't have had life insurance.

And the Steeles' plan for Danny's future was that he'd one day be a champion calf roper, like his father.

Danny was silent after his grandparents left the table, even though Kate tried to get him to talk to her. She regretted not telling Danny her plans first—the fact that she hadn't was just one more indication that she needed to be on her own with her son. Much later, when she went in to say good-night, Kate found him sitting at the window. He had one arm draped around Goldie, his golden retriever. The other held a worn lasso that had been his dad's.

"Hey, guy, you should be in bed."

"I don't want to move." He pinned her with serious hazel eyes. "I heard Mimi tell Pawpaw that this move will use all our money. She said we'll go off and forget them…and Daddy."

"Danny, honey, they want us—well, you—to fill an empty hole your daddy left in their lives. That's too big a burden for you. It's just…time…we all move on."

"But, Mimi says if we stay in Fort Worth, by this winter I can enter the Little Britches Rodeo and win it like Dad did at my age."

Tensing, Kate didn't respond. During her recovery she'd watched from her bedroom window as Danny had devoted long hours to roping fence posts. That rodeo dream was the main reason she needed to get him away from the ranch. She patted Goldie, gently removed the rope from Danny's hand and motioned for him to go to bed. "I'm looking forward to getting back into the classroom, you know. This will be a grand adventure, you'll see."

KATE BRAKED THE TRUCK and a thin layer of dust settled on her windshield. For three days she'd endured Danny's sulks and Goldie's hot breath on her neck while she'd pulled a wobbly horse trailer through a dusty landscape dotted with juniper and brittle natural grass. Now she'd run out of dirt road.

In a clearing, a weathered gray cabin sat tucked beneath scraggly pines. Beside it stood an ancient corral and adjoining stall that leaned in the same direction as the wind-bent pines. Off to the right of the house, down a steep slope, sat a small, unpainted shed. Kate yanked on the hand brake, hoping against hope that she wasn't looking at a primitive outhouse.

Stirring for the first time in hours, Danny unbuckled his seat belt and scooted forward. He clutched his dog and his beloved lasso. "Why are we stopping?"

"Uh, I think this is it."

"What?"

"Our new home, silly boy."

"Pawpaw's bulls live in a nicer place," he announced.

Kate ruffled his hair. "Yes, but everyone knows he babies his bulls." It was a weak attempt at levity. And a knot tightened in her chest. Marge Goetz had said she and her husband owned a sugar-beet farm. But the high plateau Kate had seen thus far couldn't have been classed as farmland.

"Maybe you took a wrong turn, Mom."

Kate rechecked her map and shook her head. She felt Goldie snuffle her ponytail and reached back to rub the dog's soft nose. "This is it. See the red flag on the porch rail? Mrs. Goetz said our landlord would tie one on a pine where we should turn and another on our cabin."

Finally Kate cracked open her door. "It's getting late. We'd better see what's what, Danny. Today's Labor Day and school starts tomorrow. We need to unpack. I've got no idea when it gets dark here." She waved a hand toward the horse trailer. "Unload Flame, feed him, then use the hand cart to haul boxed bedding inside. I'll start with making beds." Kate hadn't wanted to bring the horse. But two of Colton's animals had had to be put down at the scene of their car wreck. Flame was left and Royce had given him to Danny.

Against her better judgment, Kate had phoned Marge Goetz and found out the cabin did have accommodations for a horse.

"I've gotta unload all our stuff by myself?"

"Yes. Well, you and me, sport."

"Can't the guy who owns this place come help us tote boxes?"

"Danny, I'm sure he's a busy farmer."

"Well, I'm just a kid."

Kate turned to her son. "We *can* do this, Danny." She hit the button for the lift that would lower her electric wheelchair to a level where she could slide from the truck seat and drop into the chair as she'd practiced repeatedly. She'd been without the use of her legs since the terrible accident on the Oklahoma turnpike that had killed her husband. Kate had been poked and prodded by a dozen doctors, none able to pinpoint a physical reason for her paralysis. No one had used the word *psychosomatic,* but Kate knew that's what some of them thought. Kindly Dr. Pearsall said he was confident that one day something would click and Kate would get up and walk. He'd given her exercises so her muscles would be ready if and when the time came. *Like right.*

After two years, even Kate had begun to doubt Dr. Pearsall's optimism. And her in-laws had long ago relegated her to invalid status.

Her chair bumped hard against the packed dirt. She unlocked the overhead clamp. Flashing Danny a confident smile, she slid from the pickup.

Seeing his mother meant business, he crawled a bit

more reluctantly from the backseat. "What if your chair won't go up that hill?"

"It's a gradual incline. Marge Goetz said the cabin owner would leave a door key under a clay flower pot on the porch. You can unlock the door." Kate didn't want him hanging back, maybe seeing her struggle. She had to do this. Returning to Fort Worth simply wasn't an option.

"Hey," he called moments later. "It's not so bad inside. It's got new wood floors and cabinets and it smells like Mr. Duffy's workshop."

Her chair crested the slope, and Kate breathed easier. Otis Duffy, Royce's handyman, made furniture in his spare time, and Danny loved helping him.

"Oops, I see my first obstacle. Steps. But speaking of Mr. Duffy, he nailed together a couple of ramps in case I might need them. Will you bring one from the pickup? Leave the other. It's possible I'll need it at school."

Danny left and returned lugging the ramp. "My old school had concrete ramps for kids who couldn't climb stairs."

"Your school had twelve hundred students for six grades. This school has only fourteen students in eight grades and they all arrive at school in a single van."

"Are they dorky? That's who rode vans to Tumble-weed."

"Daniel Royce Steele, I'm ashamed of you. I don't want to ever hear you call special-needs kids *dorky* again."

Danny's lower lip jutted. He buried a hand in

Goldie's yellow fur. "I had more than fourteen kids in my calf-roping class. Do any kids here rodeo? I didn't see any cows."

Kate hadn't asked Marge that question, although in talking about the area, Marge had called it the land of the last buckaroo. *Buckaroo* was another word for *cowboy,* and Kate hoped that meant the cowboys were all gone. "Danny, it costs a lot for rodeo gear and things like entry fees."

"Pawpaw and Mimi will give us money."

She straightened from securing the makeshift ramp to the porch. "No. From now on we make do with what I earn. You'll get a weekly allowance for helping me with household chores. I expect you to save part, and the rest will buy feed and pay vet bills if you want to keep Flame."

"Not keep him? Flame's the best roping horse in all of Texas."

"We aren't in Texas anymore, Daniel," Kate said, aware she sounded a bit like Dorothy in *The Wizard Of Oz.* "From here on we live in a place called Owyhee, Idaho."

"Idaho stinks." Danny kicked the porch step.

Recognizing a look she'd often seen Colton wear if things didn't go his way only convinced Kate all the more that leaving Texas had been a good idea.

MARGE GOETZ PASSED A MUG of steaming black coffee to the neighbor who stood on her front porch talking to her husband, Ray. "Before you two get so deep into hashing over today's Bureau of Land Management meeting, tell me, Ben, did our new teacher get moved into your cabin?"

"Danged if I know." Ben Trueblood blew on his hot coffee and shifted his gaze to the hills where the cabin sat. His land butted up next to the farm where Ray and Marge raised sugar beets and onions. "Last week I tied red flags like you asked and left the box of folders. Chad Keevler finished the kitchen and new bathroom that the board approved. Out of curiosity, why wouldn't she get here? You said she sounded reliable." He declined to sit in the empty chair Ray offered and braced a knee-high boot on one rung instead.

Hearty, sandy-haired Ray dusted off his work jeans before dropping into another chair. "Marge is fussing because I had to take her SUV to town for engine work, leaving her without wheels. The board hired the Steele woman on Marge's recommendation. Since Sikes's reserve unit was called to active duty and left our kids teacherless midterm last year, I think she feels…"

"Yeah, yeah," Marge cut in. "Responsible. I feel responsible. Can you blame me? We found Ms. Steele so late, the Martins already sent their twins to board with Sue's sister in Elko. The district superintendent says if we dip under twelve kids, the county will suspend our funding. By my calculations, we're at an even dozen."

"Counting the teacher's kid? Did I dream you said she's a widow with a school-aged son?" Trueblood gestured with his mug.

"That's right. Her boy's ten, the same age as Jeff, our youngest." Marge still sounded worried.

Ray patted her on the butt. "Hon, you're determined to fret."

"If homeschooling our boys had fallen to you after the army took Sikes, you'd fret, too. Not a family in the valley is anxious to go on tryin' to teach their kids at home. How much of the curriculum did you teach Clover?" she asked Ben, looking over at the elfin eight-year-old girl with long, black hair who was chasing butterflies through a cow pasture. Every now and then the child stopped to pet one of the massive, white-faced Herefords.

"Now, Marge. Sikes got called up when I was bogged down with the first lawsuit brought by that conservation group who wants the BLM to revoke all grazing leases on public lands. I had to turn Clover's homeschooling packet over to Bobbalou."

Marge scoffed. "What can Lou Bobolink teach a girl?" She used the given name of Ben's old friend and longtime camp cook.

Ben grinned. "How to make beef stew and sourdough biscuits? Hell, Marge, after the recreational ATVers jumped into the land squabble, I had no choice. Vida got sick and couldn't keep house for a while, or she might've helped with lessons. Although, Clover likes trailing the herd."

"Because you let her do as she pleases. You have, Ben Trueblood, from the day she turned up a crying bundle in your barn."

The sharp, sometimes brittle obsidian eyes jerked up at Marge's harsh accusation, but almost as quickly the lean lines of Ben's bronze face softened. "Look at her.

She's happy. And a damned sight brighter than some folks give her credit for. Clover's got a way with animals like nobody I've ever run across. One day she'll make a great veterinarian."

"Not without education and discipline," Marge said.

Ray cleared his throat. "Don't rag on Ben, hon. Everybody knows Clover's way better off with him than those teens from the Shoshone or Paiute reservation who dumped her at his place."

"Leave it," Ben said, cutting Ray off. Ben had been born on one of those reservations. No one had to tell him about the harsh existence faced by those two kids he'd caught sight of running from his property that icy night.

"Marge, I'd like to devote more time to Clover. But I figure the best thing I can do for her is fight like hell to hang on to a ranch Bobbalou and I started carving out of this unforgiving land when I was fourteen. I've never blamed Clover's mother, whoever she is. I broke free of the bad crap that perpetuates itself on reservations. Percy and me, we had Lou, and he knew to leave the res and buy his own land. It's not as easy for kids today, what with our land being gobbled up or fought over."

"This land is sucking us all dry," Marge said.

Draining his mug, Ben set it on the porch rail. "Bud Martin, Percy Lightfoot, me and a scant few others are damned lucky to keep ranching the way it's meant to be done. Letting cows roam free in the tradition brought here a hundred years ago."

Ray tipped back in his chair. "It's a hard life for

men. Nigh on impossible for women and kids to survive that way, Ben."

"Which is why you don't see me trying to find a
wife."

"You need one," Marge said. "For your own sake
and to provide a bit of softness for Clover."

"Now, Marge," her husband said. "It takes a hard
man to raise four thousand cows, bulls and steers,
alongside a thousand mixed mustangs and quarter
horses without irrigation, especially now that grazing
lands are getting scarcer and scarcer thanks to the likes
of damned tree huggers and ATVers."

"That brings us back to the point I'm trying to make,
Ben," Marge persisted. "Clover needs more. More than
blue jeans, boys' shirts and chaps and being turned
loose to learn from your crew, who don't know
anything but living on the range eleven months a year.
She's never gonna be a hard man, Ben Trueblood.
That's the God's honest truth you need to deal with."
Marge snatched up his empty cup and the one her
husband had set down and stomped into the house,
slamming the screen door.

"Phew," Ray muttered. Climbing to his feet, he said,
"Let's go have a look at the beet harvester I picked up
at auction last week." As the men left the porch to
mosey toward the barn, Ray said, "I hope you don't
hold hard feelings against her for butting into your
business. The dwindling number of wives left in
Owyhee are counting on this new teacher. Winnie
Lightfoot said if we lose the school it'll be like losing
a chunk of civilization. She's right. Successful, thirty-

seven-year-old bachelor ranchers like you, Ben, are anomalies. It's families that bring in businesses to sustain a ranch community. We can't afford to lose another church, grocery, hardware or feed store."

Ben glanced at Ray in bemusement. "Marge isn't the only one on a soap box, I see." He sighed. "Hell, Ray, it takes time to socialize—time I spend trying to prevent our public lands from breaking up. The committee needs to say what's more important, keeping a million acres from being overrun by environmentalists and all-terrain fanatics, or me hunting up a woman who may or may not civilize me."

Ray flushed crimson to the roots of his sandy hair. "Enough on that subject. I can't imagine you with a missus anyway."

"Why not?" The comment rocked Ben back. He didn't *want* a wife, but he didn't think he was so objectionable. "I own a home. Granted, I'm rarely there. But it stays decent thanks to Vida. I don't drink or gamble. I cuss a little," he confessed, tugging an earlobe.

"You have to *want* a wife. Finding someone to fit your lifestyle won't be easy. Might be, if you didn't run a straight-up buckaroo outfit, or if Owyhee had an excess of single women…which it don't. Or if we didn't depend on you to represent us in this land fight and organize our Rope and Rides so we'll have funds in our town coffers to pay a sheriff and hang on to a clinic, such as it is. It's a cinch taxes don't cover our needs."

His friend stopped Ray from droning on. "I get the message. It's best all around if we keep this new teacher happy. We'll build the town up by showing we're prosperous enough to warrant a school, and other revenue will follow."

"So, does this mean you'll swing past your old line shack and see if Ms. Steele arrived?"

"Aw, dang it! You led me right into that."

"Yep."

"Why can't Marge take your pickup now that you're home?"

"She would, except her quilting club meets here in a half hour. I'm not asking you to sweet talk the woman, Ben. Marge hasn't heard a word since the teacher left Texas. We've gotta be sure she arrived so kids can start school tomorrow."

"It'll be dark soon. Who's to say if I blunder in there after dark that a Texas woman won't shoot first and ask questions later?"

"I'd give a dollar to see that." Ray grinned, pumping Ben's hand as they prepared to part. "Letting a little lady blow your ass off would seriously tarnish your image, Ben."

"You saying it couldn't happen?"

"I s'pose it could. The old Western books I've read set in Texas generally have feisty females who don't take guff off cowboys. Max Brand's books."

Ben hesitated fractionally before waving to summon Clover. "Is that how Marge describes the teacher? A feisty, no-guff type?"

"Marge only chatted with her by phone. Saw a fax of her credentials. They're so good, some on the board wondered what's wrong with her. I mean, why was she hunting a teaching job so late in the year? Daryl White was sure she ran afoul of the law. He ran a background check. Nothing came up. Guess if you don't want to stop there we can wait to see what Bill Hyder says after he drives the van tomorrow. He's this month's driver volunteer."

"You took me off bus detail, I hope." Ben boosted Clover into the backseat of his Ford pickup's king cab.

"Yeah. You've got your hands full wading through lawyers. Of course, since this woman is the new widow in town, I could assign you Bill's rotation for the hell of it."

"Don't you dare. Tell Marge I'll check on her teacher. I'll call after I see what's what." Ben crawled in his truck and gave one of his half-cynical smiles before shutting the door and starting the motor. He muttered to the child in the backseat, "Clover, girl, I hope you like the new teacher. 'Cause God's truth—I'd be the happiest man in Owyhee if I never had to cross the school threshold until you graduate."

"No school, Ben," the little girl said firmly. "I'm gonna go with Bobbalou."

"We'd both like that, but…there are laws, princess."

"You don't like laws." She bounced against the seat. Strands of long black hair flew like errant smoke. "I'll run off from school."

"No you won't." Ben sighed. "It's lawmakers I don't like, Clover." *And he didn't like being squeezed off his land.* He'd much prefer to keep running his cattle without any fences. But, Ray and Marge were right in one sense. It was a hard life. From the minute Clover had landed in his barn, she'd been the bright spot in his harsh existence. From the get-go he'd approached raising her the way he did foals and calves. While it had seemed to work for a while, this past year he'd seen signs that she needed more. Their short-lived teacher, Sikes, had said Clover should be tested, maybe sent to a special school—one for mentally impaired kids. What kind of teacher said stuff like that about a sweet little girl?

Clover was a—free spirit, maybe. His fault, not hers.

Reaching back, Ben smoothed her long bangs with his fingers. "You'll like the new teacher, princess. I bet she's gonna love you." He sounded fierce, and recognized desperation in his statement, as if repeating the words enough would make them come true.

Darkness had covered the purple hills by the time he bounced his heavy-duty Ford up the rocky slope to his remodeled line shack. A big Chevy sat outside the cabin, which was awash in light. *Well, he had Marge's answer. The teacher had arrived.*

He saw they'd turned out a horse. Dang, the corral needed shoring up. Ben mentally added a note to ask Chad up to repair it. He would've driven on out again if the front door to the cabin hadn't opened. A boy and a dog ran out and down the porch steps.

Letting the Ford idle, Ben stepped out on his running board. "Hi, there," he called over the strident barking of a lunging dog. "I'm Ben Trueblood. Marge Goetz asked me to verify that the new teacher got moved in. You'd be her son, I imagine."

The gangly kid gripped the dog's collar, but Ben

wondered for how long. "Glad to see you've got protection. Tell your mom the van arrives at school around 9:00 a.m."

Before he could halt her, Clover crawled over the seat and shot out his door to plop on her knees in front of the dog, who quit barking and licked her face even as Ben's heart jacked up into his throat.

He glimpsed a second silhouette at the door. The teacher? If so, she wasn't much taller than her boy. What had made him think she'd be burly? Probably Ray's talk about feisty Texas women who handled guns.

"Marge would've welcomed you," he called, "but her car's on the blink. I own this place." He circled a hand. "Any problems, tell Clover at school. That's her." He stabbed a finger. "Princess, let's go. We have to eat yet and get you a bath. Tomorrow's a school day."

Clover kissed the dog's nose, got up, waved to the boy she'd been chattering to and skipped back to the pickup. Ben had no more than lifted her in when the boy lost his hold on the retriever. In the semidarkness Ben saw a yellow streak zoom toward him. To make matters worse, the boy flailed his arms and chased his pet. The animal may have cottoned to Clover, but no one would mistake his bared teeth as a sign of affection for Ben, who felt those teeth sink into the soft leather of his left boot. Shaking his foot, Ben ultimately managed to close his door.

Triumphant, the dog gave a last growl and trotted back to his master.

KATE HAD CAUGHT ONLY SNATCHES of what their visitor said before Goldie went berserk. She'd levered herself out of her wheelchair and braced on the door casing as Dr. Pearsall said she could do now and then. She'd witnessed the unfolding scene and was glad the tall, lanky stranger managed to escape without being bitten. All she needed was to be told by her landlord to get rid of Danny's dog. She'd caught that the man's name was Trueblood and that the girl talking to Danny was his daughter. Oh, and Marge Goetz had car trouble.

After Goldie trotted meekly back to Danny, Kate watched the truck's taillights fade. She found it odd the man hadn't come to the door. Although, on second thought, she was glad. In the soft light shining from inside his pickup, she saw he wore the garb of a conventional cowboy, not a farmer. This cabin could be part of a ranch, she mused, sinking back into her wheelchair.

The last thing she wanted was for Danny to get friendly with a cowboy.

"Good watchdog," she murmured to Goldie as the retriever bounded into the house.

CHAPTER TWO

KATE DID NEED HER SECOND RAMP at school to get her to the front door, which she unlocked with an old-style brass key Marge had included in the box of student folders that had been left on her kitchen counter.

The folders were a disappointment. No grades had been posted from the previous year and family information was sketchy. And there were eleven folders instead of fourteen. The number of students had dwindled even before Kate started. Schools closed when enrollment dipped too low.

That concern and the general anxiety that went with a new job had seen her sewing curtains for the cabin long after Danny and Goldie had gone to sleep. She would've hung the curtains, but she needed Danny's help. The realization that she'd be more dependent on him than she would have liked troubled her, too. Danny was only ten. Was she expecting too much? Melanie Steele would say yes. Last night Danny had worked without complaint. Today, though, he was grouchy. Kate was glad to leave him standing by the pickup. His absence let her savor the pleasure of entering her first classroom in too many years.

It was a typical country school. A square box with weathered siding. The central cupola at the top of the peaked roof no longer held a school bell. The single main room fanned into wings on either side, housing the boys' and girls' restrooms. Wood floors were oiled a dark umber. Five short rows of desks with space to walk between occupied the center of the room. Kate counted desks for twenty students, but with Danny she would only have twelve.

A huge oak desk stood at the front of the room and behind it a massive chair. What did it say to students, Kate thought: *I'm the boss?*

She loved that the chalkboard was black, not green or white as in newer schools. It ran the length of the wall behind her desk. The U.S. flag stood in one corner and alongside it was a black potbellied stove. Dry wood had been stacked under one window.

As she passed the wood, Kate sniffed the pungent pine scent. The air smelled mustily of smoke, wood oil, chalk dust and industrial-grade soap. Closing her eyes, she soaked in what, to her, was the aroma of knowledge and opportunity. She had attended a similar school in rural Kansas, the one where her mom had taught until she'd died of a ruptured aneurism. Kate had always wanted to follow in her mother's footsteps. She belonged in front of a classroom.

Laughing, she threw up her arms, hugged herself and twirled her motorized chair. The sound echoed in the empty room, prompting Danny, who'd finally wandered in, to exclaim, "Mom, what's wrong?"

She sobered. "Everything is right for the first time

in ages, honey." Seeing his skepticism, she held out her arms. He cast a furtive glance toward the door to make sure he wouldn't be observed before he accepted the hug. Then he pulled away fast.

"I hope you aren't gonna do that in front of the other kids."

"I won't embarrass you, Danny. Are you worried kids here might bully you because you're the teacher's son?"

"I dunno. Maybe. In Fort Worth all the kids knew Pawpaw. They thought it was cool I got to live at the Bar R-S where all my friends trained for junior rodeo. Here…I'm nobody."

"Just be yourself, Danny. I know you'll make friends."

He turned away.

"Wait, will you open the window? Oh, and put that monster teacher's chair in the closet, please. You know, I wouldn't turn down help in tacking up a bulletin board."

He brightened, did as she requested, then worked feverishly to help Kate cover a small canvas board with red construction paper. Danny stapled on letters that spelled Welcome To School. Yellow happy faces peeked out from between letters. "It's simple," Kate said, "but it's bright and cheery."

"Yep, it's nice, Mom."

Finding a piece of chalk, Kate rose out of her chair and wrote *Ms. Steele* in printing and cursive on the blackboard.

A loud crunch of tires outside alerted them to

someone's arrival. Kate set the chalk in the tray and parked her wheelchair behind the desk. To anyone walking in the door, it would appear she was sitting in a regular chair.

At the door, Danny shouted, "It's the van with the other kids."

Kate's confidence slipped. She caught herself rubbing damp palms down her slacks. "Let them follow their normal routine, Danny." Calmly, Kate opened her book bag and pulled out papers.

"What should I do?" Danny asked.

"Pick a seat?" Kate waved at the desk he stood beside.

"What if some other kid sits there?"

"Oh. Good point. What do you think you should do?"

"Go back to Fort Worth. I hate it here." He spoke with such fervor Kate winced.

"Honey, I agreed to work a full school year. In May I'll reassess. Until then, we're staying. Why don't you ask the van driver what time he or she plans to return to pick up the students."

"It's a he," Danny muttered, brushing past two boys who were timidly approaching.

Kate pasted on a smile. "Welcome boys. Take seats near the front of the room for now. Once I take attendance I'll assign seating based on your grade."

The duo, freckle-faced carrot tops, plopped down in the second row. Two giggly blond girls followed. All four appeared nervous.

The next five to straggle in tried to act cool and

aloof. Three older boys waited to see where the girls who trailed in their wake decided to sit. The boys then put as much distance between themselves and the girls as humanly possible.

Kate noted that the last two students slipped in silently. The girl was possibly the youngest of the group. In a few years she would be stunning. Lustrous, straight black hair fell to below her shoulders. Eyes so dark they were almost purple studied Kate from beneath thick lashes. By comparison, the boy seemed bland. His black hair was cropped short, his liquid eyes somber. If Kate had to describe the color of his skin, she would call it flat tobacco, whereas the girl's glowed like burnished copper. Kate had one Hispanic name on the list from Marge and two Native Americans. Checking grade levels, she concluded these two were her Native students.

Which meant the girl was her landlord's daughter. Last night she'd barely glimpsed the child down beside Danny and Goldie.

Danny returned, trailed by a stocky man.

"You sent the boy to get me, ma'am? I'm Bill Hyder. Dave, there, is my youngest boy." The van driver crushed a battered straw hat between work-scarred hands. His gaze lit proudly on a husky, toffee-haired teen who slumped in his seat.

Kate smiled, hoping to put the man and his son at ease. "I'm Ms. Steele. I forgot to ask Marge Goetz if I should stagger dismissals by grade levels."

Bill shook his head, relaxing some. "All grades get out at two-thirty. I hope that's okay. It saves on fuel and vehicle wear and tear. Plus, our driver volunteers pull double duty between farming, ranching or jobs in town."

"Your board employs *me,* Mr. Hyder. I'll abide by their rules. Two-thirty it is. Have a nice day." She'd perfected a smile of dismissal.

He jammed on his hat and ducked out.

Kate beckoned to Danny. "Class, I'd like you to meet my son. Danny is in fifth grade. After he sits down, I'll take attendance. Please raise your hand as I call your name. Then we're going to have a two-page quiz. Simple questions designed to show me your skill levels in reading, math and science." She expected groans or outright objection, but the room remained eerily silent.

The first sound was an audible gasp from the students after she completed attendance and motored out from behind her desk to hand out tests.

Kate hadn't planned to explain her condition. The collective gasp changed her mind. "I was injured a couple of years ago in an auto accident."

A boy Kate had already handed a test to raised his hand.

"Yes? You're Terry Goetz, have I got that right?"

"Uh-huh. Did my mom know you were crippled?" he blurted, then yelped when the boy seated beside him, his younger brother, Jeff, socked him in the arm.

"Ow!" Terry scowled at Jeff. The other kids sat in shocked silence.

Kate felt shaky and needed a minute to collect her thoughts. She eased around the last seat in Terry's row and headed up the next aisle, continuing to pass out tests. She had been right—Clover Trueblood was her youngest pupil. The girl had just turned eight. Kate recalled that Clover's record hadn't made it clear if she was in second or third grade. Kate set a test designed for second graders in front of Clover. Kate's hands were empty now and it was time to deal with Terry Goetz.

"Terry," she said quietly, crossing to her desk. "Do *you* think it's necessary I be able to walk in order to teach?"

"I dunno," the boy mumbled. "Depends on what you teach. Uh, I didn't mean no offense, but me 'n' Ron Quimby and Mike Delgado are probably gonna go to the consolidated high school next year. Sports are big there. Our last teacher, Mr. Sikes, he hung a basketball hoop on the back school wall and was teaching us how to make hook shots and blocks." Terry slid lower on his spine.

"Basketball?" Kate repeated, stopping behind her desk. "It so happens I rarely miss watching an NBA game on TV. Naturally I can't run with you on the court, but I bet I can help you. These tests are timed by the way," she said in the same even tone. "Does everyone have a pencil?"

The kids scrambled to open their backpacks, and Kate saw she'd done the right thing in not coming down hard on Terry. She'd find a private moment to make him understand that the term *cripple* was hurtful.

"These scores won't be recorded," she assured them. "And accuracy is more important than speed. Is everyone ready?"

A blond girl named Shelly Bent raised her hand. "If we miss a lot of questions, Ms. Steele, are you going to move us back a grade?"

"Good question. The answer is no. Your most recent school year was interrupted. I'll use these scores to see where you need help."

That seemed to put them more at ease. At least they all sat forward and prepared to turn over their papers. "If that's it for questions, you may begin," Kate said.

She checked her watch for the start time. She'd learned from her mother the art of watching students without seeming to. Midway through the test, she noticed that a bird had flown in one of the open windows and was hopping along the sill. Kate didn't know what kind of bird it was. It had gray feathers and a yellow underbelly and throat. The bird cocked its head and warbled, sounding almost flutelike.

Kate saw she wasn't the only one captivated by the bird. Clover Trueblood set down her pencil and slipped from her seat. She answered the birdcall with an uncanny repetition of the flute sounds.

Or maybe the bird had warbled again. Not wanting to disrupt the whole class, Kate rolled toward the girl. She thought Clover would scare the bird, but that didn't happen. Clover walked right up and planted an elbow on either side of the creature. They both trilled again. Thinking it must be a tame bird, Kate went closer. Her arrival startled the bird and it flew away.

The girl whirled, fright widening her eyes. Kate offered a gentle smile. "Clover, did you complete your test? If not, you need to go back to your seat."

Without speaking, the child sidled around Kate.

"I'll allow you a few extra minutes. Later maybe we can discuss the bird."

Clover bounded back to her seat, but not before she lifted her chin and gazed straight into Kate's eyes. Kate wasn't sure whether she felt confounded or challenged. It was an unsettling experience.

Back at her desk, she noticed that several students were done. "Shelly, please collect the tests beginning with eighth graders. I'm allowing Clover an extra five minutes. She had a slight distraction."

It pleased Kate to see that her landlord's daughter was hunched over her desk, her pencil flying across her paper.

As students handed their tests to Shelly, they began to whisper among themselves, especially the Keevler sisters and Meg Wheeler.

"Jeff—Jeff Goetz," Kate called. "Will you and Adam Lightfoot pass out these books? I've attached names on sticky notes. They're reading texts. I'd like you each to begin reading the first story in your book while I glance over the tests. It's possible I'll trade books for a few of you after I check your reading comprehension. I expect I'll move some of you to more difficult books."

There was the usual disorder that went along with a break in routine. Kate found these children better disciplined than she'd expected, given none of them had been in a formal classroom since before Christmas of the previous year.

She worked quickly with the aid of an answer sheet.

Ron Quimby, Shelly Bent and her clone, Meg Wheeler, made perfect scores. Ron and Shelly were in eighth grade. They were probably working well above that. Terry Goetz missed two questions. He had terrible handwriting, but she saw no need to change his eighth-grade reader. Others in fifth through seventh grades held their own. Kate was feeling quite pleased until she reached the last test, which she knew belonged to Clover.

The girl's name was not written on the test and not one question had been answered. Quite by accident Kate turned one sheet over. Her breath caught. A perfect rendering of the bird on the windowsill stared up at her. Its feathers, the markings and intelligent eyes had been captured in exquisite detail. On the back of the second sheet was an equally complex drawing of a steer.

Stunned, she thumbed through the permanent record folders to locate Clover's. Had she missed a reference to this talent? Or a note saying the girl showed a total lack of regard for a teacher-mandated assignment? The most telling thing in the file was its brevity. All eleven students lived on rural routes. Clover Trueblood was no exception. A space for her mother's given and maiden names was blank. Nothing indicated whether Mrs. True-blood lived elsewhere or was deceased. A notation was made that Clover had passed grade one, but Mr. Sikes's progress note simply stated she hadn't been tested in grade two.

Had she been absent the day of state-mandated tests? If so, why had no one administered a makeup?

Kate frowned and tucked the artwork in the folder, then pulled a pad from her book bag to jot down contact phone numbers from Clover's record. Vida Smith, a housekeeper, was listed for Monday, Tuesday and Thursday. Her father's radio-phone number said, *message only, will return calls.* Three other numbers without names were noted for emergency purposes.

Sighing, Kate wrote Clover's father a note requesting a meeting at his earliest convenience. She put it in an envelope, sealed it and scrawled his name on the outside, then set it aside to send home with Clover.

Like most first days at school, this one passed quickly. As Kate was the only teacher, all grades broke for lunch and recess together. She was able to observe which kids paired up and who was on the outs. The older boys teamed up for three-on-a-side basketball.

From the sidelines, Kate suggested plays. She kept an eye on Jeff Goetz and Adam Lightfoot, who tossed a baseball in another part of the playground. She'd thought Danny would join them, but he moved off. Clover climbed on the monkey bars and chatted to Danny, who didn't seem to mind.

At the end of the day, Kate stuck her note to Clover's father into the girl's pack. "This is important. Please give it to your dad as soon as you get home. Tell him I'll be here tomorrow a half hour before school starts, or I'll stay an hour after class."

"Yes, ma'am." Clover skirted Kate's wheelchair and bolted for the door.

Kate levered out of her chair to erase the math problems she'd had Meg Wheeler and Mike Delgado write on the board.

She and Danny were alone again.

"Did Clover do something wrong, Mom?"

"Wrong? Oh, you mean the note I sent her father? It's nothing. Her record is incomplete so I need information from her dad. By the way, Danny, I saw you two talking at recess and lunch, after you left Jeff and Adam."

"I asked them about a rodeo. Jeff doesn't have horses, but Clover does. Her dad owns a bunch, a cavvy, she called them. She can ride any horse she wants. And her dad braids ropes. Clover said her dad used to teach a roping clinic. She knows all about slack handling, dallying, del viento, hoolihan, turnover and a bunch of other roping tricks."

Kate set the eraser in its tray. "He *used* to teach roping?"

"Yeah. Well, maybe he still does." Taking the eraser, Danny dusted it off in the waste basket. "Clover said he had to stop 'cause he spends so much time running back and forth to court. To Boise. When he's gone she gets to ride in a real chuck wagon. Isn't that the coolest thing, Mom?"

"Hmm." Kate digested the news about Clover's father spending a lot of time in court. A custody hassle might explain the girl's distraction and account for the blanks on her permanent record.

A teacher ought to know if there was a court restraining order out against one parent or the other. Mentally, Kate added that to her list of things to discuss with Clover's father.

That evening, Marge Goetz phoned. "Kate, may I call you that? During supper Jeff told his dad and me how rude Terry was today. He knows better. He will apologize tomorrow. And he'll do without TV for a few days."

"I'd planned to speak privately with Terry. He and the others wouldn't have been so surprised if I'd mentioned my use of a wheelchair in my cover letter."

"There's no reason you should have. Except we would've provided better access to your cabin and the school. My husband, Ray, worries that you'll have trouble when it snows."

"Getting around is my problem to solve, Marge, and I'll manage. When should I expect the first snow?"

"Could be another month. Two if we're lucky. It won't hurt the older boys to shovel a path from where you park into the school. I'll have Ray or one of the other board members buy snow shovels for the school and your cabin." After asking Kate if she needed anything else, the board president said goodbye.

Kate wished she'd asked if Marge knew a way to reach Clover Trueblood's father. But maybe he'd show up in the morning.

The next day, Kate rousted Danny from bed early so she'd be at school in the event Trueblood chose to come for a morning meeting, but he didn't show. Clover got off the bus. Entering the room alone, she shyly crossed to Kate's desk, where she set a peanut-butter jar filled with fragrant wildflowers.

The gesture and the child's almost palpable anxiety touched Kate. "Why, thank you, Clover. These are beautiful. Do they grow wild near your house?"

The girl bobbed her head. Kate's obvious pleasure triggered a sweet responsive smile before Clover spun and skipped to her desk.

Kate hated to bring up the letter she'd sent home, but she needed to know. "Clover, did you give your dad my note?"

"Yes, ma'am." She sat, but didn't look at Kate.

"What did he say after he read it?"

Fine black hair hid Clover's face. "Nothing."

"Is he picking you up from school today?"

"Uh-uh. I'm riding the bus and Miss Vida's staying late to fix my supper 'cause Ben's got a meeting in town."

Kate closed her eyes and pinched the bridge of her nose. "Do you always call your father Ben?"

Clover shrugged, clearly puzzled. "That's his name."

"All right. Not to worry. I'll write him another note. Or, better, I'll phone and leave a message."

The morning reading assignment netted Kate two more drawings from Clover—a dark horse with an oddly trimmed mane and a dog that looked like Goldie. Kate had Clover read out loud. She read about every fifth word, seeming easily distracted.

While the students were eating lunch at tables out back, Kate took a minute to call Ben Trueblood and was connected to an answering machine. "I understand if you're busy," she said, rushing to beat the time-out tone. "Perhaps I didn't convey the urgency of my request to speak with you in my first note. We need to conference ASAP about your daughter." The tone bleeped, so Kate clicked off, annoyed that she hadn't repeated her offer to come in early or stay late.

THURSDAY AT SCHOOL was a repeat of Wednesday.

Frustrated, Kate again attempted to impress on Clover that she really needed to meet with her dad. "This is my cell-phone number," she said, making sure Clover saw her stuff the note in a zip pocket of the girl's red backpack. "Please tell him he can call me any evening. I'm up late."

Blinking a couple of times, Clover dashed off to meet the van, leaving Kate with her day's work—more art. Today there was a likeness of Kate seated at her desk and below it a sketch of the boys playing basketball. The last drawing was of a wizened man bent over a campfire, his features and arthritic hands compellingly lifelike.

If she didn't see or hear from Ben Trueblood soon, Kate intended to load Danny in her pickup and follow Bill Hyder to Clover's home. She'd wait for him there.

Kate spent a large part of the day observing Clover. She seemed a happy child, always humming to herself as she flitted about. And flit she did. Simple things caught her attention. Clouds. A fly. Colorful rocks.

The other kids didn't exactly avoid her, but neither did they include her in play. And for some reason she chose to shadow Danny. Curiously, he let her, probably because she knew a lot about horses—Danny's greatest love next to calf roping.

As she watched the kids at lunch, it struck Kate that if not for her pretty hair and girlish features, Clover could pass for one of the boys in her slant-heel boots, faded blue jeans and Western shirt.

Clover wasn't disruptive in class. She listened attentively when anyone, especially Kate, talked. However, small things had her leaving her seat. A ladybug marching across a neighbor's desk. Oak leaves that blew in and skittered across the floor when Meg Wheeler came in late. And of all things, a honeybee that Clover guided out the classroom window because she said its family was waiting outside.

Clover's verbal skills were fine for her age and she gave detailed answers to the questions Kate asked. But she stubbornly chose not to do written assignments and she only read a handful of words on a page. Kate didn't get it. The kid was an enigma. And so was the elusive dad, whom Danny pronounced "real cool." According to Danny, buckaroos, as Clover called her dad and his crew, were the greatest because they lived in tepees on the range. They did nothing but ride horses, herd and brand cattle.

Kate didn't share her son's admiration for the man. Clover was a beautiful child who had somehow fallen through a huge crack in the education system and it was Kate's job to see that her student got the help she needed.

Frustrated, Kate left a terse message saying that if she didn't see him Friday, she was going to call the district superintendent's office about his child. "I understand what it is to be a working, single parent. I'll be at school until six o'clock."

Danny overheard the last part of her call. "Are we

staying late again tonight? If we stay till six that means I've gotta feed and exercise Flame in the dark."

"Not tonight, Danny. I'm ready to go home now. Tomorrow, bring a book along to read. If Clover's dad spends long hours out on the range, it's up to me to remain flexible so that he and I can meet."

"You said Clover wasn't in trouble. So why do you need a meeting?"

"Danny, I can't discuss another student with you, and I'm sorry you have to stay with me. You know, if Clover's dad makes this meeting, you'll have to sit in the truck until he and I finish talking. Our meeting is confidential."

"Br-oth-er! You think I can't keep a secret? I was with Mimi when she bought Pawpaw that fringed leather jacket for Christmas, and I didn't tell."

"This is different, honey. All students and their families have a legal right to privacy."

"Not me. You're my teacher *and* my mom. You know everything there is to know about me."

Kate couldn't resist teasing as she hugged him. "But you're perfect, Danny."

He wiggled out of her arms and delivered an eye roll like only ten-year-old boys could. However, he helped her collect her papers without being asked before they locked up.

FRIDAY THE KIDS WERE ANXIOUS to be off for the weekend. "Are you going to assign homework?" asked tall, lanky Ron Quimby.

"I prefer not to assign weekend homework. Tests I

give will be on work you should be covering during class." Kate couldn't help glancing at Clover. She hadn't completed any class assignments this entire week. Well, that wasn't true. She'd done her math.

Last night, Marge Goetz had dropped by with a welcome casserole and Kate had been dying to ask the older woman about Clover's father but didn't feel she'd been at her job long enough to probe for such information. After Marge had left, Kate had looked up dyslexia in a teaching textbook. Kate wondered if that was Clover's problem. But the text said a dyslexic child would have difficulty with reading, spelling *and* numbers, so that didn't describe Clover.

Class ended in a stampede out to catch the bus.

"Danny, I'm going to grade papers," Kate told her son. "Will you go see if anyone left sports equipment out on the playground?"

"Okay. Why do we hafta stay late every night? I want to ride Flame. Why doesn't Clover's dad show up?"

"I've no idea."

Kate spent a half hour going over the day's work. From the sporadic thump on the back wall, she knew Danny had gotten sidetracked shooting baskets.

At the sound of footsteps, Kate's head shot up. In walked the most arresting man she'd seen in Lord only knew when. He was lean, not too muscular and oozed masculinity. He wore narrow-legged jeans tucked in tall snakeskin boots that jingled faintly and musically as he entered the classroom. Despite herself, Kate felt a tug in her belly as she watched the fascinating, hip-rolling gait of a born cowboy.

The faded red neckerchief he wore had seen better days and obviously wasn't for show. Nor was the sweat-stained cotton shirt with stray strands of dry grass sticking out of one pocket and the shirtsleeves rolled up over deeply tanned forearms.

She hadn't heard a truck. Had he dropped from the sky?

As he turned to glance out the window, Kate saw that his raven-black hair was tied at the nape with a leather thong. His clean-shaven jaw gave an appearance of strength.

No matter how irritated Kate was with herself over looking her fill, she was more chagrined to see that he studied her with equal interest—and equal reluctance.

"Mr. Trueblood, I presume? I'm Kate Steele, your daughter's new teacher." Kate tried to imagine what he was thinking. How did he feel about knocking off work early to come in for a meeting he probably considered frivolous? Clover's dad struck her as a hard-nosed, no-frills kinda guy.

"I appreciate you making time to come talk about Clover," Kate said. "I'll try to be as brief as possible, but meanwhile, please be seated." She indicated a folding chair she'd brought from home for this very occasion.

He hadn't spoken since walking in and didn't now. He merely dragged the chair out a foot or so farther from her desk and sat heavily, before hanging the flat-crowned hat he'd removed at the door over one knee.

At last he cleared his throat. "Clover's a little bit of a thing, Ms. Steele. If she's caused trouble for you in class, I'd have thought as a qualified teacher you'd know ways to deal with about any problem an eight-year-old girl could dish up."

CHAPTER THREE

"I'M SORRY IF I DIDN'T MAKE myself clear in my note," Kate said, trying not to stammer. What was wrong with him that he couldn't see her only objective in asking to meet him was to help his daughter? "Clover *is* a very sweet child, Mr. Trueblood." Kate leaned forward earnestly. "This conference isn't because she's caused trouble. I need enlightening about her past academic achievement."

Ben adjusted the hat roosting on his knee and stiffened. "Marge said she gave you records on all the kids."

"She did." Kate unlocked a bottom desk drawer and walked her fingers along the hanging files she'd set up. "I'll be happy to show you Clover's record." Extracting a thin folder, she removed a sheet and slid it across the desk.

He didn't take it, or even examine it. Instead, he acted wary, or perhaps impatient, and sort of growled, "Why don't you cut to the chase and tell me what you want Clover to do? Or what I should do?"

Again reaching into the hanging file, Kate brought out Clover's work. She waved the sheaf of papers at Trueblood until he gingerly accepted it. A tiny smile flickered as he leafed through the pages. "These, uh, look pretty good to me," he finally said. He took a longer look at a drawing of Kate. "She missed those little half-glasses you've got perched on your nose. Outside of that it's the spitting image, I'd say."

"Mr. Trueblood." Exasperated, Kate snatched back the artwork. "Clover draws in great detail. The problem is that she did these and not her daily assignments." Pointing toward the window, Kate described the bird incident.

"My buckaroos will tell you that Clover's good with animals. For instance, if she says call the vet, my trail boss calls him. Sure enough, something's always wrong."

"I'd hoped you could shed light on the issue of her schoolwork. As you see, her previous teacher wrote next to nothing on her file. Mr. Sikes made progress notes on all of the other students. Did he ever talk to you about Clover's performance in class?"

Ben got up and paced to the door and back, all the while rubbing at the back of his neck. "We had a talk after Sikes got called up by his army unit. He…said… Clover needs… She's…not like other kids."

Kate removed her reading glasses and watched the struggle going on within the man. "I can tell this isn't easy for you to discuss. Does Clover's problem stem from your separation, or is it a divorce? Problems in a marriage do affect the children."

Ben's head jerked up.

"I'm not prying," Kate said softly. "I noticed Clover's mother isn't listed on her permanent record.

Clover also told my son you're at court in Boise a lot. And well, I've seen other students unable to handle a family split without counseling."

His sudden scowl had Kate stuttering. "I…ah… realize you'd probably rather not discuss the failure of your marriage with a virtual stranger, but, teachers are like doctors, or lawyers. We need to be privy to family secrets in order to help your child."

Feeling at a distinct disadvantage with Ben looming over her, larger than life, Kate snugged her wheelchair closer to the desk and sat up straight to give the appearance of being in control.

"I didn't fail," he said curtly. "At least not at marriage. I'm not married and never have been. I've been Clover's only parent since she was maybe six hours old. She was left on my doorstep, or rather, on a pile of hay in my barn, by her parents—a couple of kids I saw running out of my barn. But if you're looking to blame somebody for whatever the hell she's doing or not doing, lay it on me." Making a fist, Ben thumped his chest.

"There's no need to swear." Kate sounded heated, too. "This meeting isn't about affixing blame, Mr. Trueblood."

"Funny, it sounds like that to me, *Ms.* Steele. Why don't you just spit out what it is you want Clover to do?"

"All right." She tightened her laced fingers. "She's having great difficulty with reading. At first I thought she might have dyslexia." When he seemed shocked to silence, Kate added, "Dyslexia is where a person has problems with left versus right, or sees certain words backward. But information I located on dyslexia indicates a child would also have trouble doing math. Clover is a whiz at addition and subtraction. And her drawings aren't indicative of a directionally challenged child. It's hard to imagine that no one worried about this earlier."

"A teacher, you mean?"

Kate shrugged. "Last year she should have started reading chapter books. In fact, she recognizes only a few simple words and doesn't try to sound out others."

"After Del Sikes left, the district sent materials for homeschooling. I was pretty tied up, so mostly my trail cook looked after Clover. He knows cattle and cooking. Well, he knows a lot more than that when it comes to nature and land and what makes people tick. You could say Lou saved me and my friend Percy Lightfoot from running wild or worse." He'd begun to pace again.

"I see, I think. Well, I'll need to evaluate her to find out where she went off track. It's odd she missed learning to read, since she is proficient in math. If her problem turns out to be a more serious one, I assume the district has a psychologist who can administer those tests. It'll help, Mr. Trueblood, if *you* begin preparing her for my evaluation."

"Preparing her how?"

"Sit down with her every evening. Make Clover read to you. Make her sound out difficult words. As a parent you'll be tempted to blurt out the words, but don't do that. She has to figure them out herself."

"I'm no teacher," he said as he walked his hands

around and around the brim of his hat. "Shouldn't you be the one working with her?"

"If reading's too difficult for Clover, she's probably too embarrassed to raise her hand in class and ask me for help. I'll give you three basic storybooks to take home. When she's mastered these, here are the names of three more books I consider easy second-grade level. A library ought to have them." Kate tore out a sheet of notebook paper and jotted three titles, then stuck the page in one of the storybooks and offered them to her visitor.

Ben reluctantly took the books. "I'm already spread too thin," he said.

"Reading is vital. Surely we can agree on that."

If he responded before he spun away and strode to the door, Kate missed his words.

A strange man, she thought. *But, damn fine to look at.*

Upset at the flutter of interest that tripped through her, she stuffed the papers in a drawer. That same lazy way of moving Ben had was what had first attracted her to Colton. *Never again.* No cowboy or buckaroo—or whatever the term in the area—was going to turn her head.

Kate noted that the basketball had quit thumping the wall behind her. Through the side window she heard Trueblood's deep baritone mingled with the children's higher pitched voices.

It wasn't until she started her wheelchair motor, backed up and angled toward the window that it dawned on her—a streak of vanity had kept her from escorting Clover's father to the door.

You didn't want him to see you stuck in a wheelchair.

Kate grimaced. She would have hated seeing pity in his eyes.

As Danny's voice reached her through the open window, Kate realized he hadn't sounded this excited since they left Texas.

Handwheeling her chair to where she could see and not be seen, she discovered two things—the source of Danny's pleasure and the reason she hadn't heard the crunch of Trueblood's tires on the pumice drive. A black gelding and a small palomino mare grazed under a stand of trees. Clover and her dad had ridden horses to this meeting.

Kate wished she could hear what Trueblood was telling Danny to keep him so totally enthralled. The trio had moved again, out of Kate's range.

She didn't have long to wait for an answer, however. The father and daughter swung into their saddles and cantered off. Danny tossed his basketball in the air, caught it, then loped toward the school, a jaunty swing to his step.

"Mom, Mom!" Danny burst through the door and whirled one direction then the other, searching for Kate, who hadn't wanted him to catch her at the window.

"I'm at the cupboard taking inventory of construction paper. It won't be long before the holidays and I need to be thinking of an art project that will interest all of you kiddos. Toss that basketball in the bin with the others and we can leave. Oh, will you grab my tote? I didn't finish grading papers before Mr. Trueblood arrived."

"Mom! I'm trying to tell you something. Ben…uh, Clover's dad said I can call him that…he braided the coolest rope out of horsehair. He curries the manes and tails of his horses and sorts out strands by color. His rope looks like an old diamondback rattler. Clover's learning to braid, but she can't do patterns yet." Danny hardly took a breath between sentences.

Kate watched him dash about the room, doing what she asked. Usually she had to remind him several times. Not tonight.

"Guess what else? They do have a kind of rodeo here. They call it a Rope and Ride. Ben said all of their events are judged by Old West rules. I'm not sure what that means exactly. It's next spring. Will you take me?"

"Oh, Danny, I have no idea where they'd hold such an event."

He followed her out, his feet barely touching the ground as he waited impatiently for her to lock the door and motor down the ramp. "I can get directions. 'Cause that's the other thing. Will you take me to their ranch tomorrow? Or, I could ride Flame over. They're gonna brand calves. They're late because of a drought. Clover said we can ride washes looking for calves that got separated when they moved the herd to a winter land lease. What's a land lease, Mom?"

Kate stopped levering herself into the driver's seat. "A land lease is pasture a person can rent from the government. Although, I don't know what that has to do with this conversation. Danny Royce Steele, why on earth wouldn't you have come in and asked my permission before you made such elaborate plans?"

His chin jutted stubbornly as he connected the lift clamps to her wheelchair. "I knew if I came in and asked before they took off, you wouldn't think about it. You'd just say no. Please, Mom? All I've done since we got here is help set up the house. I did everything you asked. This will be so cool. Besides, yesterday when I talked to Mimi, she said Flame will get fat and lazy if I don't work him."

Kate couldn't ignore the change in Danny's spirits. It was like daylight from dark. Until now it hadn't really sunk in how downcast he'd truly become since the move. After talking to Ben, he looked like his old, happy self.

But letting him spend the day with cowboys made Kate's head ache. She tried again to discourage him. "Danny, I have Clover's address, but finding their ranch without a map could prove impossible on these back roads. I think you should wait."

"I know where they live. You remember the road we turned off of to find the cabin—the fork with the first red bandanna? If we'd kept on that road we'd have gone straight to the Rising Sun. That's Ben's ranch. His brand is neat-o. Clover showed me how to draw it the other day. She said Bobbalou named the ranch and drew the brand. I think it used to be his land, or something."

"Who on earth is Bobba...whatzit?" his mother asked.

"Their trail cook. His real name is Lou Bobolink, but everybody calls him Bobbalou. He's Paiute Indian. Uh, maybe Ben is, too." Danny hesitated, pondering that. "Did you see how he ties back his hair? Gosh, do you think Clover's an Indian? She said Bobbalou is sorta her pawpaw."

"The politically correct term is *Native American*, Danny. I'd say it's very likely Clover and Adam Light-foot are native. The Paiute are probably one of the local tribes."

"It doesn't matter, does it, Mom?" Danny turned toward her with a slight frown as Kate parked at their cabin. "If they're Ind...uh, what you said."

"No, honey, *that* doesn't matter." What did matter was how Ben Trueblood had invited her son to take part in branding without consulting her. That was so typical of something Colton would have done—never mind the impact it might have on others.

"So then it's okay if I go spend the day with Clover? You'll trailer Flame, huh? We hafta get up early. Clover said they start branding at five-thirty."

"A.m.?" Kate gasped, but it was drowned outby the grinding of the lift as it lowered her wheelchair.

"Yes, in the morning." Danny laughed. "That's day-break here, Mom. Pawpaw and me were out feeding his stock at daylight in Texas."

Kate squelched a sigh and handed her book bag to Danny to carry inside. She wasn't a layabout type, but this weekend she'd planned to grab an extra hour's sleep, followed by a leisurely breakfast to celebrate the successful completion of her first week on the job. "I have to give this more thought, Danny. Don't bring up the subject again until after I fix supper and we eat. I'll make a final decision after you shower, before you go to bed. Have you thought about Goldie? She'll miss you."

"She's a cow dog. I'll take her along."

"Not if you didn't clear it with Clover's father. All ranches operate differently, honey. If the Truebloods' cattle aren't used to being worked by dogs, it could even be dangerous. What if Goldie startled a rogue steer, or a not-so-nice mama cow?"

Danny dashed ahead to let out the dog from the screened back porch. The two then raced back around to the front of the house, where Kate was unlocking the door. Danny had two possibilities worked out. "If you've got Clover's phone number, I'll call and ask about bringing Goldie. Or, we can take her, and if Ben says she can't stay, you'll have company while I'm gone."

"*If* I decide in favor of your scheme, you'll be stuck with the second of your suggestions. The number I have for Clover's dad is for messages only. Also, you're forgetting I said no badgering, Danny, or it's an automatic no."

"Bro-ther!" He snapped his fingers at Goldie and the two headed for the corral. "I'm gonna exercise Flame, then feed him before supper."

Tension edged up the back of Kate's neck. If he'd asked to go anywhere else, she was sure she'd have said yes without qualm. But cows and roping? This was why she'd left Texas.

She went straight to the kitchen, turned on the oven, then pulled a premade dinner out of the fridge. Kate wished she did have a home phone number for Trueblood. She wouldn't be shy about giving him a piece of her mind. He had no right to meddle in her life—to expect a kid Danny's age to accept or decline an invitation. But maybe that's how people operated here. Clover seemed awfully independent for her age. Come to think of it, was Ben even her legal guardian? It sounded as if he'd claimed her like a pound puppy. He'd sure flared up at the mention of a failed marriage. As if someone like him never failed at anything. Still, he had to be commended—single parenting wasn't a picnic.

Kate found herself wondering why Trueblood wasn't married. But, that was counterproductive. Besides, it had nothing to do with her.

Throughout dinner of meat loaf, mashed potatoes and sliced tomatoes, Danny spoke little, but watched his mother warily.

"I'm not going to bite you if you talk," Kate finally said before serving the custard dessert. "I'm so relieved to have made it through the first week of school. But, Danny, you hear the kids' perspective. How would they rate my first week? Be honest. I know kids talk about teachers on the playground."

"Aw, Mom. It's not fair to ask me to be your snitch just 'cause we're related."

The spoon Kate was using to dip custard wavered and a blob fell on the table. She made two nervous attempts to clear the mess, but it slid off and hit the floor. Goldie trotted over, licked the spot clean and wagged her tail as if asking for more. Kate sent the dog back to her corner.

"I thought things went well," she said, pressing Danny. "Can you give me complaints without naming names? Otherwise, how will I fix the problem?"

Danny took the bowl and scooped out his own custard. "In a word, Mom, basketball."

"What about basketball? I've devoted every break and most lunch hours to helping Terry, Ron, Mike and Adam sharpen their game."

"That's the trouble. Ain't none of those guys lookin' to be the next Kobe Bryant."

"*Ain't* is not a word recognized in this house, young man." Kate sat back in her chair. "I'm being pushy, you mean?"

"Don't get mad, but…yeah."

"I thought they wanted to make the high-school varsity team."

Danny turned red to the tips of his ears. "If you let on I said this, I'm gonna be so busted. They just wanna look cool. For the girls, see?"

"Girls?" Kate felt like a parrot, but she must've missed something.

"Shelly, Meg, Mary and a couple of their friends hang around acting dorky when the guys make baskets. It's…like, so gross." He made a face as he finished his custard and shoved back from the table. "I'm going to go shower. I know I'm not s'posed to ask, but…you are still thinking about taking me to the Rising Sun Ranch?"

The pleading in his eyes, mixed with an emotion that said he wasn't holding out much hope, made the decision for Kate. She gently pushed back the lock of blond hair that drooped over his right eye. "It'll be lonely here all day without you, sport. But, I need to prove I can get along on my own. I guess tomorrow will be a good test."

"Really? Yippee!" He hugged the stuffing out of her, then danced around until his shouting and Goldie's barking had Kate calling a halt.

KATE SET HER ALARM for four o'clock. Even so, Danny was up before her. She heard him outside hooking Flame's trailer to the pickup. As she stifled a yawn, an image of Ben Trueblood's handsome face came to mind. She didn't want to feel this squiggly anticipation in her stomach at the prospect of seeing him today, but it was there.

Because she cared about the impression she made in the community, she took pains to use a curling iron on her broomstick-straight hair. She added a touch of color to her lips so she wouldn't looked washed out in the red blouse she teamed with jeans. *Not that she planned to get out of the pickup.*

"Mom!" Danny slammed the front door and thundered down the hall. "Aren't you up yet? I need something for breakfast."

"And a lunch," Kate said, meeting him and Goldie in the hall. She hoped Danny wouldn't notice or comment on her makeup. As a rule she didn't wear any.

"Clover said Bobbalou cooks biscuits, corn and meat or beans at lunch. All the buckaroos eat in shifts around a fire pit. It sounds like they do that all the time, not just at roundup like at Pawpaw's."

"I doubt they eat outside *all* the time, Danny. Mrs. Goetz said winters can be severe on this high plateau. Which reminds me, we need to find the box with our jackets and gloves."

"Uh-huh, they live with the herd all the time," Danny insisted.

Kate didn't argue further. Frankly, it was too early. "How does toast, juice and instant oatmeal grab you?"

"Fine, can we just hurry? I already loaded Flame."

They ate quickly and on the drive over Danny talked nonstop about all of the things Clover had told him about the Rising Sun Ranch.

As Danny had said, the road ended at an iron arch with a replica of their brand. A half-sun with twisted wrought-iron rays. The house was tucked deep in a grove of pines, a long, low structure made of logs. As houses went, it was fairly plain. Kate imagined how it would look with baskets of hanging geraniums above the split-rail porch, or beds of blooms along the winding walkway.

She followed the road to where it dipped over a knoll, and took in the seeming chaos beyond the house. Three stock trucks were being loaded with bawling steers. Men on horseback swung ropes to cut certain calves out for branding at a smoking, portable forge.

Danny bounced excitedly on the seat. "Drive down there, Mom. I wanna watch those guys rope calves. Wow, they never miss." He hauled his rope from under the seat. Goldie positioned her front paws on Danny's knees and yapped, clearly as eager as Danny to join in the fray.

"Honey, it looks like a madhouse. Leave Goldie with me while you go find Clover and her dad to ask if it's okay for Goldie to stay."

"There's Clover." Danny spotted the girl riding the same palomino as yesterday, only without a saddle. He climbed out of the pickup and ran to meet Clover. The little mare was fast and the girl was glued to her back. The scene put Kate in mind of the erratic years she'd spent following Colton from rodeo to rodeo. Her stomach knotted. The memories were not happy ones.

AT THE FLAMING FORGE, one of Ben's crew called his attention to a pickup and horse trailer idling on the slope above them. "Who's the pretty woman, boss?"

Ben turned in his saddle to see who Justin Padilla meant. "What the hell? That's Clover's teacher."

Padilla whistled through his teeth and cocked his flat-crowned hat to block the sun coming up behind the woman's rig. "I might've stayed in school past tenth grade if my teacher had looked like that," said the lanky buckaroo. "Bobbalou mentioned you had a conference yesterday. You must've made quite an impression."

Scowling, Ben nudged his gelding with the blunt flower rowel of his left spur. They were a signature buckaroo piece, but a spur that didn't hurt a horse.

He could have done without Justin, Zach Robles, his stock manager, and Enrique Quijada falling in to accompany him. Women were so scarce out on the range that a buckaroo crew could all spot a pretty one a mile away. Ben's entire crew was single and loved the freewheeling life, even though they knew it was disappearing. To a man, they spoke of finding wives one day and settling down. Even Ben, at times, grew weary of the constant battle to save the land.

Just now he considered ordering his men back to their jobs, but that would've caused more ribbing and speculation.

Kate had her window rolled down, enjoying the warmth of the morning sun on her face as she surveyed the rugged beauty of the landscape. The clatter of approaching hoof beats pulled her attention away from lavender hills. The sight of four big men on horses bearing down on her had Kate grabbing Goldie's collar with one hand and drawing her arm inside the pickup.

The retriever lunged across her lap, but Kate maintained a firm grip.

Controlling his uphill gallop, Ben stopped short of the vehicle. He tipped his hat, but didn't remove it as his men did. "Are you lost, Ms. Steele?" He leaned a brown forearm across a sheepskin-wrapped saddle horn. Belatedly, he introduced his crew.

Kate ducked around the still-growling dog. "I brought Danny over to help. Well, it's debatable how much help he'll be." She couldn't suppress a smile, then noticed there was no sign of recognition on Ben's face. "Uh…wait…you did invite him to chase strays today, didn't you?"

Another set of hooves clattered up the trail, now blocked by three foolishly grinning males. The way they didn't take their eyes off her made Kate nervous. Clover nudged her mare through the crowd. Danny, riding behind her, slid off over the palomino's rump when the girl stopped.

"Mom? What's up?" he asked, his face a mask.

"Suppose you tell me, Danny. Did you not lead me to believe that Clover's father expected you here at sunup?"

His face fell and he hung his head.

The men guessed at the situation and clustered around the boy. "Ma'am, that would probably be Miss Clover's doing," said the burliest of the riders. He was also the one closest to Clover, and playfully slapped her backside with his hat.

"Ben, you said Danny could come ride with me one of these days," Clover protested. "What's wrong with today? He doesn't need a cavvy horse, 'cause he has his own. His daddy used to win rodeo buckles."

"How many?" asked the youngest buckaroo. "Hard to win more events than the boss has."

Kate's heart dived. Colton's mom shone his trophies and buckles weekly. Danny viewed them as the measure of a real man. And now, here was another... Mentally she withdrew and let the conversation flow around her. She heard Danny declare his dad was Colton Steele, and the men acted suitably impressed. Except for Ben.

"Clover, I don't hold with stretching the truth to suit your fancy," he said. "I ought to send you home and send your friend packing."

Kate couldn't have agreed more, except that Danny was fighting to hold back tears. And, darn it, her son shouldn't have his day ruined through no fault of his own. Her mother's instincts burned hotly. "Is that open for negotiation?" she said, shading her eyes.

The question gained her a closer inspection from Ben's hooded dark eyes. The look sent hot prickles up Kate's back.

"Justin, Zach, Enrique, quit ogling Clover's teacher and go load that second stock truck," Ben snapped.

"Look who's ogling," Zach Robles grumbled. But they tipped their hats to Kate and prepared to go. Only Justin rode right up to her window. "If you ever need anything done that takes more muscle than you or the boy have, sing out. Here's our radio-phone number. Bobbalou keeps it in the chuck wagon, but we're never far away. Won't take but a few hours to mosey out your way, ma'am."

Not to be outdone, Zach and Enrique underscored Justin's offer.

As the last of his men finally rode off, Ben all but had steam coming out his ears. "What kind of negotiations? I wouldn't have expected a teacher to condone Clover's behavior."

"It's your call, of course, but Danny and I did get up with the chickens to come here, false pretext or not. Maybe I'd be less testy if I hadn't missed my morning coffee."

"What the hell," Ben muttered. "Unload his horse. The kids can go search washes for strays. Leave your rig here. I'll show you where to find Bobbalou's chuck wagon. He keeps a coffeepot hot all day."

Clover slid off the palomino and gazed up at her dad. "You'd better bring Ms. Kate's coffee up here, Ben."

"Do I look like a waiter?"

Clover stabbed a finger toward the Chevy's roof

where Kate's wheelchair was usually connected to the hydraulic lift.

Ben nudged his hat back, but still had no idea what he was looking at.

Kate mentally cringed. She knew it was inevitable he learn of her disability, but she'd purposely left her wheelchair back in her driveway to await her return. Caught now by such vanity, she waited for the pity that was sure to follow.

"Is that some kind of newfangled winch?" Ben wrapped his gelding's reins tighter around his wrist as he studied the apparatus.

Clover punched his chap-covered leg. "It lifts Teacher's wheelchair on and off the pickup. Oh, but your chair is gone, Ms. Kate. Did it fall off on the way here?"

All the pity Kate had wanted to avoid rained down on her from Ben's horrified expression. Instantly, she was back to feeling less than competent and her reaction was more curt than the situation warranted. "I don't need backhanded hospitality, or your coffee or pity, Mr. Trueblood. I'll be on my way as soon as Danny unloads Flame."

Picking up on her tone, Goldie planted her feet in Kate's lap and growled and barked at the man reining in his shifting horse. With some effort, Kate boosted Goldie into the backseat, before adding through gritted teeth, "All I need is a promise that a responsible adult will see to it my son and his horse get home safely."

"We can work that out." Ben sounded as brusque as Kate had. "I offered coffee with Bobbalou to be polite.

I can't waste time socializing if that's what you thought. I have calves to brand and steers to get to market. I meant no pity, but I'm sorry I didn't know what that contraption was." Back stiff, Ben walked his horse a few yards down the trail then set off at a gallop and never looked back.

Danny backed Flame down the ramp. He handed the reins to Clover and they shared a mystified glance before he secured the tailgate.

Kate felt guilty for sounding shrewish, but she'd been stung. Call it pity or sympathy, what she'd seen in the man's eyes magnified her physical limitations. And she'd be damned if she'd let him put himself out for her. "Danny, I've changed my mind. Be at the arch at five o'clock sharp. I'll return for you and Flame. Clover, tell your dad he won't lose any work hours on our account."

"Aren't you gonna leave Goldie?" her son hollered to be heard over the grind of the truck's shifting gears.

She was, oh, so tempted. Goldie did not like the owner of this ranch. And she should thank Trueblood for reminding her the feeling was mutual and extended to Kate. He wasn't interested in being neighborly, and it was fine and dandy with her. Maybe after today Danny would recognize that Clover's dad and other buckaroo types weren't men worth emulating. "I'm taking Goldie."

"She can stay next time," Clover consoled Danny.

Kate nodded. But under her breath, covered by the noise of a revving engine, she said, "There won't be a next time if I have anything to say about it."

Still ticked, she drove the big pickup and trailer under the arch. With any luck, she would get through the school year without another face-to-face encounter with Ben Trueblood.

CHAPTER FOUR

BEN DISMOUNTED ON THE FAR SIDE of the forge. Partially concealed by smoke, he was able to observe the departure of Clover's teacher in relative obscurity.

His first impression of Kate Steele had been that of a more fragile woman than her name implied. Today as he watched her turn her big pickup and horse trailer around on a dime and gun it up the road, she earned his grudging respect. He felt like a damned idiot for not figuring out what the device atop her vehicle was for. School board members, of whom he was one, had left it up to Marge Goetz to vet candidates for the job. True, they hadn't had a stampede for the post. Still, what had Marge been thinking? And Clover? She should've told him.

The teacher was long gone before Ben found an opportunity to manage a word with Clover apart from Danny Steele.

"That scene this morning with your teacher was bad. I can't believe you didn't tell me about her condition the day we rode to school for my meeting with her."

"What's her con-dition?" Clover slid out of her saddle and squinted up at her dad, all the while edging toward the chuck wagon.

Danny had ridden into sight and it was obvious Clover would rather join him than make time for this conversation.

"I'm referring to her not being able to walk and having to use a wheelchair to get around."

"Oh. I guess I didn't think it mattered."

"It sure does. We…the school board, well, I probably wouldn't have donated our line shack as a place for her to live if I'd known she couldn't walk."

"Why? Danny said his mom loves the cabin."

"That's not the point."

"Can I go? Justin assigned Danny and me this lunchtime, and we're both hungry as bears and thirsty. We've been running washes and it's hot."

It was hot at the forge, too. Ben wiped sweat off his forehead with his shirtsleeve. "Go on. It's not you I should be talking to about the liability that woman could turn out to be for our town."

"You're using big words. What's a li…lib'l…that word you said?"

"*Liability* is a big problem, Clover."

Having started to mount her horse, the girl dropped back to the ground and glared at Ben. "Take that back! Ms. Kate's not a problem. She's the smartest, most beautiful woman in the whole world."

Removing his hat, Ben slapped it against his hip until dust flew. He knew some of the crew heard Clover's raised voice. Zach quit what he was doing to listen. Lately Ben had butted heads with Clover in private, which suited him because he was a private man. Marge Goetz would say he shouldn't let Clover talk back. But kids were entitled to an opinion. It just took him by surprise that she'd developed such strong sentiments for the woman in only a week.

Too far away to hear the heated exchange, Danny hailed Clover from the chuck wagon. She acknowledged his wave, but before she joined him, she lowered her stubborn chin and idly dug her boot toe in a pile of cinders someone had dumped out of the forge. Almost shyly, it seemed to Ben, she said, "My teacher smells better than anybody and she wears pretty blouses and long skirts. I wish I looked like her."

Surprised at such a thought coming from his little tomboy, Ben could only stand slack jawed as she mounted her horse in a flying leap and galloped the short distance to where the teacher's son waited.

Ben wished he could say he hadn't noticed how good Clover's teacher smelled. The other day as he'd entered the schoolhouse for his meeting, he'd picked up on the usual wood oil, chalk and disinfectant—until he'd walked up to Ms. Steele's desk and had been rocked by the seductive scent of cedar and cinnamon. It had hit him like a one-two punch.

Worried as he'd been that day, he hadn't been able to turn off that portion of his brain. The same thing had happened again this morning when that arousing scent had drifted through her open window and it had had the same effect on his anatomy. *Dang.*

Ben knew that was part of the reason why he'd been pissed at Zach and Justin's blatant flirting with the teacher. Hell, he shouldn't—didn't—care who flirted with Kate Steele. He and she had nothing in common. They were as different as two people could be.

And none of that had anything to do with why the school board that had hired her should now try to replace her before they ended up with a lawsuit on their hands.

He waited until all three shifts of his crew had eaten lunch before he rode to the chuck wagon and rang Marge Goetz on the radio-phone. "Marge, it's Ben. I'll get right to the point of my call. When you offered Kate Steele our teaching post, did you know she was dependent on a wheelchair?"

"No. But even if I had, it wouldn't have mattered."

"It should have. That cabin has no handicap amenities."

"Has Kate complained? When she and I met, she sounded fine with living there."

"No, she hasn't complained, but…"

"Then don't go hunting trouble, Ben. The kids like her. That counts most. Listen, Ray just honked to let me know he's ready to drive to town for groceries. If we need to vote on adding handrails or something inside the cabin, bring it up at the next meeting. We'll see if we can afford to have Chad Keevler spruce it up."

Ben was left staring at a dead phone. Obviously Marge didn't understand the urgency. The board only met quarterly. And he thought they still owed Chad for the electrical and plumbing he'd done to add a real kitchen to the cabin.

Next Ben called Percy Lightfoot, a fellow rancher, good friend and third board member. "Percy, Ben. I just learned the teacher we hired uses a wheelchair. I phoned Marge, but she was in a rush to get to town. I'm not sure I made clear to her the pickle we could be in if Kate…uh…Ms. Steele gets hurt at the cabin or at school. The district will be liable. At either place she's twenty miles from our physician's assistant. Say she's seriously hurt, we all know Nate Ramsey's only connected to hospital doctors in Boise via satellite."

"Yeah, so? It's the same for any of us who live here. Anyway, Adam said she stands to write on the blackboard."

"She can stand? Hmm, I was thinking maybe we should cancel her contract. So, is her condition temporary?" Ben asked the question around a fried chicken leg he'd helped himself to. He rarely broke for lunch, but the chuck wagon was filled with tempting smells.

"Beats me, Ben. We can't cancel her contract. She's protected by the Federal Disability Act. Wait, Della Quimby's here helping Winnie can the last fall peaches. The women are saying Ms. Kate is teaching the boys a lot of new basketball plays."

"Basketball? How in the world—"

"Don't know. And don't care. You won't get my vote to fire her. I guess you've forgotten how we couldn't find a teacher for love nor money after Sikes's reserve unit got called up. And if memory serves, Marge didn't exactly have a cast of thousands to choose from. We were down to the wire, Ben."

Jarred by guilt, Ben mumbled that he wasn't suggesting they fire her—which of course was precisely his intention. "If we're stuck with her, maybe board members need to consider looking after her more. With winter around the corner, she'll need firewood hauled. If she doesn't have snow tires, or has never driven in drifts, someone had better volunteer to deliver her supplies."

Ben heard his friend talking to his wife and Della. The sound of steam hissing from one or more canners drowned out what the women were saying in the background. Ben tossed his chicken bone in the trash and wiped his hands on the blue bandanna tied around his neck. The scarf often did triple duty, but mostly served to keep him from choking on trail dust the times he went out with his buckaroos.

Percy came back on the line. "The women say you've got a dandy plan. I've never met Adam's teacher, mind you, but Winnie and Della overheard kids saying she's pretty. Now, Ben, since you live closest and as you're the only bachelor on the board, the women hereby volunteer you to watch out for Ms. Kate. You or your men. I'll bet Justin Padilla would trip all over his boots for a chance to help a good-lookin' woman."

Sputtering through Percy's braying laughter, Ben couldn't believe his friend would toss him to the wolves and then hang up. But, he did.

Jamming the receiver back into the box, Ben scrubbed both hands over his face. He heard a snicker and peered through his fingers to see his cook and longtime mentor, Lou Bobolink, standing there scratching his chin. "You got women trouble, Ben? Hallelujah! Never thought I'd see the day."

"Very funny, you old coot. It's not the kind of trouble you're thinking. I got chasing skirts out of my system years ago. This has to do with Clover's new teacher. We've had a couple of clashes and, dang it, now Della Quimby and Percy and Winnie think I'm the board member who's gotta make nice with her."

Eyes that held the wisdom of seventy-one years studied Ben closely. "You should tell the teacher the truth, Ben. We both know what's really bugging you. Clover told me many times you put off meeting with the woman."

Ben swung out of the creaky wagon and landed on the ground. "What I'm going to do is advertise in the area paper again for a tutor for Clover."

The old man followed his younger friend's vault to the ground, his nearly white plait of hair slapping his back as he landed and his knees gave way. Ben sprang forward to keep him from falling. "Dammit, Bobbalou, all we need is for you to break a damn leg. Then I'd have to give up land advocacy work and fill in as camp cook."

"Quit using my old bones as an excuse to change the subject. I told you the day would come when—"

Ben cut in. "I need to hire someone to spend a couple of hours a day with Clover."

"You tried that when Sikes stopped by to suggest Clover might need remedial classes and you got all huffy. You can't pay a qualified person enough to drive out here four or five days a week for a couple of hours a day. Unless maybe you ask the new teacher if she'd like to earn extra cash. She might consider it."

"I can't do that, Bobbalou. She thinks I should sit

down every night with Clover. She sent books home and a list for more from the library. The woman's got no sense and she's clueless about what life's like here. Uh…do you suppose Jock Dewey at the paper down-river kept a copy of the ad I ran last winter?"

"Last time you ran the ad you didn't get a single taker. Have you heard of anyone new moving into these parts 'cept the teacher and her boy? He's a nice kid, by the way. Was real mannerly at lunch. I figure that's his mother's doing. You got any idea where the mister in the family is?"

"Dead. Marge reported to the board by phone that she'd offered our job to a widow from Texas who had a ten-year-old son. Teacher didn't ask us to foot the bill for relocating her. I wonder why she left Fort Worth. Big cattle country. Her son said his granddad owns a spread. I know the boy is keen on competition roping. Boy asked if we have a junior venue. His dad made a name in bronc riding. I figure that's why Clover invited him here today. She wants someone from Owyhee to beat those Jordan Valley ropers. But she's in the doghouse with me because she didn't ask me first."

"So I guess that's why you're making the boy's mom drive over here again at five o'clock to pick him up."

"What are you talking about? I told her we'd see Danny gets home. I said it even before I found out she's disabled. Which brings up another thing, did Danny happen to say if she's always been lame, or did she have surgery and the chair's temporary?"

"Kid didn't say. All I know is I heard Zach and Enrique talking about the hydraulic lift she's got on her pickup. How much do you suppose that cost? Don't imagine it's cheap enough to use awhile and then discard."

"You're probably right." Ben removed his hat and jockeyed it to a better angle as he stared off toward the cabin, which now served as Kate Steele's home. "You've gotta hand it to her, Bobbalou. Takes guts for a woman in her fix to drive a big dually for a thousand miles, pulling a horse trailer. She must have left family behind to take a job sight unseen. I'll bet few women would have the fortitude to do that."

"Yeah," Bobbalou drawled. "Guts and pretty blond hair is a package Zach, Justin and Enrique like, all right. Ya know, Ben, seeing how you're too busy to take on those extra chores you say Percy thinks you should do, pawn them off on the crew."

"Oh, like she'd thank me for siccing lovesick bucka-roos on her."

"What do you care? You don't even like her."

Stalking to his gelding, Ben cinched the saddle tight. "I don't remember saying I didn't like her."

"Humpf! It's plain she's got you running scared as a jackrabbit in tall grass."

"And you know why," Ben flared.

"I do at that. So, when are you gonna do something about that, Ben?"

"Right now. I'm asking Jock to rerun that ad for a tutor." He climbed back in the wagon and made the call. Crawling out again, he wound the reins around one hand and led the gelding away. His old friend grabbed Ben's elbow.

"Some things you can't outrun. For years you've said you'll make time. When, Ben?"

"I don't know. I hope by Christmas the BLM will have completed the resource management study. The judge gave ranchers a reprieve by refusing to revoke land leases like the watershed project conservationists demanded in their lawsuit. Things got tougher at the last hearing when they teamed up with lawyers paid by rec-reational land grabbers. Every time I think we're gain-ing, they turn up another endangered species. As of last week, three rivers crucial for watering our herds are being scrutinized as possible scenic river designations. You know I didn't raise my hand to represent ranchers' interests in this fight. If I fail, my hassle with Clover's teacher won't matter. She'll be out of a job. We'll all be moving on and Owyhee will become another ghost town."

"All the more reason for Clover to learn good now."

"Yeah, well, I feel squeezed in all directions, and you're not helping."

"I can't help, only you can, Ben. What's the worst that'll happen if you spill everything to this teacher?"

"I'll tell you. Expose a chink in my armor and law-yers for the opposition will steamroll every ranch left in this valley. I tried my best to let someone else, anyone else, to take on the state. No one did. I've got no choice except to muscle this through. You know it's a constant struggle."

Lou let his hand drop. "Who would've thought

wrangling over grazing on public lands would take years, not months? When this argument hit, you were carrying Clover around in a sling. Then the most important thing was to keep her fed and dry. This problem she's having in school is a horse of a different color. I failed you, but the minute I set eyes on her, I vowed I…we'd do better by that little girl."

"We have. She's never known poverty. She's never been ignored, or worse, by a half-crazed alcoholic teenage mom. You didn't fail me, and Clover will be fine. Jock's running my ad for two weeks. I'll knock off early today, escort Danny home, then I'll go see Vida. Maybe she can spare an extra day a week. I need to ask if she sews, too. Of all things, Clover wants some skirts and blouses."

Bobbalou's wrinkled face split in a grin. "It was a matter of time. She is a girl."

"I know that. But she's never had an interest in dressing like one…until today. She hit me with wanting to look pretty like her teacher."

"Instead of asking Vida's advice, you should talk to the teacher. Vida must be ninety if she's a day. What does she know of frilly duds?"

"She's in her late sixties. Younger than you."

"Well, she dresses like an old fuddy-duddy. Mark my words, Clover's not gonna want to wear anything Vida sews up. She'll probably use gunny sacks."

Ben started to respond, but his attention was drawn to rapid hoof beats mixed with the excited voices of children. Clover and Danny drove two mangy cows and three half-grown calves into a holding pen his buckaroos had just emptied. "Would you look at that," Ben said with pride. "Those little rascals flushed out some calves we missed."

"Look how red their faces are. Better take them water before they get heat stroke and then you're left to explain to that boy's mama."

Ben waved the two junior calf hunters over to the chuck wagon. "You did good, princess," he called. "Where were those fellows hiding?"

Clover jerked a thumb toward Danny. "He spotted them way down in Cedar Draw. I said no way—weren't any cows in that brush. Danny was right and I was wrong."

Ben handed them each a dipper full of water. "Drink slow," he cautioned Danny, who grabbed the ladle and was swigging water down.

"It tastes good."

"I know, but you don't want to down cold water too fast when you're overheated. You're likely to upchuck all over."

"What about our horses?" the boy asked. "It was a long climb driving those pesky cows from the canyon to the pen."

"Good man, thinking of your horse." Ben poured a bit of water into an oak bucket and passed it to Danny, who'd puffed up a full shirt size at Ben's praise.

"You've both done a fine day's work. I say we cool your horses out on a leisurely ride back to your place, Danny."

"But Mom's coming to get me. She said for me to wait out at your arch."

"She did say that," Clover put in. "I don't think she was happy with you, Ben. She said you shouldn't lose any work on account of her and Danny. I forgot to tell you till now."

Ben recalled how pissy he'd acted and couldn't blame Danny's mother for striking back. He glanced at the boy. "Has anyone from the phone company been out to hook up your cabin phone?"

"No, and I talked to Pawpaw and Mimi so long the other night I killed Mom's cell phone. She said we hafta go without one until she finds time to drive to town. Maybe she went today."

"Only two phone men in town," Bobbalou said. "And they take weekends off."

"A woman and boy alone need a phone." Ben swung up on his horse. "Mount up, kids. There's only one road a vehicle can travel from there to here. We'll set out now. With luck we'll get there before she leaves. I may as well see if I can figure out what's up with your phone."

Ben set off to let his crew know he was leaving the ranch. When he returned, he heard Danny say, "I hope we beat Mom. I wanna see just how far it is. Justin said he'll teach me soft-loop roping next Wednesday. I know Mom won't bring me. If it's not too far, I'll come by myself."

Ben shook his head. "It's not that our ranch is so far from your cabin, Danny, but I wouldn't let Clover make that trip alone."

"I could," she said staunchly.

"No."

Ben's voice was sharp enough for Danny to ask "Why not?"

"It's off the beaten path for one reason. For another, this is rattlesnake season. It's cooling down. Snakes come out to sun themselves. Your horse may unexpectedly startle one and the road's not good. Gopher holes. I've seen a horse step in one, throw his rider and the horse runs off. Clover, we've talked about why smart buckaroos travel in pairs when trailing a herd."

"But Danny needs practice with roping. They don't have any calves at his house."

The boy laughed. "There's Goldie. But Mom would throw a fit if I practiced roping her."

Ben's eyes constantly searched the roadbed for the dangers he spoke of. "Why wouldn't your mom bring you Wednesday? She did today."

"Yeah, but she doesn't like me roping."

Although he was curious, Ben didn't want to pry. Clover had no such compunction. "Why not, Danny, if your dad won lots of rodeo events?"

"I dunno. I know Mom yelled at my grandma. Mom said there's more to life than winning trophies. Later, Mimi, that's what I call my gram…she said it's why Mom made us move, so I won't be near rodeos. I qualified for the Little Britches Rodeo this year. It's after Thanksgiving. Mimi's gonna ask Mom if I can fly to Texas. Fat chance. Mom won't even let Mimi buy me a cool new roping saddle for my birthday."

Ben figured there was more going on in the Steele family than just a disagreement over rodeos. The yearning in Danny's voice triggered his own memories. At

Danny's age, Ben had longed to get off the reservation. His mom had been like an albatross holding him back. Then she'd died, and for a while Ben had gone wild and had done exactly as he'd pleased.

All Danny wanted was to compete in calf roping. If Ben was on better terms with Kate Steele, he'd be tempted to tell her it was better to loosen the reins on a boy. Time together was precious and often too short.

"Hey, there's our cabin," Danny announced, pointing as he urged Flame into a fast trot. "We don't live far from your ranch at all," he said excitedly. "I'll bet it's shorter going over that hill." He pointed.

"Is it?" Clover asked her dad.

"It would be if not for the river. Remember crossing the bridge? The banks holding that river in are steep. And downstream five or so miles the river dumps over Antler Ridge Falls."

"I've seen the falls from below. Bobbalou said it almost dried up during the drought," Clover informed Danny.

Kate rolled out onto the porch as the three trotted their horses into the small clearing. Goldie streaked out to greet Danny, who flung himself off Flame. Boy and dog wrestled goofily in dirt and pine needles.

"I was just getting ready to come after Danny." Her eyes rose in apology to the man atop the dancing black horse.

The kids both chased after Goldie.

"Bringing him home was no trouble." Ben's wandering gaze traveled over Kate's disheveled hair. "The kids worked hard flushing strays. I didn't want them to overdo it. We would've called to tell you, but Danny said your cell conked out and no one's been out to connect the house line."

"I meant to see about that today. I got busy after I dropped Danny off and, well, the day just flew."

"I'll take a look at the phone if you'd like." He looped his reins around his saddle horn and lazily surveyed the cabin. "Chad Keevler made a lot of improvements since I used to bunk here. This was just a two-room shack with plank floors. I've gotta say, those curtains you hung at the windows civilize the place. Gives it a homey feel."

He couldn't have said anything to please Kate more. She'd waited so long for a place of her own. A year after marrying Colton, about the time she'd found out she was pregnant, she'd been teaching in Mesquite near the rodeo grounds where her husband had often performed. A fellow teacher had had a small house to sell. Kate had phoned Colton, excited about the baby and the house. His response? "We're not wasting our money, babe. First, you're gonna quit that crummy job and travel with me. I'm entering more events. If we've got any down time between rodeos, we'll bunk with my folks."

Kate should have left then, but she'd thought that after she had the baby, Colton would see how hard it was to take a child on the road and he'd change, settle down. But that hadn't happened.

Goldie barked, bringing Kate's thoughts back to the present. She gestured toward the door. "I've spent all day assembling the furniture I bought in Fort Worth.

Would you like to come in and see what a difference a little furniture makes?"

She sounded so eager to show off her handiwork, how could Ben refuse? He removed his hat and peered inside, unsure what to expect. He wasn't one to neighbor a lot.

"I'll have a look-see, but I'm no authority." Cupping his hands to his mouth, Ben called to his daughter. "Clover, I'm going inside to check your teacher's phone. Stay close, I won't be long."

Kate let him pass then she stretched behind her to close the screen door.

Feeling awkward, Ben wasn't sure if he ought to reach over her to help. She managed okay, but he'd noticed the smaller front wheels of her wheelchair hadn't crossed the threshold easily. Still, she hadn't made an issue out of backing up a few inches to try again.

It wouldn't take much to fix the problem of the threshold. Ben ran a nervous hand through his hair. But she hadn't asked for help, he reminded himself.

She passed him the dead phone. "Have a seat if you'd like. Ignore the empty boxes and tools. I'll have Danny help clean up. I'm not sure when trash pickup is. I should've asked Marge Goetz. Or, you probably know." Kate wondered why he didn't come into the light to fiddle with her phone.

"Only town folks have trash collection. Out here we load our refuse every couple of weeks and run to the county landfill." He handed back the phone. "You can probably add that to the trash. It's a goner." As he advanced farther into the room, Ben's attention was claimed by a wood-framed three-cushion futon and smaller matching one. Then he crossed over to a pair of bookcases that leaned drunkenly. Their top shelves lay on an equally lopsided coffee table.

Noticing his frown, Kate felt her joy at having tackled a difficult project fizzle. "I don't know what I was thinking, inviting you in to see what must look like a mess to you." Irritated at herself, she started to wheel around him and open the door again.

He stuck a hand out, stopping her. "Look, you've got it wrong. What I am is amazed at what you've accomplished. To tell you the truth, I've never met anyone… uh…who has to use a wheelchair. I'm afraid of saying the wrong thing, or, you know, stepping on your toes. Oh, hell!" Ben shut his eyes and pinched the bridge of his nose. "I even goofed with that."

Kate laughed. "You're refreshingly honest, which is more than my in-laws ever were. My mother-in-law refused to see I could be anything but an invalid."

"But you need extra assistance with some stuff." He wiggled the bookcase.

"You've got no idea how maddening that can be. But, yes. Those damned bookcases outfoxed me. I see now I should've bought four two-shelf cases instead of two four-shelf ones. I'll need Danny to set them against the wall and to install and fill the top shelves."

Her frustration was palpable. Ben knew that feeling and it was on the tip of his tongue to confess about his own shortcoming that Bobbalou had needled him about earlier.

The moment passed when Kate slammed a hand down on the wobbly coffee table and said unhappily, "I had so much trouble assembling this piece I stripped the threads on a bolt. I can't fix it and the company didn't include extra parts."

"I keep a canister of spare screws and nuts and bolts in the barn. Next time I'm over this way I'll drop one off. Mind if I check the size screw you need?"

"Oh, please. I'd hate the table to collapse if I ever have company."

He knelt to examine the table, placing him at Kate's level, and she was so surprised by the zing of awareness racing through her that she backed up.

Ben's work shirt pulled tight across his broad shoulders and his hands were well-shaped and sure as he felt along the wood.

Kate tugged at the snug neck of her blouse, refusing to admit it was the man hunkered at her feet who was to blame for her sudden hot spell.

"It looks like two bad bolts," he said, pushing erect again. Immediately he stepped around her and crossed to test the durability of the bookcases. "What you've done here is solid. If you care to let me know what height to put the top shelves, I'll screw the runners in place."

"I hate to impose. I know cowboys don't like to do anything that doesn't involve a horse or cow."

"That's true of a straight-up buckaroo. My life changed drastically once I had Clover to care for. I learned to do a lot of things I'd never done before. Change diapers, for one."

"Weren't there ways to find the baby's mother? Surely the law…"

"I saw her. She and the boy made enough noise to be sure I did. I first thought they were stealing equipment to pawn for booze. I know all about that. I lived on the res as a kid. No one objected to my petition to adopt a baby—everyone knew she'd be better off with me. Bobbalou named her for the clover hay the kids bunched around her."

Kate listened to his matter-of-fact explanation. "You're some special man," she said softly. "I've known a lot of cowboys. I can't think of one who would have kept a baby for love or money."

"I understood your husband was a cowboy."

"A rodeo cowboy. Yes, he was."

"Danny never said how his dad died. I'll guess he got throwed."

"Thrown," she corrected automatically. "But it wasn't a horse that killed my husband." She was quiet a moment, as if thinking back in time. "I should have said no to traipsing from rodeo to rodeo, three people crammed in a dinky trailer. My husband thrived on the adulation, though, and our marriage was soon… troubled. Colton accused me of being jealous of the buckle bunnies, but it wasn't just them. The day of the accident it poured, canceling the rodeo. We got into an argument over Colton accepting money from his folks for Danny to take roping lessons. He wasn't quite eight."

Kate sighed. "The argument ended when I had to take Danny to his lesson. When I got back to the trailer,

Colton was entertaining one of his latest admirers, who seemed to get younger at each rodeo. I should've walked out." She shrugged. "I…just blew up. It was ugly. His groupie fled, and we yelled at each other. I was mad, so was he. With that much rain, he shouldn't have hooked up the trailer and horses, but he was hell-bent on making the next rodeo in Oklahoma. I refused to fight around Danny, and once we picked him up, Colton clammed up, too. But we both knew our marriage was over."

"I'm guessing, the weather caused you to wreck."

Kate nodded slowly. "I took refuge in sleep, and Colton was too angry to wake me when it was my turn to drive. I have no idea how we landed upside down in a ravine. Thankfully, Danny and Goldie were asleep in the back of the Suburban we owned then. I woke up to screams, feeling like Alice falling down the rabbit hole. My own screams. Danny's. The horses. Both had to be put down. I smelled burning rubber, and when I next came to, I was in a rural Oklahoma hospital with my in-laws sobbing over me. They said troopers didn't know how I got Danny and Goldie out. They said Colton mercifully died instantly."

Kate gazed blankly at Ben. "Is death at thirty-two ever merciful? We would have divorced. I… His parents don't know that. But even if I never walk again, I got off easy."

Ben sensed the guilt she'd heaped on herself. Clearly, the mood in the room had shifted. It was probably best if he left. "The school board wasn't aware you had special needs, Ms. Steele."

"Please, call me Kate. I hope people notice I'm trying real hard not to have any special needs."

"Kate, then, and I'm Ben." He cleared his throat. "I'm on the board. Some of us have concerns about the makeshift ramps you've set up here and at school. Come the first snow you'll need a rail along with covered parking, or your hydraulic lift will freeze. We have to make a wish list. My ranch is closest, so I guess that's why the…ah…others elected me to help out. Next time I'm in town, I'll pick up a working cell phone and have your house line connected."

She read determination on his face. Capitulating with a graceful shrug, she said, "I'll accept help in those areas. But I don't like not giving you anything in return."

As she hung the suggestion out there, it crossed Ben's mind to seize the opportunity to say he'd trade her if she'd tutor Clover. But pride kept the words from spilling out. And the longer the silence stretched, the more uncomfortable they both were.

"Well," he said at last, "I need to round up Clover and head home." On his way to the door he gathered her boxes. "I'll stack these on the porch. When I find those bolts, I'll load the cardboard in my pickup to take to the dump."

"I…uh…thank you. At least let me fix you and Clover supper tonight. It's getting late and, really, I'm a good cook. A meal is little enough in exchange for all you've proposed."

Ben's first inclination was to bolt. The eagerness in her voice starkly contrasted with the lingering sadness in her eyes. That made him reconsider, even though good sense told him it was probably a mistake.

"Ma'am, no buckaroo worth the name would turn down a home-cooked meal."

Kate relaxed and smiled. "*Ma'am* is worse than calling me Ms. Steele. Keep it up, cowboy, and you may find red pepper in your pie."

"Not cowboy…a buckaroo. Over supper I'll explain the difference."

CHAPTER FIVE

THE KIDS WERE HAPPY WHEN they heard Clover and Ben were invited to stay for supper. Clover danced around on tiptoes. "I'll help, Ms. Kate. What can I do?"

"I have two roasting hens thawed and I thought I'd fix baked potatoes."

"I'll scrub the potatoes," Clover offered.

"That's a deal, if it's okay with your dad," Kate said, wheeling over to the kitchen doorway so Ben could hear her. He was still on the porch stacking cardboard. "I didn't invite you to eat with the intention of putting you to work."

"Fine by me." Ben smiled at his daughter. "Lou's been letting her help in the chuck wagon all summer. Clover, I'll unsaddle our horses while Danny feeds Flame. I want to check the posts on the corral while I'm at it. I see the stall leans, too. It'll need shoring up before winter winds blow. Kate, have you inventoried how much wood is in your shed?" He indicated the outbuilding Kate had feared was an outhouse the first day she'd driven in.

"Oh, so it's firewood stored there? The path is so steep and rocky I've put off checking. Why would anyone keep wood so far away from the house?"

"Varmints dig under outbuildings hunting for a warm place to get in out of the cold."

"Varmints?" Kate hesitated. "What kind? You don't mean bear or bobcats?"

"More like ground squirrels, pack rats, field mice and skunks."

"Ew." She wrinkled her nose.

"Rats, mice and skunks are the primary reason you don't want to let garbage bags pile up too long before you haul them to the landfill," he said. "At the Rising Sun, we store kitchen leftovers in sturdy plastic bags and then seal them in an empty fifty-gallon drum until someone makes a dump run. You'll get raccoons, too. Those scavengers tear through plastic bags and make an unholy mess."

"Where can I purchase a barrel? Are they expensive? Marge said my first paycheck won't be until October fifteenth." Kate frowned. "Not that I'm broke, but I'm watching pennies."

"Clover, remind me to bring Ms. Kate a drum." Ben turned back to Kate. "If you raise chickens for the eggs, I recommend storing chicken feed in an airtight container, too."

Danny's laughter rang out. "Mom raise chickens?"

Kate shook a finger. "Don't you laugh, Danny. When I was your age, my mom kept chickens. Out here we won't grocery shop every day like Mimi did."

"Hey, can we get a calf? I'd be able to practice roping at home and won't have to worry whether or not you'll take me over to practice with Ben's buckaroos."

Ben didn't imagine the sudden chill that fell over mother and son, or the mulish tilt to Danny's jaw.

"Ms. Kate." Clover flung a stick out under the pines for Goldie to fetch. "Danny roped a mean ol' mama cow who didn't wanna leave a wash today. He did it real slick and from uphill. I bet he can beat Frosty Reynolds from Jordan Valley and Davy Fisher from Riddle at our Rope and Ride. Danny's way better."

Ben shushed Clover and changed the subject. "If you're planning to help with supper, princess, quit playing with Goldie and go wash."

As simply as that, Danny set out to feed Flame and Clover joined Kate inside. Ben followed Danny to the corral with his own horses and quickly dropped the saddles off Clover's mare, Glory, and Blackie.

"We saw some wild mustangs today," Danny announced as he scooped feed into a trough.

"A wild herd? Mares and colts? Any sign of a stallion?" Ben straightened from the post he'd been checking.

Danny shrugged. "The herd was way off in a canyon. Clover called it Juniper Basin. She said maybe the horses were in Nevada. It's so cool you can see three states from your pasture."

"We're used to it, I guess. Danny, back to the wild herd. In June there was a wild horse roundup. Most local ranchers in the area thought our range was cleared of wild bands. If you saw one, Clover should have alerted me. I can't let her ride out on Glory anymore. It's too dangerous. I also need my crew to trade out cavvy mares for geldings. Wild mustang stallions build a herd by raiding local ranches and stealing mares."

"Gosh, I didn't know."

"It's okay. Clover does." Ben laughed. "Hey, no long faces. I'm not blaming you. Come on, let's have a look at your firewood."

Danny looped the corral gate closed and trotted after Ben. "I didn't know what a cavvy was until Justin explained. It's neat how you shave funny marks in a horse's mane so the crew can tell if it's a snaffle-bit horse, a two-rein type or straight-up bridle mount. My grandpa's wranglers bring their own horses to roundups. Enrique said guys who work for you get to pick six or seven horses every day to ride. Is it true buckaroos don't own anything but their own clothes and a saddle?"

"That's right. The ranch owns the *cavvietta*. That's a Spanish term for all the horses the buckaroos ride. We shorten it to *cavvy*. Buckaroos travel light, Danny. They operate like drovers you see in old Western movies. Your grandpa's wranglers probably have families, maybe even own homes near his ranch. Here buckaroos are drifters. Men who live with the herd 24-7. I used to love trailing a herd, sleeping in a tepee under the stars. But our way of running cattle is becoming a thing of the past." Ben couldn't keep the sadness from his voice as he yanked open the shed door and gazed into the gloomy interior. "I'll need a flashlight to see what's stacked in the corners, but from what I can see this won't last the winter. What's here seems good and dry. The cabin's been vacant awhile since I shifted to leasing grazing land on the east fork of the Owyhee River."

"Pawpaw Royce owns all his land. Clover said you're fighting with some guys who want the leased land for mountain biking and stuff. Why don't you buy it?"

"Money," Ben said after he shut the shed door. "We ranchers lease for sixty-five or seventy dollars an acre. To buy the same unimproved parcel they want six to eight thousand an acre."

"That's a lot."

"It is," Ben agreed. "And we depend on natural vegetation. What land I own outright supports four hundred cows. I could make a living with that, providing drought or disease didn't wipe out my herd and as long as I have land to grow feed. But leased grazing includes access to rivers. I can run four thousand mama cows and two hundred bulls and make a better living for me, Clover and Bobbalou. It's the only way I can afford to hire from six to ten buckaroos." He shrugged. "We all survive better."

"I hope you win the fight," Danny said. They entered the house through the back door.

Kate glanced up from the stove. "Who's fighting?"

Goldie almost knocked Danny down in her haste to lick his face, leaving Ben to repeat their conversation.

"That explains why Clover said you spend a lot of time going to court in Boise. Why I thought you were maybe involved in a custody suit."

It was plain in the silence following Kate's remark that both adults remembered the sharp exchange they'd had during that meeting. Ben preferred to ignore the comment and move on.

"Hmm, that chicken you're cooking smells scrumptious. If it's nearly done, I'd better wash off my trail dust."

"Danny, get Ben a clean washcloth and towel, please. I would, but if I leave the cream carrots and peas, they'll stick to the pot."

Standing so near Kate, Ben battled the curl of pleasure that struck unexpectedly at hearing her say his name in her sweet, melodic voice.

Kate smiled at him. "Clover's setting out silverware as we speak." She gestured to an alcove in the compact kitchen. "I need to apologize for inviting guests to eat and then squeezing you around a card table. There are only two chairs, so I'll use my wheelchair. Danny… grab the step stool out of the close. Your backside is skinny enough for that."

Ben frowned. "We shouldn't have stayed and put you out."

"Do you have something against cozy?" Kate teased.

"Guess not. We're used to being crammed in a chuck wagon with six or so sweaty buckaroos. Isn't that right, Clover?"

"Yeah. And I told you Ms. Kate smells a lot nicer than our buckaroos."

Kate turned a deep scarlet, though she did her best to act nonchalant when Ben shifted from boot to boot and laughed nervously. "She did say that," he admitted, going redder. "Clover, some things are best kept between us. You embarrassed Kate and me."

"Why? It's true," Clover insisted.

Ben looked at Kate apologetically. "Before you got here, Marge Goetz said I should work on discipline with Clover. I admit, I haven't paid much attention to manners. Probably I've left too much to Bobbalou."

Danny bounded back into the room and handed Ben a blue towel and matching washcloth. The boy began regaling his mom with the story of his first lunch in a buckaroo chuck wagon.

Excusing himself, Ben left Danny chattering. When he came back, a baked potato sat steaming on each plate and vegetables and rolls sat on the counter. Kate leaned out of her wheelchair, attempting to pull a hot roasting pan out of the oven with a folded dish towel.

Ben rushed to her side, grabbing pot holders off a hook. "Let me get that. It's heavy. Yeow, and hot. You need oven mitts, Kate." He lifted the roaster onto the top of the stove.

"Thank you," she said a bit stiffly. "Cooking is something I've managed to do up to now without anyone's help."

Too late Ben recalled a remark she'd made about her in-laws treating her like an invalid. Not knowing how to rectify matters, he passed Kate the meat fork and the heavy platter he found lying on the counter.

Kate took both, but once she had them, she had no idea how to go about transferring the roasting hens onto the platter. Her hands were already full. She sat weighing logistics, afraid she'd burst into tears.

Over her shoulder, Ben said quietly, "This looks

like a two-man job. Why don't I hold the plate while you fork out the birds, or vice versa."

"I...uh...have a lot to learn about my limitations when it comes to cooking for more than Danny and me."

Once the chickens were on the platter and carved, the next problem was trying to find room for too much food and a crowd of four at the shaky card table. Ben's knees barely fit beneath it and his left leg kept banging the metal strut on the arm of Kate's motorized chair. Time and again they interrupted each other to apologize.

Finally, Ben held up a hand. "Look, if we keep apologizing for something we can't change, this great meal you've fixed will go cold before we eat it."

"You're right. You and Clover are being good sports. I'm sorry." Kate stifled a laugh. "There I go apologizing again."

Ben rolled his eyes at the two kids, who broke out in giggles.

When their plates were empty, Kate glanced around. "Who saved room for apple pie?"

"With pepper?" Ben teased, reminding her of her earlier parting shot.

"No pepper, but no ice cream, either," she lamented. "I can offer the kids more milk and you coffee. It's prepared, but the coffeemaker needs turning on. I think you're closest."

Ben had seen where it was. Rising, he reached around to press the switch.

"Thanks. You're pretty handy in the kitchen, Ben." Kate began stacking plates.

Rather than take the dishes out of her hands and risk making her feel inept, Ben merely propped a hip on the counter to stay out of her way. "Danny and I talked some about how my way of ranching differs from his grandpa's. By the way, Kate, you'll need a cord of wood. I'll bring you a load of kiln-dried pine when my order comes."

Kate set the dishes on the counter. Grasping the edge of it, she pulled herself up to the sink so she could run water and set the dishes to soak.

It took all the willpower Ben could muster to leave her alone. He made a mental note to see if Chad thought he could install an automatic dishwasher.

"I hope you've run out of words and aren't just standing there feeling sorry for me."

"Actually, I was thinking you put me in mind of buckaroos. They're self-reliant and fiercely proud of their way of life in spite of hardships. Horse throws a shoe, they forge a new one over a campfire. A shirt rips, they sew it with a bone and horsehair. A saddle breaks a cinch, they weave a new one. It's hard to housebreak a buckaroo. You remind me of the independent part, Kate."

A plate slid out of Kate's hand and it was pure luck that it didn't break. "You've pegged me wrong, Ben. This is my penance." She dropped back into her chair and swiped the hair out of her eyes. She didn't know where that statement came from and hoped Ben would let it pass.

But he figured out what she meant. "You need to meet Bobbalou. He drilled into my head that blaming yourself doesn't do anyone any good."

Kate didn't look convinced.

"Kids, why don't you go play awhile, until we fix pie," Ben suggested.

Clover and Danny bounded up from the table, calling to the dog as they raced into the other room.

"I know about the self-blame game, Kate. I was fourteen when reservation cops banged on the door one night and informed me they'd found my mother dead in a ditch next to the road that led to town. OD'd. I knew she had a big problem and often I talked her out of going out on the town. That day we argued. She was already drinking when I got home from work and discovered she'd stolen the money I'd been saving to buy new boots. I'd been working off the res for Bobbalou. She cried and carried on, swearing she'd pay me back. A song and dance I'd heard too many times. I pushed her out the door and said, go carouse with your friends. So…she went."

"Oh, how horrible for you, Ben. But…you were just a boy." For a few awkward moments neither of them spoke.

Kate was sorry she'd made them both remember painful incidents they'd rather put to rest. She motored to the fridge. "Pie plates are in the cupboard below the coffeepot. Do you mind putting four of them on the table? I'll bring the pie. Danny," she called, "come put out clean forks for everyone."

The kids seemed to understand that something had caused tension between the adults and Danny, the worrier, tried to lighten the mood. "Ben, tell my mom about the cavvy marks and how your buckaroos can find Rising Sun horses even if they get mixed in with a wild band. And war knots. They're so cool, Mom. Justin showed me how to tie one in Flame's tail so it'll keep my rope from tangling when he swishes his tail. Justin said I can't leave the tail knotted or else it can catch on a corral rail. And Mom, did I tell you they have roping competitions here? But they're not really rodeos. Zach says they're sporting events. Isn't that right, Ben?"

Prickles ran up the back of Ben's neck. He wasn't surprised when Kate set the pie down hard on the table. "Danny..." she began.

Clover added her two cents. "Bobbalou says our Rope and Ride's not for sissies in SUVs. They toss a rope or two then put on their Nikes and drive back to the city. Our competition is for real horsemen, Ms. Kate. And women, too. When I'm ten I'm gonna enter."

"Are you two ganging up on me?" Kate asked.

"I think Clover's trying to clarify that our event is for sharpening skills," Ben said. "And it's a fund-raiser. Entry fees offset taxes the town lost when the mines closed. Our trophies are hand-woven ropes, or saddles. Say Danny was to win in his division, he might come home with chinks. You probably call them chaps. On our range they're necessary protection for riding through sagebrush."

Kate cut generous slices of pie and passed everyone a wedge. Taking hers last, she let her fork hover as she casually inquired, "Ben, don't you think Danny should pursue a fallback career?"

A cinnamony apple wedge refused to go up or down his throat no matter how many times he tried to swallow.

"I'm not being snobbish," Kate assured him. "I'm asking because I'd like Danny to hear that every roper can't be a star. For every man who makes money on the circuit, there are a hundred who die broke. Ranching has ups and downs, too. I haven't been here long, but I have kids at school who are scared of what will happen to them and their families if you lose the lease rights in court."

Ben pushed back his unfinished pie. "We appreciate the meal. Clover, finish up. I'll fetch the horses."

Danny swallowed his last bite and jumped up. "Ben, I'll help Clover bring Glory and Blackie to the house."

"I didn't mean to insult your occupation," Kate said once the kids were out of earshot. She backed up to give Ben room to exit the cramped alcove. "I just don't want Danny entering roping competitions. I don't care what you call an event. A rope and ride, a stampede, a big loop contest—all spell rodeo."

"Maybe you should have taken a teaching job in the city, Kate."

"Marge Goetz told me they raised beets and onions around here. I expected farmers, not cowboys."

"It's your call, of course, what your boy does. Can I just say I don't know a single kid who entered our event while young who's run off to chase rodeos. In fact, most have turned into hardworking men."

Kate motored to the porch, holding Goldie. Ben's words were a glaring reminder that Colton had never really grown up. He'd spent his adult life chasing rodeos.

Ben grabbed the saddles he'd left on the porch. One stirrup caught on Kate's makeshift wheelchair ramp and dislodged a two-by-four with a bang. Goldie tore loose from Kate and barked wildly at the noise.

Irritated, Ben passed Clover her saddle. He stopped to reset the board. "Those should be secured by lag bolts before you kill yourself. I'll pick some up at the feed and supply next time I'm in town."

"I suppose you're going to town while I'm at school?" Kate said.

"I generally go when I find time. Is there something else you need?'

She seemed to hesitate a moment. "No, nothing. I just thought if I tagged along, maybe I'd meet the parents of some of my students. They must wonder about me. About my competence to teach." She indicated her chair.

"Marge read your résumé to board members, so they know you're qualified. But if it's socializing you miss, say it straight out and I'll set something up. Or Marge can."

"No, that's not it. I just…never mind."

Settling his saddle on Blackie, Ben made short work of cinching it tight. Clover had already mounted Glory. Ben itched to get underway, but light from the house fell on Kate Steele's delicate, bowed shoulders, defying her recent assertion.

"You made plain how you feel about rodeos," he said. "How about carnivals? One's due at our fairgrounds soon." He named a date, the first Saturday in October. "Most residents in the valley go. There'll be craft exhibits and such. I'm taking Clover. You and Danny are welcome to ride along."

"Oh, I don't know." Kate's fingers dug into the arms of her wheelchair. "Danny would probably love it, I'd better stay home. I'd hate to hold you back."

Ben heard the ripple of longing in her refusal. "I can load your chair in the back of my pickup. The fairground is flat."

"Really?" She hesitated only a fraction of a second longer as she watched him swing up on the big black horse. "If you're sure I won't be a burden. Oh, but don't you have someone special you usually take?"

It crossed Ben's mind she was asking in a roundabout way if there was a woman in his life. Lately it seemed everybody was bothering him about the same thing.

"I may be a simple buckaroo," he snapped, "but I've got a good grasp of yes and no, Kate. I'm surprised with all the words in a teacher's vocabulary, you'd rather beat about the bush."

At first Kate gasped, then she laughed. "Yes, then. Yes, I'll accept your invitation to take Danny and me to the carnival."

Tightening his hold on the reins, Ben whirled Blackie on his hind legs and barely flashed a backhanded wave.

Clover was in a chatty mood on the ride home. "I had the funnest time tonight. When can we do it again?"

"Is *funnest* a word? If it isn't, you'd better not let

your teacher hear you describe an evening at her house that way."

"She said she gave you books I'm s'posed to read. Ms. Kate said to remind you, Ben. She asked me 'bout my favorite book. I don't know if I have one. Do you, Ben?"

"No. Uh, I don't, princess." They'd reached the bridge over the Owyhee River. A breeze skittered leaves from a nearby oak across the planks and moonlight sparkled off the water swirling below. The bridge was too narrow to ride side by side, so Ben dropped back. And hung back for the remainder of the ride home while he mulled over what he'd do if no one answered his ad for a tutor.

Clover dismounted at their barn. "The video you gave me last Christmas is 'dapted from a book—*The Black Stallion.* Vida said so. I could've told Ms. Kate it's my favorite."

"Does Vida read to you?"

"Nope. We watch TV or she brings videos. Her daughter, Teresa, works at a video store. Vida gets stacks every week. I like when she brings ones with horses. But she mostly likes lo-ove stories." Clover singsong-ed the word and rolled her eyes.

It dawned on Ben how little attention he paid to what went on around his house when he wasn't there. Vida Smith had raised nine kids on her own. Her husband had died in a farm-implement accident when her youngest had been a toddler. She'd kept things together by taking in laundry, cleaning houses and raising a huge garden that had fed her brood. A son and a daughter still lived in the valley. Ben's main concern when he'd hired Vida was that she could mix formula, clean house and was honest. He hadn't asked if she'd had formal schooling. Now he had to worry whether or not she allowed Clover to watch inappropriate movies.

Ben had worked his butt off to build a ranch to be proud of, but he'd fallen down in other areas. Talk about guilt.

CHAPTER SIX

As KATE TURNED HER SCHOOL calendar to October, she knew she couldn't put off testing Clover's reading and comprehension skills. She hadn't seen Ben since the night he and Clover had eaten at her place. She'd gleaned from talking to Clover that her dad had made several trips to Boise and Clover still hadn't seen the books. But before Kate could assign her other students work, leaving her free to test Clover, Sarah Keevler threw up at her desk, narrowly missing Jeff Goetz, who sat in front of her.

The girl was mortified. Her sister Mary leaped from her seat, shouting, "Yuck! Next time don't eat such a big breakfast, Sarah."

The school had no phone and, unlike city kids, the students didn't carry cell phones. There was also no couch or cot where a sick child could lie down. Kate sent Danny out to their truck to look for Flame's horse blanket.

"My dress is icky," the girl wailed, "and I think I'm gonna puke again."

"Quick, Mary, help your sister into the restroom," Kate instructed. "Will someone wet paper towels at the sink and bring them to me along with a wastebasket so I can clean this mess?"

At first no one moved. The kids had all left their seats and stood as far from Sarah's desk as possible. Kate heard a few mutter, "Gross."

"Yes, it's gross," she agreed, "but it could have happened to any one of us. I'm sure those of you who live on farms have seen worse."

If they had, no one said so. It was Clover who rushed to the classroom sink to wet paper towels. On her way back to Sarah's desk, she remembered to grab the wastebasket.

"Thank you, Clover." When the girl took some of the towels and knelt to wipe the floor, Kate tried to stop her. "Oh, sweetie, you don't have to help."

"I like helping. 'Sides, I don't see how you can reach the floor from your chair."

Clover's acute observation pointed up a definite shortcoming in Kate's ability to handle this job.

The girl seemed to sense Kate's thoughts and gazed at her with sad, wise eyes. "It's okay, Ms. Kate. Ben says ev'r'body needs a helping hand sometime."

The words reminded Kate of Ben's offer to help her out with repairs at the cabin. She hadn't heard boo from him since, although the cardboard stack on her porch was gone and the corral boasted a few new slats.

Kate smiled at Clover. "Here comes Danny with the blanket. Would you help him spread it on the floor over there." She pointed to a corner. "I'll seal this ruined textbook in a plastic bag. Here, one of you older boys go toss it in the big garbage bin outside." She addressed the other students. "The rest of you can drag your desks away while I help Sarah. You all have assignments, so don't let me hear any chatter while I'm in the bathroom. Understood?"

Kate's wheelchair barely squeezed through the outer door of the girl's washroom. The school board had obviously never considered the possibility of special-needs kids, let alone a teacher. Mary Keevler peered out from the first of three stalls.

"Sarah didn't barf again, but she's hot and smells worse than our uncle Hank's pigs."

Kate heard Sarah burst into tears.

"Let's get Sarah out of that dress," Kate suggested soothingly. "It's lucky I wore a suit today. Sarah can wear my blouse. It'll practically be dress length on her." While Mary helped her sister, Kate slipped off her jacket and blouse. "Mary, do you want to sit with Sarah, or join the class?"

"I'm sorry I said she smelled like a pig." Mary's apology sounded perfunctory. "Sarah's not gonna die, is she? Mama read about some boy in the valley who got appendicitis. It ruptured and he died. The article said the boy barfed all night."

Kate's own stomach lurched. "Sarah," she called, "does your stomach hurt?"

"No, I feel icky all over and my head hurts."

Kate sighed with relief. "Mary, it's probably a virus. I expect everyone on the van was exposed, but just in case they weren't, I'll drive Sarah home. Do you think your parents will object?"

"No. I just want to go back to class."

Mary left, and once Sarah was cleaned up and wearing Kate's blouse, Kate led her to the makeshift bed. One crisis successfully over. Kate owed Clover thanks for helping to bolster her confidence.

Lunchtime presented another problem. Leave Sarah inside by herself, or let the other students stay outside without supervision?

Again, Clover seemed attuned to Kate's dilemma. "Ms. Kate, if you need someone to keep Sarah company, I'll stay inside today."

"Clover, that's kind of you, but I was about to ask Mary to stay with her sister."

"No!" Mary protested. "Shelly and Meg asked me to help plan decorations for Shelly's Halloween party. Her mom needs to know by tonight. She's going to the party store in Boise."

The three girls wore such hangdog faces Kate almost gave in, but she'd come to realize they tended to behave like primadonnas. "Girls, you're holding up everyone. You have two choices. Mary can stay with Sarah, or all three of you eat in, and you can do your party planning here."

Shelly, the most spoiled of the trio, complained, "That's so not fair. The boys will be outside. I'm inviting them to my party, so we hafta find out what games they'll play."

Clover tugged on Kate's arm. "Sarah wants a drink of water."

Kate glanced at the girl curled in the corner. Sarah hadn't moved a muscle as far as Kate knew. She asked Sarah anyway. "Are you thirsty?"

The girl nodded, struggling up on one elbow. "I didn't want to bother anyone."

Terry Goetz pointed to Clover and made opposing circular motions beside each ear with his forefingers. This caused Meg, Mary and Shelly to titter.

"Stop that, Terry. Girls…you, too."

"Clover's freaky, Clover's freaky," Dave Hyder chanted. "She talks to animals and claims she knows what they're thinking. You should ask Clover to your Halloween party, Shelly. She's spooky enough."

That brought another round of laughter, but Kate was glad to see Danny didn't join in.

"Those are unkind remarks, and for making them you'll all lose ten minutes of your lunch hour," Kate announced. "I'm going to get Sarah some water. If there's not total silence while I'm gone, you'll forfeit an additional ten minutes."

Kate took her time filling the paper cup, letting them stew. She'd just handed the water to Sarah when several loud bangs sounded out front, rattling the window panes.

Sarah nearly dropped her water. "Ms. Kate, are we having an earthquake?"

"No. I don't think so."

The kids, being curious, surged to the door. Demanding order, Kate wove through them and cautiously opened the door. She was shocked to see Ben Trueblood and another man hammering nails in a substantial ramp, one with a double rail.

Ben straightened as the door opened. "Sorry if we're disturbing you, Kate. I told Chad this would be the best time to come. I thought you'd have the kids outside for lunch. This is Chad Keevler, by the way. He's built a second ramp for the cabin. If you're going straight home after school, I'll set it for you."

Kate nodded at Ben with thanks, then rolled her chair all the way out on the stoop. "Mr. Keevler, I'm Ms. Steele, your daughters' teacher. I'm happier to meet you today than you know. Sarah's not feeling well."

"Sarah's sick? Did you call Teri, er, my wife?"

"Call her?" Growing exasperated, Kate turned to Ben. "What is the procedure? The school has no phone and mine's shot. There's no cot for a sick student like Sarah…."

"Ben, you sit on the board." Chad wiped his hands down his coveralls. "Teri and I haven't even attended a meeting since our funding got cut. Is this the result?"

Mary Keevler elbowed her way past the students hovering around Kate. "Daddy," she shrieked. "It's awful. Ms. Kate said I have to stay in at lunch just because Sarah's sick. Shelly asked Meg and me to help plan her Halloween party. Tell Teacher it's not fair to punish us."

Chad had stripped off his baseball cap and now helplessly twisted it between work-scarred hands. He obviously wasn't used to being the family disciplinarian.

Kate let him off the hook. "If you have the time and means to take Sarah home, Mr. Keevler, that will solve today's dilemma. I'll arrange to purchase an extended-range cell phone, which hopefully will alleviate future problems."

"Ben?" Chad deferred to him. "That'll mean putting off the work you contracted me to do at the cabin for at least a day."

The students were losing patience. "Are we going to get any time to eat?" Mike Delgado demanded.

"Mike, at the moment I'm attempting to get Sarah home," Kate chided.

"What's that got to do with us?"

"You just lost ten more minutes from your lunch, young man. Another word and it'll be twenty." Her scowl had Mike stepping back and the others falling silent.

"Chad, you see to Sarah," Ben said. "Kate, we used to have a half-time traveling nurse and a teacher's aid to cover lunches and recess. We lost extras when the mine shut down. The board will have to work something out if we're going to keep this school open. Go on with the kids. They should grab time outdoors while weather allows. Today's report said we're in for a cold snap."

Kate took Ben's advice and dismissed the students for lunch.

Jeff Goetz high fived Adam Lightfoot. "My dad says it'll snow before Halloween. If they close school for snow days, we can sled in the canyon out back of your house, man."

"Snow? But, it's barely fall." Kate turned in her chair to look over at Ben and the top button popped off her suit coat. She grabbed it before it bounced onto the stoop, but didn't quite get her lapels closed over her bra. "Blast! I hope I have a safety pin in my purse." She clutched the edges of her jacket together. "Sarah vomited on her dress and is wearing my blouse, Mr. Keevler. Her own clothes are in a plastic bag."

Ben glimpsed plenty of pale cleavage before Kate clamped the jacket under her chin. Their gazes collided, his scorching, hers embarrassed.

Doing his best to control his physical response, Ben reached up and dropped his wraparound sunglasses over his eyes. He knew it was an honest male reaction, but it irked the hell out of him that this wasn't the first sexual stirring he'd felt for Kate Steele.

"Why don't I…uh…go ride herd over the lunch bunch while you…uh…" Awkwardly he gestured toward the front of his own dusty black shirt.

"Thanks," Kate said meekly, still doing her best to suppress a flush. "I'll do that." She maintained a death grip on her jacket while trying to motor back into the classroom. "It might as well be Friday the thirteenth," she grumbled, wondering what, if anything else, could go wrong.

Chad Keevler preceded her inside and knelt next to his daughter, talking softly to her.

"I'm taking her home," Chad called. "Thanks for all you've done. My wife, Teri, will launder your blouse and get it back to you. Sarah Rose says she doesn't know what she'd have done without your assistance, Ms. Steele."

"All part of being a teacher." Kate stopped sorting through the contents of her purse, which she'd emptied onto her desk, and watched him scoop Sarah into his arms.

What if Sarah had passed out from dizziness in the bathroom? Kate couldn't have lifted her. Maybe she wasn't suited for teaching full-time, at least not in a rural school. Discouraged, Kate propped her head in her hand and closed her eyes a moment.

Ben stuck his head in the school door.

"No pin?" he asked, seeing that her desk was littered with junk from her purse.

The rasp of his deep voice in the quiet room had Kate jumping out of her skin. "Who's watching the kids while you're sneaking up on me?"

"Whoa!" He held up a hand. "I merely came to ask if the metal clippy doodad Clover has holding her hair out of her eyes might work in place of a pin."

"Sorry, Ben. It's been a tough day. I don't know if it will work, but if Clover's willing to part with her hair clip, I'll cross my fingers it's strong enough to hold. I usually have a pin with me."

He disappeared. Soon Kate heard the scrape of Clover's boots. "I'm sorry you're having a bad day, Ms. Kate. I have a sweater in my backpack, but Ben says it's probably too small for you." The girl extended the clip.

Kate tested the spring in the big silver clip and, finding it taut, pinched the lapels of the cherry-red jacket together just above the empty buttonhole—half an inch above her bra. She breathed out carefully, then smiled at the solemn-faced child when the clip held. "Hey, Clover. If I don't make any sudden moves, I believe this will get me through the day. You had a clever idea. Thank you."

"You're welcome, but it was Ben's idea. He didn't want you to stay embarrassed."

Teacher and pupil stared at each other for a second or two, then Clover turned to leave.

That was when Kate realized she was about to lose a golden opportunity. "If you're not in a rush to get back to the playground, Clover, I think we should talk a minute about what went on earlier with Dave Hyder and Terry Goetz."

"That's okay. Ben and Bobbalou say I have a gift and others don't understand."

"A gift?" Kate paused. "But weren't you just guessing that Sarah was thirsty?"

"No, ma'am. I knew."

"How?"

She shrugged. "I can't 'splain how."

"So, when Dave said you talk to animals…" Kate purposely didn't complete the sentence.

"He's wrong."

"I thought as much." Kate's relief bubbled out.

"We don't talk like you and me…." Clover mumbled. "Bobbalou says my brain's like a radio. It sometimes picks up animal stations."

"Oh. ESP, you mean?" Studying the child with the fathomless black eyes, Kate thought back to the bird calls and the captured honeybee. "Extrasensory perception is a term applied to a small number of people who sense things that the rest of us are unable to. From another dimension. Oh, I know you don't understand exactly, but there have been studies done proving the condition exists. If you have ESP, Clover, you're one of a special few."

Dark eyes glowed, and the girl smiled. Kate had never noticed before, but Clover had a deep dimple in her left cheek. Returning the smile, Kate said fervently, "Maybe if I just knew how you communicate with birds and honeybees, I could easily teach you to read."

"Ask Bobbalou or Ben to tell you 'bout birds and bees, Ms. Kate."

"This sounds like a very interesting topic." Ben's dry voice floated through the back door.

"It's not what you're thinking," Kate said, flustered. "Has anyone ever suggested that Clover be tested for ESP?"

Ben was familiar with the term, but he was afraid testing would provoke more teasing from the other kids. "Don't you need my okay for psychological testing?" *Mr. Sikes had told Ben the district needed written authorization.*

"Yes, of course. But, it may help…"

"You need to bring the kids back inside," Ben said curtly. "A cold north wind has kicked up."

Kate checked the time. "Oh, yes, please send them in."

"One thing first. Chad transferred the other ramp and plywood for your carport to my Ford. I'll go get started shoring up Flame's stall if you bring Clover home with you instead of sending her on the van with Bill Hyder."

"Sure. I'll be glad to." Kate still felt stung by Ben's curt tone. "I'm sure you're busy with your chores," she said coolly. "You've done so much for me. I'll hire a handyman to do the rest."

"It's my cabin. I'd be done by now, but Chad was tied up on another job."

"Uh…all right, then. But I need to go to town to get a phone before the phone mart closes. Is it okay if Clover rides along?"

"A phone mart?" Laughter tinged his voice. "Owyhee's smaller than a small town. Stop by the cabin. I'll drive you to town and give you and Danny the fifty-cent tour."

"Okay. By chance is there a secondhand store? I really need to see if I can find a kitchen table and chairs."

"That would be Clay Bonner's Furniture Barn. Or his wife, Rosie's antique shop. It's settled then. Oh, will my working on the stall bug Goldie? I'd hate for her to kill herself trying to break through the screen."

"She's really a big softie who'll be your friend forever if you let her out. I'll give you a key to the house."

"Right. I still have her teeth marks on my boot from the day you moved in."

"She didn't know you then."

"I'll take your word. Clover, bring the key out. I'd better go round up those hooligans. They're getting loud about something."

Kate dug her house key out from the pile on her desk. After Clover dashed out, a thought pricked the bubble of Kate's growing excitement. She'd already agreed to go with Ben to the fair on Saturday. People in small towns gossiped.

Oh, but surely no one would think a sexy man like Ben would be romantically interested in a woman stuck in a wheelchair. More than likely he felt obliged to make sure she didn't wreck her wheelchair at the school or on property he owned. That's why he was being helpful. A man who moved among lawyers, as Ben did, probably worried that her in-laws might sue the town if she got hurt. And the carnival was for Danny's sake.

Kate was glad to keep her mind on teaching for the remainder of the day. It wasn't until she locked up the school after the van left that she remembered she hadn't located a reading test for Clover. The kind she could administer without Ben's signature.

At home, she had psychological tests. She could lose her job if she administered them without parental consent. But Kate doubted the school district had a psychologist if they'd lost funding for even a part-time nurse.

Ben would never sign. In the years Kate had taught, she'd witnessed more dads balk over psych testing than moms. Mothers tended to go along. But Clover didn't have a mother. And what if she didn't have ESP, but really heard animal voices? From a college psych class, Kate recalled that schizophrenic kids heard voices.

She paid close attention to Clover on the drive to the cabin, but from all Kate observed, Clover and Danny chattered like normal kids.

"Gosh, Mom," Danny exclaimed as Kate parked. "Ben fixed Flame's stall and he's working on a carport."

"So I see."

The kids exploded out of the passenger side of the pickup, welcomed by Goldie, and the three raced over to join Ben.

Kate took her time lowering her wheelchair. Feelings

she was unprepared for coursed through her—pleasure at seeing a man working on her home. Not long ago she used to imagine Colton doing just that. Fixing up their house, making it a secure haven for his family, for her and Danny. She slid down into her chair.

She wasn't watching her son's father but her landlord, who triggered feelings she'd prefer not to have. Her heart recognized how much she'd like to come home to this sight every afternoon.

Ben attached a last piece of siding to the carport frame before he slid his hammer into a loop on his tool belt and greeted the children. Looking over them, he sent Kate a smile. As he stripped off worn leather gloves, he sauntered lazily toward her, tools rhythmically slapping his muscular thighs.

Her mouth went dry, causing her to glance away.

"Hi." He dusted sawdust out of his hair and off his shirt. "I figured you'd want to change before we head into town. I need a minute to unload roofing material for your carport. By the way, I told the kids Goldie can go with us if it's okay with you."

"Fine. I definitely need to change so I can return Clover's hair clip."

"It seemed to serve its purpose." His eyes skipped over the clip, but stalled on the vee of flesh above it.

"I lived in fear it wouldn't. You've been a busy man, I see. It's amazing all you've accomplished. And the ramp you and Mr. Keevler installed at school is so superior to mine. It's ten times sturdier."

"That's good." He smiled, but still managed to look endearingly self-conscious at her praise, Kate thought.

"The ramp here is more exposed, where the one at school is protected by the eaves. I hope you'll tell me if it gives."

"I'll test it now." Engaging the joystick on her chair, she skirted him.

Ben watched her cross the uneven clearing. She'd never asked for one, but he imagined a cement walkway would make her life easier. Something else he noticed—how pretty she looked in red. Kate Steele was blessed with a vanilla ice-cream complexion and wearing red put color in her cheeks.

Ben looked down at his naturally brown forearms. Life in the sun had darkened his skin in places to near mahogany, but Kate was probably the same milky white all over.

Damn, he had no business letting his mind contemplate them lying naked together. But in some things, he'd learned, a man's mind had a will of its own.

The kids and dog loped toward him. "Climb in the backseat of my pickup with Goldie. I have cartons of shingles to drag out. Danny's mom will probably be ready to go by then."

She was. Kate had changed into worn blue jeans, a peach-colored blouse and blue corduroy jacket. Ben stood, hands itching to help as she muscled herself from the chair into his passenger seat. He forcibly held back an offer of aid. Few people wore an I-can-do-it-myself look as pugnaciously as Kate.

Ben shut her door, then manhandled her wheelchair into the bed of his pickup—if only to prove to himself that he could do something to help her. After lashing her chair down with bungee cords, he jumped behind the wheel.

On the road to town, Ben began identifying local landmarks. The section where his land butted open range and, on the opposite side, the fields where Ray Goetz raised rows of sugar beets. "What's plowed will sit fallow until Ray plants millions of onion bulbs in the spring." He turned onto a two-lane highway that wound through six miles of stark, sage-studded hills.

"Our town's nothing to write home about," Ben said as he turned off the highway and headed downhill.

Kate noticed the buildings dotting the valley were unpainted.

"Boy, it's nothing like Fort Worth," Danny said.

"No," Kate murmured. "But, we've seen towns like this one, in Texas, Oklahoma and Kansas." Colton's rodeo circuit.

"Cow towns, you used to call them, Mom."

She considered telling Ben she'd never meant that in a derogatory way, but the moment passed.

"This is High Street," he said, turning. "High and Broad are the two main drags. Numbered streets run the other way. The fairground where we're going Saturday is three miles due north of Sixteenth."

"There's the Furniture Barn," Kate said. "Ben, if I find a kitchen table and chairs to buy, is it okay to ask the shop owner to load them in your pickup?"

"I'll load them," he said. "First on our agenda should be to see about a new cell phone and ask where they are with your house phone. We renovated the cabin to sweeten the pot in hiring a teacher. I'll poll board members and see how fast we can add a phone at school. It should've already had one." He parked on the street between the feed store and Clay Bonner's Furniture Barn.

"Danny needs feed for Flame. I may as well grab a big sack of kibble for Goldie and a few bales of hay." Kate dug out her checkbook and thumbed to the page showing her balance. "I think I can swing that much." She glanced over at Ben, feeling a need to explain her dwindled finances. "A funeral, two years of doctor bills, plus the costly replacement of our Suburban pretty much wiped out Colton's life insurance. Colton wanted to drop the policy. You have no idea how thankful I am that I squeezed the premiums out of my grocery budget to keep it up." Her voice sounded remote.

"You and Bobbalou," Ben said. "I might've scrapped my policy if he hadn't kept nagging. I'm glad I listened. It made it easier to expand my policy after Clover came along, turning me from a shiftless buckaroo to a family man."

Colton had never reached that point, Kate thought.

Clover got Ben's attention with a tap on his shoulder. "Is it okay if I show Danny and Goldie the city park? And will you give us money to buy a cone at the Dairy Queen?" She pointed past Kate to the park at the end of the block. The Dairy Queen was an old-fashioned one with outdoor seating. Kate stopped Ben from taking out his wallet. "Let me treat the kids. It won't cover the cost of gas, but I'll feel less of a freeloader."

Ben started to refuse, but glimpsed her fragile pride.

"Sure." He left his wallet in his pocket. "While you tell them when to meet us back here, I'll unload your in-town transportation."

Ben went out of his way to not make her feel helpless or beholden, Kate realized, unlike her mother-in-law. The excitement she'd suppressed back at school over this simple outing returned in a rush.

They accomplished a lot in a whirlwind hour. Ben introduced Kate to Dotty Wheeler, Meg's mother. She worked at the bank. They ran into Della Quimby outside the telephone office, where Kate bought a new phone. "Both of those women are charming," Kate said as they crossed the street to search at last for a kitchen set.

"You charmed them," Ben said with a grin. "What parent wouldn't want to hear the nice things you said about their kids?"

Kate caught a wistful undertone. "Clover is the sweetest, most generous child I've ever met."

"Yeah? Still, I'm the only parent in the school who's been called in for a conference."

Since they'd walked to the Furniture Barn, Kate decided to let that comment pass. She soon found an oak table and four chairs in a corner of the store that cost surprisingly little. Happily, Kate sat and watched Clay Bonner and Ben fit the five pieces in his pickup bed between feed sacks and hay bales. Once the men were sure the wood wouldn't rub on anything, Clay turned to Ben. "Thanks, buddy, for bringing me some business. It's been slow. Real slow, lately."

The two men discussed the worsening economy.

After Clay went back inside and before the kids returned, Kate decided to bring up her concerns about Clover. "I feel guilty taking up your afternoon, Ben, when you could be reading with Clover. How's that coming?"

He circled the pickup and rechecked the knots on the ropes holding her table.

Kate decided another approach was needed. "Where is your library? Or a bookstore?"

"They don't exist. I'll take your list next time I go to Boise. I forgot last week."

The kids ran up, sticky-faced and out of breath. Clover launched her sturdy body at Ben. "Danny doesn't believe Mike Delgado's uncle sells twenty kinds of hamburgers at his restaurant. Can we eat there on the way home?"

"Twenty? Are you sure of your facts, Clover?" Even Ben seemed skeptical.

She bobbed her head, whipping her straight black hair like a horse's mane. "I know, 'cause Mike betted Adam Lightfoot, and Adam had to buy Mike a milk shake."

Ben boosted the kids into the cab. This time he couldn't stand to watch Kate struggle. He clasped her elbows and lifted her up at the waist.

She scanned his face for pity. Seeing none, she said, "Thanks."

"Don't mention it." Once she was settled, he stored her chair, then climbed in and frowned at the panting dog. "What'll we do with Goldie if we stop for burgers?"

"It's cool enough to leave her with the windows

rolled down an inch. But, Ben, if you're anxious to get home, Danny and I don't need to stop to eat. You should still have time to read one of those books together before Clover's bedtime. I've put off her reading test to give you a chance to work with her. I wish you'd told me before you hadn't progressed past the two books I gave you."

Ben ignored her remark and smiled back at the kids. "I don't know about you all, but I worked up a healthy appetite. Delgado's famous burgers, coming right up."

CHAPTER SEVEN

"THAT WAS A TOTALLY COOL PLACE," Danny declared of Joe Delgado's burger joint as they drove away. "I still can't believe you ordered banana and cream cheese on your hamburger, Clover."

"You put icky tomatoes and sweet relish on yours."

Kate broke off bits of her leftover meat and fed it to Goldie, taking care the dog didn't slobber on Ben's upholstery. "Enough, you two."

Ben eyed Kate feeding the dog. "You should have said you don't like hamburgers, Kate."

"Are you kidding? I just can't put away the amount of food you can. I don't know when I've enjoyed an evening more. Funky decor, great jukebox and stimulating company." She nudged Ben playfully in the ribs.

"What's stim-u-lating?" Clover asked.

Danny scoffed. "You don't have to ask that, Clover. We aren't in school."

"But I like to know stuff. Ben always asks people to explain things."

"I have a question." Kate glanced at the girl. "Why do you call your father Ben?"

The girl brought her shoulders up level with her ears in an elaborate shrug.

"Don't get me wrong—Ben is a very nice name," Kate declared, then shifted self-consciously as she felt his dark eyes moving over her.

"Bobbalou said Ben's not the name he was born with. Isn't that right?" Clover kicked the back of his seat to gain his attention.

Kate shot him a sidelong glance. "Of course, it's Benjamin. That's nice, too."

Clover giggled, rocking gleefully behind Ben's seat.

"Clover, dang. Between you and Lou, a man can't keep a blessed thing in his life a secret." But the words had no sooner left his mouth than he wished he could take them back. He didn't want Kate probing. Mad at himself, he reached for the knob and adjusted the heat. "It may freeze tonight," he said, abruptly changing the subject. "Danny, when we get to the cabin, Clover and I will help you spread hay in Flame's shelter. You'll want to move his feed and water in tonight, too."

"It felt quite chilly when we left the restaurant, but are you sure it'll freeze?" Kate asked. "I can't fathom a hard freeze in October."

"Can't go by the calendar. Our cattle and cavvy horses already have thick winter coats. That's a sure sign winter's coming early."

"I noticed someone had stacked a small supply of firewood on the cabin's back porch. That shed's so far from the house it concerns me."

"My wood should arrive any day. I have ten cord coming from an outfit in Mountain Home. I figure the kids and I can move what's in your shed to the porch and fill the shed with new wood. Even if the temperature falls into the twenties, it'll warm up during the day, which ought to give us time to finish before really bad weather hits."

"That's kind of you, but you must be neglecting things at home."

"Bobbalou and Zach Robles keep my ranch running. Vida Smith is slowing down some, but she sees our house stays clean. Isn't that right, Clover?"

"Yep. And she's gonna buy some material to make me skirts and blouses."

"Whadaya want skirts for?" Danny asked. "Can't ride horses or climb a fence if you're wearing skirts."

Ben had backed the Ford up to Kate's corral before Clover answered Danny. "Meg Wheeler told everyone I dress like a boy. She said it like it's a bad thing."

"Clover, Meg Wheeler is..." Kate thought better of pitting one child against another. "What I mean is, next time anyone hurts your feelings, come tell me."

A deep furrow bisected Clover's brow. "That's tattling."

"Yeah, Mom." Danny shoved open his door so that he and Goldie could get out. "Kids don't like tattle-tales."

"Danny. Clover. Wait." But the kids were gone. "Meg's thirteen and Clover is eight," Kate muttered. "And even if they were the same age, it's about learning respect." She shoved open her door and smacked Ben. "Ben, I'm so sorry. Did I hurt you?" She saw him rub his chest.

"Naw. But save your breath. The kids took Goldie out to do her business." He reached in and lifted Kate out as easily as if she weighed no more than Clover. Before she could object, he'd set her gently in her wheelchair. It was the second time her flesh tingled from the press of his hands at her waist, but Ben just kept speaking as if hauling her from the Ford was no bigger a deal than tossing hay bales.

Untying the ropes that held the load in his pickup, Ben noticed Kate hadn't moved. "Hey, Joe Delgado may build great burgers, but his coffee's terrible. I wouldn't turn down a good cup of java after I unload."

"Danny," Kate called, "come help Ben tote hay to Flame's shelter. We agreed before leaving Texas that Flame is solely your responsibility."

Danny sounded surly. He knocked into her chair as he dashed past. "Yeah, I notice a whole lot else got to be my responsibility just like Mimi said it would. I wish we still lived at the Bar R-S. All I had to do there was be a kid."

Kate heard his every word and her chest felt tight.

Ben saw how Danny's caustic remark had hit home. As she motored up to the porch, he saw Kate's shoulders hunch low. He waited for her to chastise the boy, but she didn't. Maybe because he and Clover were present. Or it could be she made allowances because Danny had lost his father. Ben didn't feel he had any right to comment. Shoot, not when he was so lenient with Clover.

"Hop to, kids," he called. "No dallying around. Let's spread this hay. It's cold as a well digger's ba...er...

knees out here. The sooner we make Flame comfort-
able, the sooner we can go inside and warm up."

And he didn't let the kids off after that chore ended.
He made them each tote a chair to the house, while he
lugged the oak table and remaining chairs in one trip.

The smell of fresh coffee and the welcoming warmth
of Kate's home hit Ben hard. How often had Bobbalou
told him a woman put her special stamp on a home?

*Just every time he started on Ben about Clover
needing a mother.*

Ben usually disagreed, thinking about the hovel he'd
grown up in. But as neglectful as his mother had been,
she'd hung colorful weavings on the walls and made
coffee on the mornings she hadn't been nursing a
hangover. She'd been fourteen when she'd had Ben.
Fourteen—just a few years older than Danny Steele.

"Ben?" A hesitant voice wafted through the kitch-
en doorway. He couldn't see Kate around the table and
chairs he held. But the sweet sound of his non-Native
American name rolling off her tongue had him relaxing
his grip to the point he nearly dropped everything.
He'd been born Hawk Trueblood, but had ditched that
and taken the name Ben.

"The kids are having hot cider," Kate said. "But
they shouldn't have left you hauling that heavy load all
by yourself. Hold on, I'll send them each to take a
chair. Or can I help?"

"I just need a minute to get my bearings." Ben heard
the low whir of her wheelchair backing up. "You want
these in the nook to the left of the door, right?"

"Right…here," Kate said as he cleared the door and staggered left.

He managed to set the table down and keep the two chairs from tumbling. The table rocked. A lot. Ben scooted it one way, then the other.

He knelt down to take a look and Kate rolled up beside him. "Is the floor uneven?" She bent so far over she almost fell out of the chair.

Crawling out from beneath the table, Ben dusted his hands down his jeans. "I see the problem, Kate. One leg is an inch shorter than the others. How did we miss seeing that at the store? I'll load it up again and take it back tomorrow. I'm sure Clay will return your money. He wouldn't sell you faulty merchandise on purpose."

Kate clamped a hand over Ben's wide shoulder as he started to push to his feet. "That explains why an oak set fit my budget. The chairs are fine. Clay could've charged the amount I paid for the chairs alone. It's as if I got the table free." Her twinkling eyes urged Ben to see the humor in the situation.

Ben found himself wanting to trace the tiny laugh lines alongside Kate's pretty pink lips. And felt a mounting curiosity to see what she'd do if he kissed away her sultry, sexy laughter.

The space between them narrowed in excruciating degrees and neither one breathed as their lips touched, startling them both.

Kate gasped. Ben turned away.

"Coffee?" He stumbled over the simple word, then made the mistake of glancing back at Kate. Her eyes were shut, and Ben almost gave in to an overwhelming longing to see what a real kiss would taste like. Instead he spun around to the counter, yanking open cupboard door after door. All of which were empty.

"Ben," Kate said, sounding slightly exasperated, "my mugs are *below* the coffeepot, remember? Where I can reach them."

He did remember and felt even more like an idiot. "It's late. We should probably take off and forget coffee. Tomorrow's a school day for Clover. For you and Danny, too."

"Stop slamming cupboards a minute, Ben. We obviously need to talk about what almost happened." Kate concentrated on her hands, which she rested in her lap. "Nothing did...but if we'd *really* kissed, would it have been so horrendous?"

He'd finally found the shelf that held her cups, but his back remained to Kate. If the expression on her face matched the hurt in her voice, he couldn't have taken it.

"Oh, forget I said anything. Have your coffee, Ben. I brewed a pot for you. We'll consider it a near miss, okay? A blip on the radar of two adults who shared a fun evening. The magic in the air is gone. I'm fine. I'm over it. Aren't you?"

No, Ben wasn't sure he was over it—whatever *it* was. But if Kate could set aside her feelings so easily, so could he.

"Can't let this coffee go to waste," he said, half turning. "I'll drink one cup, but I need to go soon. I plan to be back here early tomorrow to roof your carport. Maybe I'll find a block of wood that I can glue to the bottom of the table leg." Pouring his coffee, Ben noticed his hand wobbled. Frowning, he gripped the handle tighter. He was glad when the kids and Goldie tore into the room.

"Goldie just came in from outside, Mom. She's shivering. Feel how cold her coat is."

The dog approached Ben first, so he bent to rub her warm. "Danny, don't be surprised if you're scraping ice off your mother's pickup windows tomorrow."

"Oh, my pickup has super-duper defrosters and front-seat warmers."

"Seat warmers?" Ben handed her a steaming cup of coffee, to which he'd added cream.

She shrugged. "Someone ordered all the bells and whistles then canceled delivery. I lucked out and got the pickup as is for a great price. Hey, you remembered I take lots of cream. Thanks, Ben."

Danny opened the fridge and got out two small cartons of juice. He handed one to Clover and they skipped out of the kitchen again.

Silence descended. Out of the blue, Ben blurted, "You never said if the accident…uh…severed your spinal cord or crushed a disk or…hell, Kate, tell me to mind my own business." He swallowed a big gulp of coffee and felt he deserved the burning sensation down his throat.

"Unless one of a dozen specialists who examined me all missed something significant, I don't have any of those problems," Kate told him. "Why I can't walk is a medical mystery." She bit down hard on her lip, hoping Ben would let it go at that. Otherwise he was sure to get around to wondering if her paralysis was all in her mind. Kate had seen a psychiatrist who couldn't say for sure. "I want to walk. I've tried. I just…can't." She brushed angrily at tears.

"Dang, now I've gone and upset you. I shouldn't have said anything."

Kate saw the jerky way he set his mug in the sink and then called to his daughter. "Time to hit the road, princess. Tell Danny goodbye. And, son, check Flame's water first thing tomorrow for ice. Warm his mash. Remember what I said about saving up to buy a clip-on horse blanket. Kate, see you."

"G'bye, Danny," Clover said around a huge yawn as she followed Ben out the front door. "G'bye, Ms. Kate."

Kate motored her wheelchair over to the door, intending to explain that he hadn't upset her, but Ben's pickup was throwing gravel at the county road before she got there. *What could she tell him?*

Long after Danny and Goldie settled down, Kate was still feeling restless. She forced herself to do the exercises Dr. Pearsall had recommended to keep her muscles toned in preparation for the day this baffling condition left her.

Lying in bed much later, her leg muscles aching, Kate was angry at herself. She'd practically begged Ben to kiss her. And when he'd started to and then stopped, it had nicked her pride.

The morning Ben hadn't shown up to work on the carport by the time she and Danny were ready to leave. Thinking she must have scared him off for good, Kate began making a mental list of the things that needed to be done to winterize the place. She'd have to hire someone now. Ben had been right about the weather. It had turned cold overnight and she'd had to dig out gloves and wool caps.

As they drove down to the main road, Ben turned in. Applying her hand brake, Kate lowered her window. "I wasn't sure we'd see you this morning."

"I said I'd be over."

Her fingers tightened on the steering wheel. "I thought you were mad when you left last night."

"What gave you that idea?"

"You didn't finish your coffee."

"You looked tired. It was late for Clover. I hope to finish the carport except for attaching the roof to the cabin. Chad Keevler said he'd do that. By the way, you'll be happy to hear Sarah's better. A twenty-four-hour bug, Teri said."

"I'm glad for her sake. So, do you still want me to bring Clover home with me?"

"Please. That way I can work straight through. We got a reprieve on the snow according to this morning's weather forecast. The storm stalled off the Pacific Coast. It's anyone's guess what path it'll follow when it breaks and heads toward land."

Danny leaned across his mom. "Ben, Flame's water wasn't frozen this morning. But he sure gobbled up the warm oat mash you suggested."

"If his water didn't freeze that must mean I got his shelter deep enough. Well, I best get to work. You two have a nice day."

As she drove off, Kate glanced back at Ben in her rearview mirror. She'd lost half a night's sleep over that man. After her disastrous marriage to Colton, she'd vowed she would never fall for another cowboy—or buckaroo—again. They were all the same. Shiftless, careless heartbreakers.

But Ben was different.

Right! Kate knew the early warning signs. Oh, yeah, she was developing a thing for Ben Trueblood.

At school Kate was determined to make headway in testing Clover's reading skills, but one thing after another cropped up. It wasn't until after lunch, when all the other kids were working on projects, that she had time to devote to her youngest pupil. "Clover," she said quietly, "we're going to find out how well you read."

"I like it better when you read to me." Clover sounded reluctant.

"Reading on your own is great fun. Did you like any of the books I sent home with your dad?"

Clover fidgeted. Finally, she said, "I guess my fav'rite is the book with the puppy."

"*Harry the Dirty Dog,* you mean?"

"Uh-huh. He was white with black spots, but he got so dirty he looked black with white spots, then black all over. Nobody knew him. I cried."

They talked a bit more about the story. Kate couldn't fault Clover's comprehension. But had she read the book, or had Ben read it to her? Kate opened her folder and removed a timed test. "I like horse stories better," Clover said. "I loved *The Black Stallion.*"

"You read it?" Kate gaped. Danny had struggled with that book last summer.

Animated, Clover began relating the tale of the boy's love affair with the beautiful black horse. Her dark eyes sparkled, momentarily mesmerizing Kate. But then Clover flipped the test sheet and began sketching the stallion.

"Ms. Kate. Ms. Kate!" She blinked and jerked her eyes from the rearing horse.

Most of her other students stood by their desks, jackets on, holding book bags or backpacks. "The van is here to take us home," Ron said.

"Oh. Oh! By all means, you're dismissed. Please tell Mr. Hyder that Clover is riding home with me. Her dad is doing repairs to my cabin, ah…his cabin," she stammered. Deciding she was making matters worse, she gathered her papers. "Have a good weekend. I may see some of you tomorrow at the county fair," she added.

Danny and Clover cleaned the blackboard for her and carried erasers outside to dust while she straightened desks and packed her tote with papers to grade on Sunday.

Kate thought about supper. She debated inviting Ben and Clover. She could say she wanted to test out her new table to see how wobbly the leg was. *What a lame excuse.*

The cabin was quickly becoming the home she'd dreamed of owning. She used to lie awake nights imagining herself playing hostess to friends. Nice people, not Colton's raucous pals.

She passed Chad Keevler leaving the cabin as she

drove in. "Kids, will you look at that. Ben and Mr. Keevler finished the carport—even the roof. It looks great."

Danny drawled, "A carport is a roof, Mom." The comment tickled Clover's funny bone, and they both broke up laughing.

"All right, you two. Ben didn't expect to get the carport connected to the cabin today. Good grief, you guys are silly. Go run some of that energy off with Goldie."

The kids tumbled out. Kate had to wait for the lift to lower her chair. She used the time to watch Ben as he packed up his tools. No two ways about it, the man was eye candy. Slim hips, taut muscles in all the right places. Graceful. He probably wouldn't take that as a compliment.

Ben locked his toolbox and carried it toward his truck. He'd heard the kids and the dog and the whir of Kate's hydraulic lift—which was why he was surprised to see her still sitting in the Silverado. He let the toolbox drop and abruptly detoured. "Is something wrong?" he yelled, before reaching her door.

Kate couldn't very well admit to ogling him. But lying didn't suit her, either. "Sorry, no. I'm fine. My mind was a million miles away."

"Jeez, you scared me." He reached in and hauled her out, but didn't set her down right away. His fingers dug into her slender waist, and for an eternity it seemed as if neither moved nor breathed.

Prickles ran up Kate's spine. "I can stand if you hold me," she said, touching a finger to his full bottom lip.

His hands tightened on her. "I…ah…don't want you to fall."

"I know. But…for just this once, can we pretend I'm normal? I hate dangling like a rag doll."

The air was icy. Vapor curled around Ben's head from their combined breathing. Heeding Kate's request, he lowered her slowly, barely letting his hands slip up her body.

She hesitated touching him, but somehow it seemed right. Her eyes never strayed from his as she sneaked both hands under his open jacket and flattened her palms over his chest. She savored the moment she grew aware that he was as affected by this as she was.

"Oh, how I've missed human contact," she murmured, longing to lay her cheek over his heart just to hear the reassuring beat.

He swayed with her, and so she gave in to her wish, closing her eyes, smiling softly when his heart thumped faster.

They stood that way for long minutes neither saying a word. Goldie's barking and the sounds of their children's voices broke their interlude.

"Dang." Ben's remark expressed what they both felt about the interruption.

Kate understood when he hastily placed her in her wheelchair. She caught his hand. "Would you and Clover stay for supper?"

Ben heard the strain in her voice. He hated to decline, given the waters they'd just been testing. "Kate, I have to round Clover up and make tracks for home. I've got men due at the house within the hour to talk about a ruling handed down by a circuit judge today. I'm sorry."

"No need to apologize," she said, disappointed nevertheless. "Another time."

"I'll see you tomorrow at nine. For the fair," he said. "Say, I hope you won't feel like a rag doll if I pick you up and set you on some of the carnival rides."

"You want me to do rides? I thought they were just for kids."

"There'll be all of the regular rides you'd find at any fair. You aren't squeamish because…" He broke off sharply.

"Because of the accident, you mean?"

"Well…yeah."

"I honestly can't say. As a teen I loved rides. The wilder, the better. But I haven't been to a carnival in years. This will be Danny's first. Money was always tight."

"Tomorrow is my treat, Kate. I insist," he added, when she started to object.

The kids dashed up to tell them about Goldie flushing a raccoon.

"Look at you, covered in pine needles," she chided her son. "Goldie, too. You need to dust yourself off and brush her before you go inside."

Danny swiped the knees of his jeans and shook needles out of his hair. "I've never seen a raccoon except in pictures, Mom. Clover spotted him in a tree. Goldie treed that fat, old coon. Mom, can I go inside and phone Mimi and Pawpaw?"

His shining eyes softened Kate's attitude. "You may if you brush Goldie."

"C'mon, Clover. You can meet my grandparents over the phone."

Ben grabbed Clover by the back of her jacket. "Whoa. Climb in the pickup while I load my toolbox. We have to hightail it home."

"Aren't they staying for supper?" Danny almost tripped over Goldie as he turned to ask his question.

"Not tonight," Ben said. "Another time. Maybe Sunday," he added unexpectedly as he swung his heavy tool case into the Ford. "I meant to mention it earlier, Kate. Bobbalou called from the radio-phone to say the guys from Mountain Home were delivering my firewood today. If you don't have other plans, I was thinking the kids and I could move the wood from your shed to the back porch Sunday. Then we'll fill the shed with new wood."

There was no denying she'd love having Ben's company two days in a row. But she felt guilty, too. "I can't let you neglect stacking your own wood to help me, Ben."

His eyes darkened. "If you'd rather not have our company, Kate, that can be arranged," he said, suddenly stiff.

"No, no. That's not what I meant." She raised her eyes to his. "I thought I made it fairly plain a few minutes ago how much I *like* your company, Ben. I just don't want to be a burden."

"You're no danged burden," he snapped.

"Okay. Then I insist on fixing you and Clover both lunch and supper on Sunday. You'll all be working hard, and I'll be cozy inside, grading papers and cutting out Halloween decorations for the bulletin board."

Ben inclined his head. "It's a deal. Well, you should go in out of this wind, and I need to take off. Uh, for the record, I like being in your company, too."

He climbed in his truck so he couldn't see Kate's flush of pure pleasure. On her way back into the house, she wondered what his past history was with women.

Over dinner, Danny seemed withdrawn and almost sullen compared to his earlier exuberance.

"I'll bet your grandparents were happy to hear from you," Kate said. "Did you explain we've been without a phone for a while?"

"Mimi says it sounds wild and woolly here."

"Did you tell her it's not?"

"No. She asked why I was chasing raccoons instead of practicing roping."

Kate buttered her corn muffin and took a bite. Corn muffins were one of Danny's favorite foods, yet he picked his apart and left it crumbled on his plate. "Are you not feeling well? I hope you haven't caught Sarah Keevler's flu bug." She reached over the table to lay a palm on his forehead.

"I'm not sick. Mom, can we go back to Texas for a visit on my birthday?"

"Danny, your birthday is next month. We've barely settled here. It's too soon."

"No, it's not. Mimi said if we come home for my birthday, Pawpaw will buy me the saddle I want. She said it's a holiday weekend. Veteran's Day, or something."

"Danny, this is home now, not Fort Worth."

He shoved back from the table and ran from the room. Kate let him go, but she considered phoning her mother-in-law. Melanie's promises were blatant manipulation. Kate had seen her use the same ploy so often with Colton. Kate decided she needed to cool down. She'd call her in-laws next week.

DANNY WOKE UP GRUMPY, but cheered up as soon as Ben and Clover arrived.

"I asked my dad once to take me on that big round wheel that goes up high," he told Clover.

"A Ferris wheel?" she asked. "They're okay, but I like roller coasters and the Tilt-A-Whirl best."

"We might want to get in line for the Ferris wheel early," Ben said. "It's usually popular. I'm glad you both have warm jackets and hats and gloves. The weatherman said no snow until next week, but my almanac says to expect some today."

"The house was like ice this morning. Ben, will I have to worry about pipes freezing?"

"Remind me and I'll wrap them tomorrow when I bring the wood. Kids, today is your special treat for all the hard work I'm going to expect from you tomorrow when you'll be stacking wood."

The kids crinkled up their noses, but neither complained.

As soon as they got to the carnival, Ben guided them to the booth where Marge Goetz's quilting club was selling funnel cakes. Della Quimby was there. She drizzled hot icing on the steaming fritterlike confection.

"I'm Winnie Lightfoot," a small, dark-eyed woman said. "We've never met. Adam is loving the science project you assigned. Percy and I want to thank you for making school exciting for our kids again."

Kate couldn't have been more pleased.

"Mom, is it okay if Clover and I go to the rides now?" Danny asked. Both he and Clover finished their cakes and hot chocolate, but Ben waited for Kate's decision before he tore off tickets from the reel in his hand and passed them to the children.

"Clover, you know to go on some of the tamer rides to start since you just ate."

She nodded and ran off hand in hand with Danny.

"Those two seem to get along like a house-a-fire." Marge Goetz noted. "You two, as well," she added, jabbing Ben with an elbow.

Ben ignored Marge. He didn't want any more speculation about his growing interest in the teacher. "Would you like to take in some of the exhibits?" he asked Kate after they'd said their goodbyes. "I'm inclined to let my funnel cake settle before we hit any rides."

"Exhibits like handcrafts, I hope? I'd love to find some colorful pillows and a throw to brighten my beige futon."

He laughed. "I didn't think you'd be clamoring to see the livestock."

"Maybe later. The kids will need to wind down. Ben, are you worried that Marge will make too big a deal out of our friendship?"

Ben shrugged. "Don't let it worry you. Marge routinely gives me heck for not socializing more. She thinks Clover needs a mom." Seeing a look cross Kate's face that could be construed as wary, he quickly added, "Marge and Ray are real civic minded. They took it hardest when the mine closed and people bailed out of here. Marge has been the catalyst behind keeping our school afloat. Her theory is that families attract more families, while too many bachelors might attract more unsavory elements. A lot of longtime residents are worried that if the ATVers and other recreational-ists win this land fight, the transient nature of that group will attract businesses that cater mostly to nightlife."

"Wow, the pressure's on you from all sides. I see now why I'm living in a cabin you own. I'm sorry. But I don't need babysitting."

"That's not it. Dang it, Kate, no one is pressuring me to do anything."

They let it drop, but Kate remained distant for the rest of the day and pushed to go home early, despite the children's protests. Kate used the drop in tempera-ture as her reason.

Ben thought it had gotten colder, but he sensed she was still upset by Marge's jab.

Halfway home, Clover reminded Ben, "We don't owe you a whole day's work, 'cause you made us leave the fair early."

"About the wood, Ben," Kate said, before he could reply. "It's a job that goes beyond neighborly kindness. I've decided to ask if some of the older boys at school would like to earn extra cash to fill my shed. And Ben, I'm paying you for the wood and the delivery cost to move it to my house."

"It's not your house, it's mine," he said more curtly than he intended. "We'll be over at ten. And kids, whether or not I negotiate pay above the price of carnival tickets will depend strictly on the hours you give me and how dedicated you are." He drove down Kate's lane and dropped her and Danny off after having the final word in the matter.

An hour later it started to snow. The flakes were so big Kate was quite certain tomorrow's wood hauling issue would be settled by the weather.

CHAPTER EIGHT

THE NEXT MORNING, ten on the dot, Kate was hugely surprised when Danny, who'd been at the front window watching snow fall, hollered at her, "Mom, guess who just drove in? Ben. I think he's bringing our wood. He's got something in his pickup covered with a blue tarp."

A fire crackled in the stone fireplace. Kate had been feeding it wood from the supply on the back porch but was afraid she'd run out by nightfall. Bless Ben.

"Mom, you made me come straight in after I fed Flame and exercised Goldie. Clover's making snowballs and she's throwing them at trees. I've never had snow deep enough to play in. Can I go out now? Pretty please?"

"If Ben still plans to move wood for us, then yes. Providing you wear boots, a warm jacket and hat. I don't want you getting sick. I have no one to look after you if you're ill, Danny, and I need to work."

As if afraid she'd change her mind, Danny grabbed his hat and jacket from where they lay drying on the hearth. Kate shivered at the blast of cold air that raced through the house when he dashed out.

She flung a light cardigan around her shoulders and went as far as the front door. Snow had blown onto the porch floor, leaving it slick, so she decided to stay put. She rubbed the frost off the window and looked out. Both kids were intently listening to Ben's instructions. He gestured to the shed then made precise motions with his hands, no doubt explaining how he wanted the wood stacked. He went through the instructions twice. Kate smiled, admiring his patience. He had a nice way with kids and animals. *And women.* She couldn't forget the care he always took with her.

She watched him lift two red wagons and a snow shovel out of the truck. Immediately he set about shoveling a path from the shed to the back porch. The way his blue jeans tightened across his sexy butt as he fell into a rhythm of bending and tossing snow aside had Kate's mouth feeling cottony.

She needed to focus elsewhere. *On Goldie.* The retriever jumped in the air, snapping at giant snowflakes, making Kate laugh. When the dog didn't catch the flakes, she looked surprised and set to chasing her snowy tail.

Clover frantically motioned Danny to the back of Ben's pickup. Kate saw the little girl show Danny how to pack a tight snowball. Too late she realized Clover's intention. Both kids crept up on Ben, lambasted him with the snowballs and scampered off. *Those rascals.* But, what could she do from the house?

He straightened fast, hunched over and stripped off a glove so he could dig snow out from under his collar. Unable to hear what he shouted, Kate figured it must not be anything too terrible from the crooked way he smiled before getting back to shoveling.

His grin had her longing to join in a snow battle. Having lived in Kansas as a kid, Kate recalled measuring snow in feet, not inches. Twisting, she studied the white sky with its steadily falling flakes. If the snow kept up at this rate she didn't know if school would be open tomorrow.

Kate couldn't help them carry wood, but she could make them homemade chicken-noodle soup for lunch. She had cooked chicken in the fridge and veggies. It was a matter of tossing everything together with canned chicken broth and simmering it on the stove. If Ben was determined to work on after lunch, she had a pork roast thawed that she could toss in the oven for supper.

She worked on putting together a Halloween art project until she heard one kid clomping around on the back porch, then the other. She wheeled to the door to make sure they didn't stack the rows too high for her to reach.

Ben must have had the same idea. He sprinted up the steps just as she opened the back door. Snowy ice crystals were melting on his cheeks, eyelashes and the crown of his cowboy hat. "Whatcha need, Kate? You'll freeze in that skimpy blouse," he said, his dark eyes missing nothing.

"I heard the kids and came to remind them to keep the stacks low." They both turned to watch the children shake snow off the wood as they unloaded their wagons.

"Mom, this wood has lots of splinters." Danny picked at slivers in his hand.

"It's way more splintery than our wood at home," Clover agreed.

"You kids should be wearing gloves," Ben said. "Clover, you know better. You could catch a bad virus from pack rat droppings. I nailed boards over places they got in. What we really need is to move all the old wood out and pour a concrete slab. Hell of it is, I should've thought of that before this storm hit." He bent a wrist and wiped melted flakes out of his eyes with a strip of exposed brown flesh.

"Do you think I can find a handyman in town will-ing to pour a floor?" Kate asked. "Oh, but it's your shed. I shouldn't be making those decisions without asking your permission."

"That wouldn't matter. I just don't think we're going to get a break. Almanac shows the first snow hanging on a couple of weeks. Otherwise I'd buy cement to-morrow."

The thin sweater Kate had thrown around her shoulders slid off on one side. Kate tried to grab it, but Ben stepped close, peeled off a glove and ad-justed the sweater for her, his cold knuckles brushing her breast.

"Look at you shiver," he said gently. "Go back in where it's warm. The shed floor may have to wait until spring." Almost without thinking, Ben stroked the back of two fingers along Kate's chin.

Her hand flew up to cover his, then she glanced at the kids.

"It's okay," he said too softly for them to hear. "I know I'm a rough and tumble buckaroo, but I hope you know I'd never hurt you, Kate."

"I know that, Ben. It's just…"

"What?" He hunkered down, bracing his forearm on the arm of her wheelchair, a move that brought their faces close together.

"Nothing. Really. Nothing." She wasn't going to tell him she felt guilty for being sexually attracted to him. She hadn't slept well, worried about how attached Danny remained to Texas and wondering how Danny would feel if he noticed this attraction developing between her and Ben. And did she want it to develop? "I'll go in, Ben. I put on a pot of soup for whenever you're ready to come and warm up."

It was plain from his expression that he wanted to probe deeper, but he let it go. "Clover, before you kids fill the wagons again, I want you to go to the pickup and get some gloves to fit you and Danny."

"Danny has gloves," Kate said.

"Mom, those are my roping gloves. I don't want them getting sticky."

Goldie bounded onto the porch and shook snow and mud off her yellow coat. "Goldie, you're a mess! Danny, run and get me a towel. I'll dry her off as best I can."

Danny left a last piece of wood in his wagon. "Clover, I'm gonna help Mom a minute, I'll meet you at the shed. Bring me gloves. I don't wanna buy new roping gloves, because I'm saving money for the entry fee for your Rope and Ride."

Spinning her wheelchair to follow Danny, Kate

called after him, "I thought I settled that, mister. No roping contests."

Kate was left holding Goldie's collar. She realized both Clover and Ben stared at her with faint disapproval. "That's my final word," she said tightly. "I'd appreciate if neither of you encourage him."

Ben set Clover's wagon back out into the snow and he shooed her out. For a minute Kate thought he intended to argue. Instead, he tugged down the brim of his hat, turned up his collar and disappeared in a swirl of snow.

Goldie whined and tried to follow Ben. She hung on to the dog until Danny stomped back carrying two old towels. Knowing the routine, he dropped to his knees and dried Goldie's feet and underbelly while Kate did the same to her body. When he'd finished, he tossed the towel in her lap and unloaded the last piece of wood.

His stubborn look reminded her so of Colton, her heart actually hurt. She knew this argument wasn't over. Today, with snow piling up, it was an issue she could let go for another day. "For now just take a pair of gloves from Clover, then. Ben was right about picking up a disease from pack rats."

He kicked his way through the snow gathering on the steps.

"Remind Ben there's hot soup," she called, struggling to roll back from the doorway while preventing a recalcitrant Goldie from racing outside. Danny didn't acknowledge hearing her. That trait was so like Colton, tears stung the backs of Kate's eyes.

Accepting her fate, Goldie flopped in front of the

fire. The heat of the blaze warmed Kate's legs, relaxing the spasm that was gripping one thigh. She hadn't suffered leg cramps in a long time. Maybe it was the cold, or the result of renewing her exercises.

It was past noon when the trio tramped in again, kicking off boots and shedding wet hats, jackets and gloves by the fire. Their faces and fingers were red from weather that appeared to be worsening.

"I hope you're winding down," Kate said, eyeing the tired bunch as she ladled thick soup from a steaming pot.

The kids slumped in the new oak chairs. Ben crossed to the stove, rotating his shoulders as he went. "Let me carry the bowls to the table. Are you going to stay put, or would you like assistance into one of the oak chairs?"

"Thanks," she said, flashing him a smile. "I can manage alone. Just leave me the chair with the cushion. I'll let you bring French bread from the oven while I settle myself. Are you packing it in for today?"

"There was more wood in the shed than I calculated. It's better for burning than the newer stuff. I think if we can continue at the pace we've been working, we'll finish before dark. Hopefully."

"I wish we were done now." Clover set her milk glass down to rub her arm.

Kate had eased from her wheelchair to the seat beside Clover. "Did you make that red welt from scratching, or do you have a buried sliver?"

Clover inspected her arm. "It just itches, Ms. Kate."

"Want me to have a look?" her dad asked, setting bowls in front of Danny and Clover, who both dug straight in with their spoons. "Guess not," Ben said, winking at Kate. He made another trip from the stove to the table. After pulling apart the hot buttered bread Kate had made, he answered her original question. "Because there's more wood in the shed than will fit on the back porch, the kids are restacking it while I put the new where they've cleared."

"Is there room for all of you in the shed at one time?"

"It's bigger than it appears from outside." Ben frowned. "There's nothing I can do until spring to grade the path to make it more accessible for your wheelchair. Promise me you won't try to go down there yourself. I'll do my best to keep your porch supplied, but if you run low, phone me."

He was so serious, Kate promised. It felt good having someone care about her. "I wish I could help. You three are doing so much."

Ben set his spoon down and covered her hand. "You are helping," he said, meaning every word. "This soup hits the spot, doesn't it, kids?"

They nodded, but both of them look bushed.

"That settles it," Kate said. "I'm fixing a pork roast for supper. Ben, if it keeps snowing this hard, will there be school tomorrow? And if not, how will I know?"

"Ray Goetz will phone you if the district cancels. Frankly, Kate, I'm betting on it."

Danny perked up. "No school tomorrow? Cool. In Fort Worth we never got a day off for snow. Only once for flooding. Clover, what'll you do with a day off?"

She rubbed her arm and shrugged.

"I hope Clover curls up by the fireplace and reads a

good book. Ben, did Clover read *The Black Stallion* by herself or did you give in and read it to her?"

Ignoring her question, he carried the dishes to the sink. "Actually, if the snow continues, Clover will go with me to haul feed to cattle on our winter range."

"Ben…" Kate was not going to let him avoid the subject.

Danny broke in before she could say her piece. "I thought Zach said your cows forage."

Over the sound of running water, Ben replied, "A horse will dig through snow to find grass, but cows aren't that smart. It takes all our buckaroos, Bobbalou and me forking hay to get a herd the size of ours through a harsh winter."

"I get to drive the wagon," Clover said. "Ben, can Danny help us tomorrow?"

"Out of the question," Kate snapped back. "If there's no school, I'm staying put."

Talk turned to what Ben fed his cows. He and Danny carried the conversation.

Finally Ben straightened from the kitchen counter and stretched. "Well, kids, we've dallied long enough. I know, I know," he added when they started to protest, "a nap would hit the spot. But if the almanac is right, Danny, you and your mom will be happy to have us complete this chore."

"Mom, will you feed Goldie?" Danny hopped up and dragged Clover to her feet. "I hope our jackets and gloves are dry."

"Times like this you hafta bite the bullet," Ben said, joining them at the hearth.

"My pawpaw tells whiners to *cowboy up*," Danny said. "In roping class it was his favorite saying."

Kate waited until she heard the door slam, then braced her hands on the tippy table to lever herself up. Her right leg tingled as if she had feeling coming back. She let go of the table and lurched crazily.

"Hey, hey!" Ben ran into the room and snatched her seconds before she fell. He yanked Kate hard against his chest, then almost went down when he tried to turn her and set her in her wheelchair. Their foreheads bumped. "Jeez, sorry." He gripped the chair's armrests and found himself staring straight at Kate's parted lips.

So help him, Ben had imagined almost this very scenario after he'd climbed into bed last night. He should forget the hell how lush her lips were. He should pull up stakes and get out while the getting was good. But instead of following his good sense, Ben leaned in and kissed her. Fully and completely.

For an instant he felt her mouth freeze, but the frost didn't last. Kate's lips grew damp and pliant. Her arms circled his neck, keeping Ben off balance.

He had denied himself the soft pleasures of a woman for too long. His heart threatened to explode and his addled brain was seconds from self-destruction.

The front door slammed, and Danny yelled, "Ben, are we supposed to wait for you to split kindling? Clover says we are."

Breathing as hard as if he'd run a mile at breakneck speed, Ben had difficulty comprehending the boy's words.

Kate dropped her arms from around his neck. "Tell

him yes," she warned. "Then you'd better go. This is craziness, Ben. I don't know what's happening. Look at me. At us." She massaged her arms.

Ben answered Danny and added that he'd be right out. He made no attempt to camouflage his desire. "I have looked at you, Kate," he said, running a finger over her puffy lips. "I'm looking at you now. Get used to the fact. I like what I see." With that, he sauntered off.

It took Kate quite a while to pull herself together. While she prepared the roast for the oven, she tried to reconcile herself to the fact she had fallen under the spell of another cowboy. A cowboy by a different name. But how different was Ben?

Maybe her attraction to him was just the lure of that old dream about having a real home with shutters and a yard with trees. She and Ben already had the kids. "And a dog," she muttered, shaking kibble out for Goldie. "Yes, I'm talking about you. Tell me to stop this idiocy, Goldie girl. Tell me you don't want to share me with another dog or silly cats who are good for nothing but loving."

But Goldie just looked up at Kate with grateful eyes then dug into her kibble.

THE THREE WOOD STACKERS straggled in at sundown. The storm hadn't let up. Tree boughs drooped heavily with wet snow.

"Something sure smells good," Ben said, stamping off his boots and shaking melting snow off his hat and jacket onto the towels Kate had spread at the door. The three carried in a pungent aroma of pine.

"Mmm. You smell like wet trees. I've fixed pork

roast with apple stuffing and I've made hot coffee. Are you desperate for caffeine before supper, Ben?"

"Am I ever. I need to sit by the fire a minute and warm up. Kids," he said, watching them zip out of wet jackets, "you two worked like beavers. Yesterday I said we'd negotiate a fee for service, but I think you both earned a bonus."

Clover flopped on the braid rug next to Goldie, who hadn't been interested in moving far from the fire all afternoon. The girl sat up and shook her hair out of a ponytail, then fell back again, closing her eyes.

"She's not up to dickering, Danny." Ben clapped a large hand over the boy's shoulder. "We can leave it till later, or settle the money man to man."

"Whatever you think is fair, Ben." Danny leaned around Ben to check with his partner. "Is that okay, Clover?"

She opened one dark eye. "'Kay." She had one arm curled above her head, and Kate noticed deep scratches along the paler underside.

"Clover, hon, you've really dug the skin off that arm. I have some ointment in my medicine cabinet. Sit up so your dad and I can have a better look, please."

"I think something bit me," Clover said, sitting up and stretching out her arm.

"Ben, this looks nasty. Really swollen. It does look like a welt or bite, though." Kate inspected Clover's other arm. "I don't see any others. I thought it might be a flea, but wouldn't there be more bites? I don't think Goldie has fleas, but pack rats do. You said you found evidence of them in the shed."

"I didn't hear any scrabbling and the holes I blocked were old. Do fleas live long without a host?"

"I'm not an authority on fleas," Kate said.

"I thought teachers were authorities on everything."

"Ah. We're good at making people think that."

"Whoa, that is a mean-looking spot," he said, examining Clover's arm more closely. "Does it itch a lot?"

"It did. Now it sorta hurts." She braced her elbow with her other hand and sat as though in a stupor while her dad, Kate and even Danny examined the area.

"It probably hurts because you scratched it so much." Danny flopped down on the rug to pet Goldie.

"I have Neosporin and cortisone cream, I think," Kate said.

"Whichever you think," Ben finally said. "I generally rely on Bobbalou for healing nicks and cuts. He mixes roots and herbs in the old manner. But by now he'll be hunkered down with the crew in a windbreak out on the range. Rub on something to keep her from scratching. Tomorrow, when we haul hay out to winter pasture, I'll have Bobbalou take a look."

"Cortisone should relieve the itching. I'll go get the tube and be right back. Darn, the oven timer dinged. Supper's ready. Ben, if you'll settle yourself and the kids, I'll be there in a jiffy to dish things up."

"We all need to wash off pitch, or worse. And you kids petted Goldie. Come on, kids, shake a leg. My stomach's about to eat holes in my backbone I'm so hungry."

Danny laughed, and Kate. But either Clover had heard the expression many times, or she was really done in. Her eyes, normally bright, seemed lifeless. Kate went down the hall to find the cream.

Ben was already carving the pork roast when she returned. She hesitated in the doorway and, briefly, her hand slipped off her chair's joystick. The scene so resembled the family in her broken dream.

Ben must have sliced off the end of the roast as a treat for Goldie. The dog, still licking her chops, sat in anticipation near the table, her tail beating a tattoo on the vinyl floor.

So normal. So real. Except—they weren't a family.

Ben glanced up, saw her staring and stopped carving. "Did I take your job?" He gestured with the meat fork. "I was just trying to speed things up."

"No. I...ah... It's fine. We just have a rule that we don't feed Goldie at the table."

He nodded. "Sorry, girl," he said, transferring his attention to the dog. "You know a pushover when you meet one."

"It's okay this time." Kate sent Goldie to her bed and busied her unsteady hands spreading cream on Clover's swollen arm. "There, honey," she said, capping the tube. "Ben, I'm not going to cover that with a bandage. I think it's better to let air heal where possible."

"I'm sure it'll be better by morning if she stops scratching," he said, forking a slice of meat out on each empty plate.

Kate set the tube on the counter, washed her hands and helped serve the dressing, creamed corn and green beans.

"I'm afraid we're going to have to eat and run," Ben said right before he tucked into his food.

"Will you be okay driving home in this storm? I don't have extra rooms, but I can offer sleeping bags by the fire."

"I'm tempted. But sleepyhead there might do better in her own bed." He indicated Clover, who was almost asleep over her plate.

After a hurried dinner, Ben apologized for leaving Kate with a mess in the kitchen.

"After all you've done for me today, Ben," she said, "a few dishes are nothing." She waited in her chair near the door while he bundled Clover up for the trip home. "Promise you'll drive carefully. I feel guilty letting you go out in this storm."

He brushed off Kate's concerns with a quick peck on her lips. "I've slept out in worse weather, Kate. I know the road between here and my ranch. We'll touch base tomorrow, unless the phone lines go down. We can be reasonably sure there won't be any school."

Kate nervously watched him swallowed up by swirling flakes. She didn't feel right letting him go. On the other hand, not even the intense kiss they'd shared earlier gave her a right to beg him to stay.

LESS THAN A MILE DOWN THE ROAD, Ben wished he'd accepted Kate's hospitality for the night. He'd ridden and driven through whiteouts before, but he hated leaving Kate on her own with the power sure to go out. Danny said it rarely snowed in Fort Worth, and Ben worried that, if something did go wrong, Kate might try to drive. He couldn't remember feeling so protective about anyone other than Clover. *Well, that wasn't true. There was his mother.*

And he hadn't been able to help her. Bobbalou said that was why Ben kept people at arm's length—until Clover. Her big, baby eyes and total helplessness had instantly claimed his heart.

Ben glanced in the rearview mirror where she slumped over her seat belt. Normally she'd be bouncing off the walls, excited about the first snowfall of the season.

He was tempted to turn on the overhead light to see if she was asleep. "Clover," he called quietly. "You okay, princess?"

"I don't feel good. My arm hurts, Daddy."

Ben jerked. He could count on one hand the number of times Clover had called him *Daddy.*

"Bobbalou knows Paiute medicine. Tomorrow he'll fix you up."

Clover didn't react, and Ben had to concentrate on his driving. Snow blew straight at his windshield. He fought every mile and didn't realize how tight he'd gripped the wheel until his headlights flashed off the wrought-iron arch of the Rising Sun, and he relaxed, knowing they were home.

It still took a long time to go the last half mile. But at last he drove under his carport. Tonight he didn't mind so much entering the dark, chilly house. Clover needed to get to bed.

She didn't release her seat belt, so he went around and opened her door. The dim light showed her eyes closed and her face shiny with sweat.

Ben felt bad for turning the heat so high to defrost his windshield. Lifting her out, he carried her inside and straight to her room. He sat her on the bed and tugged off her hat, jacket and boots. Poor kid was as hot as a lit firecracker. Ben gave her a little shake. "Princess, we're home. You need to wake up and get into your pajamas."

Her eyes fluttered open, but she stared at him blankly. Then she said something that made no sense whatsoever. "Catch those fireflies, Daddy."

Thinking she was dreaming, Ben shook her harder and noticed her arm. It was hot. Brick-red. Swollen twice the normal size from her little wrist to her elbow.

Something was really wrong. He tried twice more to rouse her with no success. Fear as bad as any he'd experienced clutched Ben's chest. Storm or no storm, he decided he had to take Clover to the clinic. Ben had met the physician's assistant, Nathan Ramsey, once. He lived in rooms attached to the clinic the mine owners had built. Thank God the town council had voted to fund the clinic after the mine closed.

Wrapping Clover in a quilt, Ben rushed back to his still-warm pickup. The eight-mile trip felt like the longest he'd ever taken. He wished his old mentor, Bobbalou, had been at the ranch. Or that he had Kate with him. Only one other time had Ben felt so paralyzed and alone—the day he'd learned of his mother's senseless death.

Surely Clover's arm could be easily fixed with medicine.

He hung on to that thought throughout the drive. At

last, on knees that shook like a rough-running engine, he flew out of the Ford with Clover in his arms and pounded on the clinic door.

A sleepy Nate Ramsey unlocked the door. "Bring her in," he said after Ben poured out his story. "You had a helluva drive here. Not fit for man nor beast out tonight."

Ben lay Clover on a gray examining table. She sweat so profusely the paper cover Ramsey pulled out and tucked in at the foot was soon wet where her head thrashed back and forth. "That arm does look mean," he said to Ben, who hovered nearby.

"My educated guess is that it's a spider bite. It was old wood you were working with?"

"A spider? You don't think she picked up a sliver that went in real deep?"

Removing the glasses he'd donned, Nate rubbed his eyes. "I'll bet money on a bite. Whatever it is, her condition is beyond my expertise. I'll need to send satellite photographs of her arm to an attending physician on duty in Boise."

"You can't just give her a shot? An antibiotic?"

Nate shook his head. "You didn't see a spider and kill it, then?"

"No. Between the weather and all, my main goal was to get the wood stacked."

The physician's assistant moved a portable camera on a stand over to the bed and took photos from several angles, then punched a string of codes into his computer.

It felt like an eternity to Ben before the fax machine

in the corner whirred and Ramsey rushed over to remove a sheet of paper. "Emergency room doc thinks it's a spider bite," he said, waving the fax. "He says for me to draw blood for a culture. We'll test for venom and determine the type of poison we're dealing with."

Ben paled. "How long will that take?" His big hand dwarfed Clover's limp one.

"Six to eight hours to grow a good culture and consult with hospital lab techs. I see from your record that you have a fax at your ranch. I'll give her a tetanus shot and draw blood to test. You can go on home and give her Tylenol every four hours, with ibuprofen in between. I'll notify you when I get results and I'll relay instructions for where we go next."

"You mean, leave her like this? I can drive her to Boise."

"It wouldn't help. Not until we see what the culture shows. The tests are the same and I can do them here. At home, you need to elevate that arm. Apply ice packs to keep it from swelling worse. Doc says to wash the area thoroughly with soap and cool water. I'll do that and rig you up an ice pack."

Ben was so exhausted he couldn't think straight. All he could do was agree with anything Nathan said.

CHAPTER NINE

BEN HAD NEVER HATED SNOW MORE. The road was treacherous. He couldn't see a foot beyond his front bumper. Depending on the results of Clover's blood test, the PA said Ben would very likely have to drive her to Boise.

The radio of his pickup blasted out grim news. Disabled cars and trucks were blocking the main roads leading into the city. The announcer said most people had been caught unprepared. *No shit!*

The dash lights showed it was after midnight. Late as it was, Ben rang Bobbalou from the Ford's radio-phone. He wasn't surprised by the groggy "H'llo."

"It's Ben. How are the cattle? How are all of you?"

"What's wrong? First time you ever woke me up to ask such a stupid question. We're up to our asses in drifts. The cows are restless and hungry. I'd rather see your ugly mug shortly after daylight, hauling in a wagon loaded with feed."

"Clover's sick. The clinic PA said her temp's 104. Kid's out of her head, Bobbalou. We stacked wood for the teacher today and Clover got her arm bit. Spider, Ramsey thinks. We've gotta wait for results from blood he took. I don't have any other choice." Ben forced himself to think of his cattle. "How many cows might we lose?"

"Don't know. Zach's counting on you bringing hay. Does the doc think she was bit by a black widow? I can tell you how to fix a poultice out of chittam, aloe root, green tea and a few other ingredients. You make a paste."

"The doctor in Boise that Ramsey contacted by satellite said not to put anything on her arm until we know what we're dealing with. I wish you were here, Bobbalou."

"Bah! What do city doctors know?"

"I'd have brought her to you, but your herbs and stuff are at your place. I'll let you know what they recommend when Nate calls back. I just pulled into the ranch. Tell Zach he'll have to make do until I know when I can get away. If she's not better soon, I'll see if Percy can shake free and deliver a trailer load of hay out your way."

"I knew the part of you that's white would one day mess up the Paiute part. Will you humor this old man? Tie the fetish bracelet I made Clover for good luck when she was a baby around her bad wrist. She outgrew it, but you can extend it with one of the deer hide thongs I made you to tie back your hair. She stores the bracelet in—"

"I know where. I've seen her hide treasures in that wooden box you carved as a present the year she started school. Humor an old man, indeed." Ben felt the first break in his fear. "For Clover, I'll embrace old medicine, modern medicine or voodoo medicine. Anything that'll pull her out of this. I've gotta go, Lou. We'll touch base again after I hear something more."

This time the house seemed colder, darker and lonelier. Ben tried to ignore this sudden longing to have someone share his home, someone like Kate. That notion had hit him today after he'd kissed her. She made him want something he hadn't wanted since he was a little boy. A real family.

For a long time now he'd lied to himself about a lot of things. He'd barreled through life declaring to everyone who knew him that he didn't want or need to share his life with any woman. When friends like Marge or Winnie dared suggest he needed a wife, a woman to help raise Clover, his answer had always been a resounding, hell, no! Maybe what he'd meant and they'd all missed, including him, was that he hadn't run across anyone he wanted at his side—until Kate.

But he couldn't think of that now. Methodically, Ben followed Nathan's instructions to treat Clover. Elevate her arm. Keep the ice bag cold. Ben had asked Nate to read the instructions to him twice. The PA had said Ben could give Clover a child's ibuprofen tablet between doses of Tylenol.

Ben was reluctant to let Clover sleep in her bedroom. What if he was dead to the world and missed her calling him? To ease his own mind, he made her a bed on the couch. If he could get her to take the ibuprofen, he'd hunker down in the leather recliner. That way he'd know if she stirred. The last thing he did—to cover all bases—was dig out Bobbalou's fetish bracelet and tie it around Clover's swollen wrist.

At around four in the morning, she woke up. "Ben," she said plaintively, "I'm thirsty. Uh, why am I on the sofa? And why are you sleeping in your big chair?"

He shot bolt upright. "Princess, hi. How do you feel?" His words sounded garbled because of a yawn. The only light in the room came from a glowing alarm clock he'd brought out from his bedroom at two when they'd gotten home.

"My arm feels cold and my pillow's all wet. Did Jack Frost bite my arm like he did Enrique's toes…I forget when that was." She rubbed her eyes.

Ben scooted her quilt aside and sat on the edge of the sofa, brushing back her tangled hair. "I'm sorry that ice bag got your pillowcase wet. Jack Frost didn't bite you, princess. Something at Kate's cabin did. A spider, the doctor thinks. We're to ice your arm until tests come back and Mr. Ramsey at the clinic phones telling us what to do next. You have to keep this arm raised higher than the rest of your body. I'll go fill the ice bag and bring you something to drink. Water or juice?"

"Juice, please. My head feels like I stayed too long on the Tilt-A-Whirl."

"You still have a fever. But it's too soon to give you more ibuprofen. You should probably try to go back to sleep after drinking some juice."

"Okay. I remember it was snowing lots."

"I'll see if it still is, or if it's quit when I go to the kitchen." He took the ice bag, stripped the damp pillowcase and turned the pillow over. Ben awkwardly moved his way through semidark rooms. He felt muzzy-headed from worry, which was probably why he missed the glass when he poured the juice. Swearing, he mopped up the spill, then almost forgot to return the juice container to the fridge.

The perimeter lights he'd installed to ward off wild animals showed snow still coming down. The tire tracks where he'd driven into the carport were completely covered over now.

Back in the living room, he helped Clover sit up to drink. "It is still snowing. At least you won't miss school with this bite or whatever it is. Did you feel a sting when it happened?"

She nodded as she polished off the juice. "I think so. I kinda do."

"In the shed? On the back porch? Or at the pickup?"

"I think it was in the shed." She closed her eyes. "I'm sleepy. Can we talk tomorrow?"

"Sure. I'm glad to see you acting a little more like your old self, Clover. You had me worried when your fever went so high." Ben leaned down, kissed her forehead and tucked the quilt up under her arms. The arm that had been bitten still looked terribly swollen in the muted light. He wasn't good at praying, so he crossed his fingers and hoped rest and ice would reduce it significantly by morning. He would have liked to see it looking better now, but it was still purple-red and angry.

Worry delayed his going back to sleep for quite some time after Clover's breathing evened out. As long as she remained feverish and her arm swollen, he didn't think he could take her along to haul feed out to the buckaroos. Vida didn't drive. Ben was reasonably sure her granddaughter, who chauffeured Vida to her part-time jobs, wasn't equipped to drive in deep snow. There must be two feet out there, or more.

That was the last thought Ben remembered having. Next thing he knew, he jerked awake, his neck stiff. Clover snored softly. The room glowed in the hazy light of a wintery morning. The clock read six-twenty. He realized it was the whir of the fax machine in the room he'd designated an office that had woken him up. He left the machine on all of the time because the BLM office forwarded copies of court documents to him. Ben wasn't in a rush to get more reports from them. He shared them at ranchers meetings, but he wouldn't be calling a meeting in this weather. All his friends would be too busy trying to save their stock to give a damn about those determined to destroy their livelihood.

The machine stopped abruptly after spitting out two pages. Not enough for a BLM report. Ben got out of the chair and switched on the light. Nothing. Then Ben recalled Nate Ramsey reading off his fax number. Maybe Clover's tests had come back. If so, why wouldn't the PA have called him with the results?

He raced into the office and snatched the pages. The top one bore the clinic logo. It looked as if the second sheet stopped in the middle of a transmission. In the middle of a word. Ben grabbed the phone to call Nathan. He depressed the switch three times before it dawned on him the phone was as dead as the lights and the fax.

Phones frequently went out in bad weather. Lines snapped with the weight of ice and snow. Ben hurried back to the living room, tugged on his boots and found his jacket. Although his phone was out, that didn't necessarily mean phones in town were.

He'd memorized the clinic phone number when Clover had been a baby. Things like that stuck in Ben's head. He fired up the radio unit in his pickup and rubbed his hands together to ward off the cold. He got a squeal and a high-pitched hum, but no answer. *Damn!* Stomping back and forth outside his truck, he clicked on and off several times, then redialed to be sure he hadn't been in too big a hurry to get all the numbers fed in.

Nothing. Satellite service was gone. Ben crumpled the sheets and stared at the carport rafters. "What now?" he shouted to no one. It didn't help to kick his front tire and would have served him right if he'd broken his big toe. He wished the damned spider, if that was what it was, had bitten him and not Clover.

He pictured the wood pile, the shed, the cabin and— Kate. A solution of sorts popped into his head. Not his best choice, but… Tossing the pages on his dash, and before he argued himself out of going, he dashed back inside to get Clover.

Fortunately, she was awake.

"My arm still hurts, Daddy Ben." Her shaky statement coupled with huge tears dripping down still-feverish cheeks served to make his decision easier. He bundled her in the quilt, buckled her in the backseat, then chewed up fresh snow with his four-wheel drive. It took a harrowing fifty minutes to reach Kate's cabin.

Still it was only eight o'clock. Ben didn't take into account that she may have slept in. He grabbed the fax and bundled Clover in her quilt. Snow filled the tops of his boots before he reached the front porch.

Kate's door shook under his flat hand. All at once the door swung open so fast Ben almost fell in on top of Kate, who sat gaping up at him.

"Wow, this is a surprise. Is something wrong? How's Clover?"

"Read these." Ben shoved the papers he'd brought into her hands.

"First get Clover in out of the cold."

Ben elbowed the door shut. Despite his worry he was aware that the house smelled of fresh coffee and something more tantalizing. Bread, maybe. Home-made. His mouth watered, but he shook off thoughts of food and willed Kate to give him good news.

She scanned the two sheets then went back to the top to read a section more thoroughly. Her eyes grew big and her lips trembled. "Oh, Ben."

"What? Dammit, what?" Clearly agitated, he paced around her, dripping water from boots still caked with snow. "I...need...you to tell me what the clinic...says." His dark eyes, flooded with misery, suddenly teared up. "It's finally caught up to me," he said shakily.

"What has? I don't understand. I thought you came here upset because I put cortisone cream on Clover's arm. It's number two on this list of things *not* to do."

"I'm trying to tell you I haven't the foggiest idea what's on those damned pages," he shouted. "Clover can't read well, Kate...because I *can't* read at all!" As his admission hovered in the air between them, Ben squeezed his arms so tightly around his daughter she squirmed and gasped for air.

She pushed weakly at Ben. "You're squeezing the stuffing out of me."

"Sorry, princess." He loosened his hold, but his eyes didn't flinch from the shock he saw in Kate's. "Please!" He resorted to begging. "She's so sick. Tell me what the doctor in Boise says I hafta do to make her better."

"Oh, Ben," Kate burst out. "Why didn't I guess it's you who can't read?" She gave a dismissive wave and again bent over the pages. "There's time for that later. It says here that preliminary venom testing ruled out five spiders common to this area. An expert on the hospital staff thinks Clover's bite may be from a brown recluse spider."

Kate glanced up, her eyes shimmering. "Ben…the downside… There's apparently no antivenom available in the United States to counteract poison from a brown recluse. If you can find the spider and verify that's what it is, it will help the doctors determine a course of treatment. Otherwise you have to wait and watch her for up to ninety-six hours. I'm sure there's more, but this page stops short."

He swore again. "I'm not waiting! As a kid I had a friend who was bitten by a brown recluse. Toby lost his leg because no one could agree how to treat him. I won't let that happen to Clover." Clutching her, Ben stomped around in circles. "Anyway, how in hell can a doctor sitting on his duff in Boise know what bit her?"

Kate bit her lip. "I think what may be missing from

this page is a picture of the spider. Danny has an insect book that shows various spiders and bugs," Kate suggested. "I called him for breakfast right before you came. He'll be out in a minute. Speaking of breakfast, have you two eaten?"

"It'd be good if Clover ate so she can have another dose of ibuprofen. The PA in town said it might help reduce both the pain and the swelling. If I have any chance in hell of finding the culprit, I'd better get out to the shed and start moving wood. There's bound to be more than one spider in the woodpile. I don't suppose you'd have two or three glass jars with lids?" he asked, finally setting Clover on one of Kate's futons. "Old jelly glasses would work."

Kate thought a moment. "I have a carton full of baby-food jars I collected way back when I started teaching. All of my books and supplies were stored for years at my in-laws'. I brought everything, figuring I'd toss what I didn't need. The box is in the hall coat closet."

She pointed, but Ben was already moving down the hall. A few minutes later he backed out of the closet, juggling three jars in each hand.

"You expect to find six spiders in my shed?" Kate grimaced.

"If I have to move every stick of wood in the shed and porch to find the right one, I'll do it."

"Ben, it sounds a lot like hunting a needle in a haystack. And…is there danger of you being bitten, too?"

"I have gloves in the Ford. And a powerful flashlight. I need to get cracking. Is it okay if I leave Clover with you?"

"Of course. Um, I know finding the spider is your top priority, but I want to talk more about your reading. You must be aware that there's a staggering number of adults in this country who can't read? I can hardly believe you managed to hide this so well."

"I compensate. I have an excellent memory. I get other people to read the reports and then I'll say, okay, sum up what you think. I ask questions and store facts. Bobbalou's bugged me for years to sign up for night classes." Ben shrugged, one hand clasping the door knob. "I found reasons to avoid registering for literacy classes. I was afraid if word got out, I'd be humiliated. But I knew I had to get Clover help. I'm running an ad in the newspaper to hire her a tutor, Kate. It's just…so far no one's responded."

"You're never too old to learn to read. I'll keep your secret, Ben, but only if there's no more wiggling out of lessons." She ran a hand over Clover's forehead. "I can teach you and your dad together, honey. Would you like that?"

The girl seemed groggy again.

"First things first," Kate said briskly. "Clover, we need you at one hundred percent. For now, let's move you to the futon farthest from the fire. Ben, another thing this report says—no heat near her bad arm. It hastens pitting of the skin." Kate didn't add, *and accelerates tissue destruction.* She'd discuss that later with Ben, out of Clover's hearing.

Clover dragged herself to the other settee. Goldie

left her braid rug to sniff the girl. The dog ended up whining and laying her chin across Clover's lap.

Danny wandered out of his bedroom, oblivious to the fact they had company. "Mom, I finished the puzzle Mimi sent. Hey, I didn't know you guys were here. Has it stopped snowing? Do we have to go to school?"

"No." Kate pulled him aside and began explaining about the spider. Ben was already on his way out. Kate darted a worried look his way, but the door was closing so he didn't see. She should have said to be careful. What if he got bitten, too?

"I know right where that book is." Danny ran to the bookcase.

"Danny, breakfast is ready. Clover's still not feeling so hot. I'll fix trays and you two can eat in here."

"I'm gonna help Ben find that mean old spider."

"You'll do nothing of the sort."

Danny pulled on his jacket and cap and tucked the book under his arm. "Mom, I've gotta go with Ben. Yesterday me and Clover did see a spider. I remember telling her maybe it was a black widow. But then we saw it was brown. I know right where it crawled out of sight. I can show Ben."

"Danny, no!" Kate cried. "It's too dangerous. Let Ben look. He's an adult."

Donning a stubborn set to his jaw, Danny ducked around his mom's wheelchair and was out the door. Panicked, she motored over to the open door and yelled, "Danny, I said do not go in the shed. Stop!"

"I'm not scared of a stupid old spider," he shouted, slipping and sliding in the snow beyond the porch.

Fear ricocheted through Kate. She should have stopped Colton from driving in the rainstorm. Now Danny was heading for danger. The papers from the clinic crackled in her shaking hand. If Clover had been bitten by a brown recluse, the prognosis was bleak. There was a probability she'd develop necrotic lesions. *Death of the skin,* the fax said in bold black letters. Following, in parentheses, was a description of the rotting flesh that would need to be cut away by a doctor every day as the lesions spread. A continuous course of antibiotics might help avoid bacterial infection, but two out of three victims required plastic surgery to close deep holes caused by the lesions.

Overwhelmed by fear for Danny and Ben, Kate aimed her wheelchair at the ramp. "Danny, please wait. We need to talk about this." She saw him trudging down the path Ben had shoveled yesterday. The snow was less deep there and he widened the gap between them.

Telling Goldie to stay with Clover, Kate spun back to shut the door then gunned her chair down the ramp. The smaller front wheels hit a mound of snow at the bottom and lurched to the side, throwing her off balance. She couldn't budge the darned thing.

Kate saw Ben take a flashlight from his pickup. Why hadn't he heard Kate shouting? Danny opened the shed door.

Visions of her son's body covered in gaping wounds filled Kate's mind. She forced herself out of the chair, then stumbled forward on legs that hadn't carried her for over two years.

BEN ELBOWED HIS PICKUP DOOR closed, turned and saw
Kate fall. Making a guttural sound, he dropped every-
thing and bounded toward her through knee-deep snow.
"Kate, what in hell are you doing? You've got no boots,
no jacket." Ben half hopped, half waded through drifts.
The fact Kate wasn't in her wheelchair hadn't sunk in.

His shout penetrated the fog of fear Kate had been
operating in. All at once she comprehended where she
was—lying in the snow at least ten steps from her
chair. *She had walked.* Her legs felt like sponge rubber
now. The realization had her babbling, sobbing and
struggling to stand again.

Panting hard, Ben reached her side and swung her
into his arms. He tried shifting his grip to dust her off,
but she was too covered in snow for him to make any
headway. The wind whistled around them, and dammit,
he couldn't even tell if she was injured. "Kate…honey,
talk to me. Why are you out here? Is Clover's fever
back? Did she convulse? The PA said she might." Once
that fear hit, Ben started waddling uphill like a duck.
For every step forward, his boots slipped and carried
him back two.

"Ben, Ben." Kate pounded at his broad chest.
"Clover's okay. I left her with Goldie. It's Danny. He
insisted on helping you find the spider even after I told
him no. I think worry drove me to…" Her eyes glistened. "Ben, I walked. Alone. Several steps. Oh, but
you need to stop Danny."

The boy either heard the commotion or else wondered why Ben was not in the shed. When he came back
outside and saw Ben carrying Kate, Danny let out a yell

and scrambled up the path. "Mom! Mom! Oh, no, did she fall outta her chair? I'm sorry, I'm sorry," he sobbed. "It's my fault, Ben. I didn't listen."

"Stop, Ben," Kate urged. "Did anyone hear me? *I walked.* It's crazy. It happened just like Dr. Pearsall predicted. I walked!"

Ben didn't stop until he reached the porch. Barely glancing behind him, he ordered, "Danny, bring your mom's wheelchair. And calm down. Apparently she's fine."

The sheepish boy quickly complied. He wrestled the chair up the ramp. Inside, he watched in amazement as his mother stood without anyone's help.

Even Goldie left Clover's side, trotted over and nuzzled Kate's wet ankles.

Ben and Danny watched her hobble to the empty futon, where she sank down and kicked off her wet slippers.

Ben whooped. He and Danny shared high fives.

"My calves are tight in spots and floppy as Jell-O in others, but mercy, it's truly a miracle." Strong emotion clogged her voice and Kate wiped her eyes. "I refuse to cry. I want to laugh and turn cartwheels. But there'll be time to celebrate my good fortune later—once Clover's well."

Danny threw his arms around her. "Please, Mom. I know I can help Ben find the spider. I looked up brown recluse in my book, see, it's right here." He grabbed for the book, which had fallen to the floor. "I think it's the one me 'n' Clover spotted yesterday. He coulda bit her.

He fell off a piece of wood she set on the stack. I know about where he crawled real fast outta sight."

Her son sounded so earnest, Kate blindly accepted the book. She shuddered, looking at the picture, but found herself relenting. Clover lay like a zombie, her swollen arm dangling. Kate was afraid the bite had begun to blister.

Ben saw it, too. He walked over, knelt down and kissed the little girl. "Hey, princess, are you feeling yucky again?"

She bobbed her head. "I'm hot and my arm hurts somethin' awful."

Kate closed Danny's book with a snap. "You two, go then. Shoo. Ben, how much ibuprofen can Clover have? I'll see if I can coax her to eat a little of the breakfast I fixed." She held out her hands, inviting Ben to help her stand.

He did, with admiration and trepidation. Ben wasn't at all sure he ought to let loose of her, but when her smile came out like the sun, he slowly withdrew his support.

Kate took six steps before her legs buckled, forcing her to grab hold of the back of a chair. "I was afraid it was a fluke," she said, tears running down her cheeks.

Ben rushed over and kissed her on her wet, trembling mouth. He didn't seem to care that the kids were nearby. "I thought maybe it was due to adrenaline rush," he said huskily. "But, hey, look at you. You're still on your feet."

"When it comes down to it, we're quite a pair, aren't we? You have to learn how to read from A, B, C, Ben, and I need to start walking with baby steps."

"Huh?" Danny glanced up from studying his book. "Ben can read. Everybody but babies and little kids can."

"That's not true," Clover said, rousing. "I can only read a few easy words. I wanted to tell you, I was afraid you'd make fun of me. Meg Wheeler says I'm dumb."

"Honey, you're a smart little girl," Kate said, "and Danny won't tease, and he won't tell…anyone." She slowly worked her way back across the room to sit beside Clover. "And you will learn to read. So will Ben."

Ben set his hand on Danny's shoulder and turned him toward the door. "I'm actually glad my secret's out. It's a weight off my chest, I can tell you."

"Why didn't you learn in first grade like ev'rybody?" Danny asked, looking up at the man he admired.

"I guess you'd say I didn't grow up in a learning-friendly environment. But that's a whole other story for another day."

The two stepped out into a storm that finally showed signs of lessening. Ben's parting comment made Kate wonder about his childhood. He'd mentioned a bit about his mother, but she realized how little she did know. One thing was certain. Ben was a compassionate, caring dad.

No matter what his background, Ben Trueblood had grown up to be a good man. A man worthy of a woman's kisses. And, Kate mused, someone who could teach Danny a thing or two about how to be a real man.

But she was forgetting one thing. She didn't want

Ben to give Danny ideas about becoming a buckaroo. Should their relationship move forward, Ben would have to promise her that.

She smoothed a hand over Clover's fine hair, and the little girl snuggled in close. "I love you, Ms. Kate," she said sleepily. "I saw Daddy Ben kiss you. I hope you're gonna marry him and move in with us. We don't have any bad brown spiders at our ranch."

Kate opened her mouth to tell Clover that she and Ben were just friends. Glancing down at the girl's swollen arm, she decided it would be better not to say anything to upset Clover. And in reality, it might just be the fever talking.

Struggling to stand, Kate made her way to the kitchen to get juice and an ibuprofen tablet. But the girl's fantasy came back to Kate after she'd changed into dry jeans and a sweatshirt and sat grading papers. Because the truth was, Kate kept conjuring up the same fantasy of the four of them as a family.

CHAPTER TEN

MIDWAY THROUGH THE MORNING, Kate's right thigh seized. Her leg went into spasms that hurt so bad tears came to her eyes. Thankfully, Clover had dropped off to sleep after she'd eaten a bite of breakfast. Kate would hate to cry in front of a child who was dealing with something potentially worse than muscle cramps.

Goldie, bless her heart, got up and paced over to Kate. The dog made sympathetic noises and pawed lightly at Kate's knee. "It's okay, girl. I overdid a good thing. What I need is a good masseuse. I'm sure this weather doesn't help atrophied muscles that suddenly want to work again." Kate wished she'd been a little more faithful about doing her exercises.

She was still attempting to ease the cramp when Ben and Danny returned carrying three jars.

"Kate? Did you fall again?" Ben set down his two jars on the table and stripped off his leather gloves. He dropped to his haunches and rubbed Kate's knee.

She lifted the hem of her sweatshirt to dry her eyes. "I hate this waterworks. I'm dealing with leg cramps, Ben. The doctor in Fort Worth warned me to lay off caffeine, which worsens cramps. I must've had four cups of coffee today. I've also been hit and miss doing stretching exercises. But enough about me." She glanced tentatively at the jars. "I hope you guys screwed those lids on tight."

"Yep," Danny reassured her. "Didn't we, Ben? Now we hafta check these spiders against the picture in my book. Goldie, get away from those." The dog had left Clover's side to nudge his nose against the jars Ben had set on the coffee table.

Kate passed Ben the book. "You look. I'm squeamish."

The man and the boy lined the three jars up and dropped down on their knees. Neither noticed Kate scoot away.

"I think we got him." Ben pounded Danny's back. He turned to Kate. "We moved every stick of wood in the stack where Danny thought he saw a spider zip out of sight. Come look." He tapped a page. "Danny's book shows the brown recluse with funny marks on his back, exactly like this fella."

Danny leaned in. "The note under the picture calls them fiddle or violin marks."

"I figure we can let this bitty black spider go," Ben said. "I'll take the two brown ones in for Nate to see. They could hang out in pairs like black widows. Males and females may have different markings."

Kate surged forward. "You listen to me. You will not turn a spider loose so he can end up back in my woodshed or in the house, Ben Trueblood."

He and Danny both studied her as if she'd sprouted

two heads. "Mom is such a girl when it comes to bugs and stuff," Danny confided.

Ben handed Danny the jar containing the black spider. "Be a good buckaroo. Go away from the house. Make his demise quick and humane."

Kate would much rather have Ben handle the spider, but this gave her an opportunity to speak her mind. She waited until Danny closed the door first. Ben was inspecting Clover's swollen arm.

"Ben, since I volunteered to take on the job of tutoring Clover and you in reading, there's something I'd like from you in exchange."

"I'll pay whatever you say the going rate is, Kate. I don't expect you to teach us for free."

"It's not money I want." She made sure he was paying attention. "I don't want Danny involved in rodeo-type competitions, so please stop saying things like you did a minute ago to encourage him."

"That's a tough promise. Our Rope and Ride is the equivalent of a regional rodeo. It's a big deal for ranchers and town folks. People come from miles around. Competing is about the only fun buckaroos have. Young kids like Danny learn valuable techniques by hanging over the fence, watching experienced buckaroos."

"My son isn't a young buckaroo. He's going to college, so he can have a job with more security."

Ben's eyes narrowed. "Stuck in some office, you mean? Relegated to a cubicle where he can't tell if it's snowing out or if the sun's shining? That would smother the life out of most ranch kids."

"And men accuse women of being overly dramatic. There are lots of jobs besides ranching that don't involve being in an office all day. And Danny might learn to love one of them."

"Learn to love what?" Danny had come in the back door and caught the tail of their conversation.

"The career you decide to pursue," Kate clarified. "At your age, if you study hard, there's no limit to what you can do. The world is your oyster."

"Huh?" He appealed to Ben for clarification.

Ben knew from experience that some boys fell in love with ranch life from the cradle. Danny already exhibited all the signs. Obviously his mother didn't see them, or she chose to ignore them. But the time to point that out to Kate wasn't in front of the boy. Given the chance, Ben thought he could change her attitude. So he dropped the subject for now, gesturing instead at his sleeping daughter. "Kate, will you do me a favor? Ride with me to the clinic? Our PA is connected to the hospital in Boise via a more powerful satellite. If information flies back and forth fast, you may catch something I miss. As well, you can ask Nate to prescribe a muscle relaxant to help with your legs."

"Are the roads passable? It's snowed more since you drove to town yesterday."

"The county has a plow. I expect Jim Wilson's been out since dawn. With phones down, I do need to swing past Percy Lightfoot's and ask if he'll haul a load of hay to my cows. I've got no idea how many days this arm of Clover's will keep us housebound."

"I'd go, but we have Goldie and Flame. What time do you think we'll be back?"

"The dog can go along and Danny can feed and water his horse before we go. Can't say how long we'll be."

"Okay. I'll fix us sandwiches. You two haven't eaten a thing."

Danny took off like a shot to tend to Flame.

"You seem hesitant about going along," Ben said.

"I'm just uneasy about riding over slick roads."

"I don't intend to crash, Kate."

She eyed him sadly. "I doubt anyone ever intends to, Ben. But accidents happen."

"That was a thoughtless remark. I'm sorry, Kate." He closed the gap between them, leaned over her and cradled her face between chapped hands. "I'd love for you to come with me, Kate, but I won't pressure."

His concern for her when he had his own problems touched Kate. "I'm the one who should apologize. This isn't about me. It's about getting Clover treatment. I want to be there for you, Ben. And Clover."

Kate knew her words had pleased him by the kiss Ben delivered. Neither seemed willing to break contact until they heard Danny kicking snow off his boots.

"To be continued," Ben promised, taking a deep breath.

From the passionate light smoldering in his eyes, Kate didn't doubt him for a second. "I think you just left me too weak in the knees to try walking out to your truck."

"I'm not letting you try," Ben said, reluctantly releasing her from his embrace. "I'll carry Clover out first. Put Danny in charge of our specimens. Then if he takes out your wheelchair, I'll carry you to my pickup."

"Don't forget Goldie. Ben, are you sure you want all the fuss and bother of having us go along? Me in particular," she clarified, as she sat in her wheelchair.

"I want you with me," a sleepy voice said from the couch.

Kate and Ben both turned to look at Clover. How long had she been awake? Had she witnessed their kiss?

"My arm feels hot," she said, throwing off the quilt. "Tell Mr. Ramsey I want a shot to make the hurt go away."

Ben's brows puckered.

"You want a shot?" The question came from Danny, who'd just walked in. "Wow, Clover, you're brave. I don't know any guys who'd ask for a shot."

"I hope it's that simple," Ben mumbled, leaving Kate to bundle his daughter up again.

Once Ben took Clover to the truck, Kate made sandwiches. She tried to get across to Danny the seriousness of Clover's fate.

"I know Clover might get worse, Mom. It says so in my book. Don'tcha think if I tell her she's brave now, she'll remember that later when she needs to be lots braver?"

"Maybe. I'm proud of you for thinking of that, Danny." She hugged him, but he wiggled out to go snap a leash on Goldie's collar.

"I didn't think of it on my own, Mom. It's what calf ropers learn in Pawpaw's class. Ya gotta believe you can win whether or not you hurt."

That was news to Kate. But perhaps Royce pushed such an attitude to extremes. That would explain why

Colton had constantly felt he had to challenge his last win by asking for rougher bucking horses at each rodeo.

Ben returned for Kate and the lunch. "It's snowing again. Are you having second thoughts?" he asked, holding out her jacket.

"No. Danny raised a point and now I'm trying to figure out what separates someone who's self-assured from someone who is flagrantly cocky."

"Uh-oh. I hope you're not tacking that last label on me."

She laughed as Ben zipped her jacket then swept her up into his arms. "Fishing for compliments, eh?" She felt the low rumble of laughter in Ben's broad chest as he charged with her through two-foot drifts.

Ben set her in the passenger seat, shut her door and rounded the hood to jump in his side.

"If this weather keeps up," Kate murmured, "school will be closed tomorrow."

"The board builds ten days into the calendar for inclement weather."

"Can you recall a time you've used all ten?"

"I have to admit I rarely pay attention, and after Sikes left, the kids were home anyway." He glanced at Kate. "I hope you're planning to stick around."

"She'll stay this year," Danny said. "I know, 'cause I wanted to go back to Texas, and Mom said she'd signed a contract for a year and we're staying till May, period."

"You're not renewing for a second term?" Ben briefly took his eyes off the road again to look at Kate.

She read in his glance something deeper than interest on behalf of the school board. "I said I'd reassess in May, Danny."

"But, if you leave, who'll teach me and Ben to read?" Clover asked.

"If you work hard, you'll be reading at grade level before May."

"Ow, ow, ow." The girl leaned forward and stuck her swollen arm over the seat for Kate to look at. "It hurts and itches all at the same time, but I'm not s'posed to scratch."

Ben had just made a hard right turn off the highway. "Three more miles and we'll be at Lightfoot's ranch."

"Where's your ice pack, hon?" Kate asked the girl. "That might help the itching."

"At your cabin. It stopped being cold."

"Princess, you'll have to wait and see if Winnie has a spare ice bag," Ben said. "If not, we can fill a plastic baggie with snow. Hang on, it won't be long."

The words were no more out of his mouth than he passed beneath a wrought-iron gate similar to his. A hill to the left of the barn was crisscrossed with sled tracks.

"Their house is a twin to yours, Ben," Kate commented.

"You have a good eye. They are alike, but our floor plan is flipped. Winnie found the plans in a house magazine. Chad Keevler and Percy built this house. I helped and saw things I liked. I bought the plans from Winnie."

"I'd love to see what they've done inside, but this is no time for a social call. It takes too much effort to get me out and Clover's feeling worse."

"Look, Mom," Danny said. "They've got two big dogs coming out of the barn with Adam. And there's Jeff Goetz." Danny wrapped an arm around Goldie, who'd seen the dogs and started barking ferociously.

"Winnie will be disappointed," Ben said. "Visitors are a treat for ranch wives. But I know she'll understand."

"I hope so. Teachers are supposed to be equally accessible to the parents of all students, but this is our third outing together. People may try to make more out of it. You know what I mean?"

He parked next to a mud-spattered pickup, got out and snorted a laugh. "Winnie and Della Quimby volunteered me to look out for you, Kate. Those two and a few others have been trying to marry me off for ten years. They'll be jumping for joy to see they've finally found a woman I'm interested in."

He left Kate to ponder his words. *How interested was he?* They'd kissed, sure, and she liked Ben—a lot. Kate thought about him when he wasn't around. But she'd made one huge mistake in her love life. With Colton she'd let galloping hormones lead her into marriage, but even the great sex had faded when Colton had made it plain that variety was the spice of life. She'd told herself his conquests didn't matter, but they did. She should have heeded what a stove-up rodeo bum had once told her—you can't tame a rodeo cowboy, and it was a foolish woman who thought she could. The dream of finishing in the money at the next rodeo, or the next, had a greater pull on most men than any wife or mistress.

But Ben seemed more settled. He had a home. By his own admission, though, he and Clover rarely spent time there. Clover said straight out she'd rather be out on the range trailing the herd than at home.

Kate was a homebody. If ever she married again, she wanted a man who put home and family first.

Ben reappeared faster than she expected. Winnie Lightfoot, who had a trim figure and hair much like Clover's, stepped out on her porch and waved.

Kate waved back. "Oh, good," she said to Ben, "you got an ice pack. Clover, hon, maybe this will make your arm feel better until we get to town." Kate turned and shooed Goldie away in order to settle Clover more comfortably.

She missed the smirk Winnie flashed Ben and had no way of knowing she'd been the hot topic of their conversation. For Kate's sake, Ben had denied that the teacher had gotten under his skin. His best friend's wife had scoffed and said if Kate mothered his sick child, he'd be a fool to turn her loose.

Ben considered that as he backed down Lightfoot's lane. Some time ago, he'd dated a divorcée who'd owned a coffeehouse in town. It had failed when the mines had closed. Ben hadn't been all that sad to see Liz go. She'd had no interest in Clover, which didn't set well with Ben. Before Liz, the Baptist preacher's grown daughter had come home. She'd lavished a lot of attention on Clover, who was two years old at the time. But it turned out Grace was more interested in converting Ben than marrying him.

Bobbalou said her aim was to save all heathen

Indians, which was probably exactly how she'd put it. The last time Ben ran into Grace in Boise, she was a missionary home on furlough from the jungles of Bolivia. As Winnie rudely pointed out, Ben's history with women pretty much sucked, and she insinuated that he harbored unrealistic expectations. Ben disagreed. He wanted a lover who was interested in being a full partner in all aspects of his life. But maybe it wasn't realistic to expect a woman to endure the ups and downs of ranching, especially if land leases were revoked. A man stood to lose—most everything.

Kate Steele was under Ben's skin, but little things gave him pause. She was dead set against letting Danny mess with roping and she'd admitted she had no firm plans to stay past May. Ben was falling for Kate, but Clover was already smitten with her teacher.

"You're quiet," Kate said, interrupting his meandering thoughts. "Is it the worsening weather? Are you afraid we might not make it to town and back?"

Removing one hand from the wheel, Ben rubbed the back of his neck. "We're getting some nasty fog along with flurries. Makes driving a pain. Winnie had a short-wave radio on. Reports are this storm is blowing through fast. The weatherman said a Pacific jet stream ought to shove the snow north and bring warm winds next week."

"Good. I'd hate for the kids to miss much more school, since last year was mostly a loss."

He looked sheepish. "Clover being the worst of the lost sheep, huh?"

"Perhaps. And depending on her course of treatment for that bite, she might have to miss more school."

"Are you saying they haven't learned how to treat these bites in the twenty-five years since my friend Toby tangled with a brown recluse?"

"I don't know that, Ben, since you didn't receive the entire transmission. I'm saying, from what I read, treatment may take weeks, not days."

He fell silent again. The only noise in the cab came from the rapid swish of the Ford's wiper blades.

There was a light on in the clinic and one other vehicle parked out front, beside the PA's car.

"Kate, you'd bog down in your wheelchair. Let me carry Clover in. Danny can stay with her while I come back for you."

"I hate making you run back and forth. Maybe I can walk in, with help."

"Not until Nate examines you and we're sure walking's not damaging your muscles."

"I don't see how it could, Ben."

"Maybe, but maybe not. If Nate clears you, I won't argue again."

"Oh, okay. You'd better go. The other patients have come out."

"It's Leonard Mackey. His is the oldest ranch in our valley. He suffered a heart attack last year and his sons have taken over day-to-day operations. Clover, I'll come around and get you out after I have a word with Len and Bess. I hope he didn't try to help his sons in the storm."

He slammed the door and hurried over to the older couple.

Kate saw him grasp the older man's arm and take the key from the woman Ben opened the passenger door and carefully seated the old fellow, then helped his wife in. It gave Kate a warm rush to watch Ben show such concern for the older couple. He closed the car door, but didn't move until Mrs. Mackey had safely backed up the slope.

"How far does she have to go to get home?" Kate asked when he returned. She helped Danny restrain Goldie, who wanted out the minute Ben reached in for Clover.

"She has sixteen miles to the ranch. Half on gravel. Bess is a tough ranch wife. Apparently Len suffered what Nate termed a ministroke. Luckily, Nate had samples on hand of a medication cardiologists in Boise added to Len's others. Bess can drive straight home without stopping at the drugstore."

"Why didn't one of their sons drive?"

"They're out trying to save their cattle from dying. On a working ranch, Kate, saving the cows takes priority over almost anything."

"Before a man's life?" Her tone said what she thought of that. "Danny, snap on Goldie's leash and take her out for a minute before you go in with Ben."

Ben should have left Kate to her delusions. He didn't. "Frankly, Kate, it's a toss-up over the importance of cattle versus a ranch owner's health and wellbeing. If our cows die, we can't pay for doctors, medicine or mortgages and food. Cattle around here are as precious as a rancher's life's blood."

So it was true that people ranked below steers. She wondered what he'd do about Clover if doctors couldn't cure her quickly? But that wasn't fair. He'd spent a whole day turning over wood to find the spider. Still, Ben hadn't liked asking his friend Percy to deliver hay to his herd. It reminded Kate of all the times her father-in-law had expected Melanie to cancel their plans because one of his prize bulls had developed an ailment. Kate had realized then why Colton had lived his life expecting the world to revolve around his wishes.

Danny brought Goldie back. Kate toweled her feet and belly and sent Danny on into the clinic.

"Would you mind carrying the two jars of spiders?" Ben asked.

"You're kidding, I hope."

"I told Nate we had spiders. He needs to verify the markings and I need to carry you."

Her heart pounded harder at the thought of holding the jars. "I'll do it for Clover."

Ben laughed. "I'm teasing, Kate. I'll get out the jars and set them on the running board. Danny volunteered to come fetch them."

"And maybe slip and fall? I stand by my first offer, but if you drop us both, Ben Trueblood, I'll kill you."

"I believe it. I've seen what you can do in an adrenaline rush, Kate. Once I put the jars into your hands, close your eyes."

She did. Still, cold shivers ran up her spine. But maybe this would help her get over her spider phobia. She'd come here to make a fresh start in her life, but there were a number of areas that needed work. For one, she wasn't being fair to Ben about his stock. They did represent income. His life's work.

"We made it," he whispered in her ear, bending to place her in a chair next to Danny.

Kate opened one eye. "Take the jars, please, Ben. I can only cross so many hurdles in a single day."

He whisked them away. "Thank you, brave lady. Nate," he called, "take these spiders with our new schoolteacher's compliments."

Grinning, Nate Ramsey shook Kate's hand before he took the specimens. The two men each held up a jar and shook the contents. They eventually agreed that Danny and Ben had identified the brown recluse.

"Danny, my man." Ben extended the jar with the harmless spider. "You're our expert spider terminator. This fellow earned the fate of his little black buddy for no reason other than he dared take up residence in your mother's woodshed."

"That's right." Kate looked her son in the eye. "And no letting him off easy because we're miles from home. Dogs and cats have homing radar. Who's to say it's different with spiders?"

"Aw, Mom. For a teacher, you're not very smart. If I shook this guy out on the branch of that tree outside, he'd crawl under the bark and it'd be his new home."

"Says you. One book on insects does not make you an expert. I read your book. It says most spiders are poisonous. Luckily, very few have fangs long or strong enough to penetrate the human skin."

"I read that, too. All right, this guy is history."

While they were having their mother-son debate, Nate contacted the doctor in Boise via satellite phone. He listened mostly and scribbled on a yellow pad.

"Okay, this is what you can expect," he said, hanging up. "See this blister already forming inside the bruise? Doc called that a bull's-eye. The core will get bigger as it fills with blood. Within a day it'll rupture and form an ulcer. That's bad. You'll need to get her to the hospital when that happens. Staff there will cleanse the ulcer with povidone iodine and soak it three times a day in sterile saline. That's essentially sterile salt water, Ben. You heard me tell the on-call doc, it's snowing again. He said to tell you they will undoubtedly have to surgically cut away dead skin as the ulcer expands."

With each bit of information Nate dispatched, Kate noticed the muscles in Ben's back grow more tense. He was standing outside Clover's room and Kate was in the one directly opposite waiting for Nate to examine her legs.

Ben seemed so alone that Kate slid off the end of her table and hobbled over to him with some difficulty. She ran a hand up his back. "If you're worried about what to do with Danny and me, maybe I can contact Marge Goetz and ask if she'll arrange for someone to take us home."

Nate picked up the satellite phone again. "I need to let the outpatient department know what time you expect to be there with Clover, Ben. A rough estimate is fine. They're aware of weather conditions."

"Hang up," Ben ordered gruffly. "I'm not taking her. At least not yet."

Nate objected vocally, and Kate dragged Ben down the hall. Lowering her voice, she hissed, "Ben, what he says corresponds with the information they faxed you. You're catching this early, and it's good you know for sure the type of spider. With early treatment, her ulcers might not spread."

"An open sore is easily infected," Ben argued, his jaw thrust out. "Hospitals are full of germs."

Danny came back inside the clinic. "Where is everybody? Hey, does anybody care that it's snowing harder?"

"Another reason not to drive to Boise," Ben said. "In no time it'll be dark. Nate, will you check Kate now? I'd like to get underway while we have daylight." He lifted her with little effort and deposited her back on the examining table.

Choosing a new chart, Ramsey began writing as Kate explained about the accident. As she talked, he handed her a gown and had her remove her boots and jeans. "I've read case studies on miracle recoveries such as you seem to have experienced. But I've never seen one. Your muscles are weak when palpated, but that's understandable if you backed off physical therapy. You need to notify Dr. Pearsall to send us your complete records. I can give you a few muscle relaxants to tide you past the worst spasms. If Ben wasn't in such a blooming hurry to leave, an ultrasound treatment on your hips and legs would do wonders."

"How long will that take?" Ben inquired from outside her door.

"Ten minutes per side."

"We can spare the time."

When the treatment was over, Nate said, "I'll list this in your chart, Kate. You might want another treatment in say, two weeks. Your insurance should cover it."

"My legs feel better already," she said, working her jeans on underneath the gown. "Maybe I won't need the pills."

Nate left the room and returned with a small packet as she zipped her boots. "It won't hurt to have them on hand."

Kate thanked him, stuck the pills and the invoice to send to her insurance company in her pocket and prepared to leave. He forestalled her. "If you have any influence with Ben, I wish you'd talk him into taking Clover to the hospital."

"I'll try," she promised.

She kept her word to Nate after they'd settled Clover in Ben's truck. "You didn't tell the Nate about your friend, Toby. I know his experience has you worried sick, but there's been a lot new in medicine since then."

"I meant what I said. Hospitals aren't clean. The one where Nate wants to send Clover just had a rare staph infection. People died."

"Oh."

"I have a plan, but I need your help."

"If I can help, you know I will," she said, facing him.

"Come home with me. Stay with Clover while I ride out and collect Lou Bobolink. I didn't say anything back there, because doctors are at odds with the old methods of healing."

"What kind of old methods?" She sounded wary.

"Last night when I phoned Lou and mentioned Clover had been bitten, he tried to tell me how to make a poultice. I'll give Bobbalou twenty-four hours, Kate.

I swear if Clover's not improved by then, I'll take her to the hospital."

"Ride out to camp? But…you just told Nate it'll be dark soon, and dangerous to travel even on the highway. I don't know, Ben… Are you sure?"

"I could reach our winter lease blindfolded. It's not a hard decision for me. I'd trust Bobbalou with my life."

"I think you should do what the doctor in Boise told Nate. They've had years of schooling, Ben. Remember, Dr. Pearsall was dead-on about my case."

"If you won't stay with Clover, Kate, I'll bundle her up and take her out to Lou."

Kate huddled in her jacket. Dusk had crept in and the wiper blades had difficulty sweeping aside the wet snow. "With all you've done for me, I wouldn't feel right telling you no. Danny, Goldie and I will stay tonight. One night, Ben. Tomorrow we have Danny's horse to look after. And if Clover isn't better, you have to go to Boise."

CHAPTER ELEVEN

"ARE YOU REALLY GOING TO STAY all night at our house?" Clover aimed her sleepy question at Kate. "The only person who has ever done that is Ms. Vida, when Ben has important business."

"I'm staying, Clover. This time his business is to get help for you." Kate sent Ben another sidelong glance that said in her estimation help was in Boise.

"My arm feels giant. It's hot 'n' itchy. And my leg hurts, too."

Kate reached into the backseat and stroked Clover sympathetically. "It'll be time for more ibuprofen before you go to bed."

Danny roused. "Where will I sleep, Mom? Uh, I just thought of something. Maybe I can ride out to the camp with Ben. I'm not a bit sleepy."

"Not on your life, mister! Besides, having someone tag along might hold Ben back, Danny." It was a convenient excuse. It scared Kate witless to think of Ben out there trekking through darkness and deep snow. No way could she bear it if Danny were with him.

"Danny, I'm counting on you to help your mother." Ben had read Kate's mind—she did not want her son going along.

Everyone's spirits picked up when Ben reached the Rising Sun arch. "Sorry about asking you into a cold house, Kate. I have a generator, but I don't like leaving it operating if no one's home. I'll fire it up. Between it and the fireplace, it shouldn't be long until the worst of the chill is off. Stay here until I get a light on."

"All right. Danny, walk Goldie along the fence line."

"Okay. But I'm hungry. When's supper?" Danny and Ben had devoured the sandwiches Kate had made on the drive to town, but that was a long time ago.

"I'm not hungry," Clover said listlessly. "My stomach wants to throw up. Am I getting the flu like Sarah Keevler had?"

"Oh, honey, it's probably nausea from the spider venom," Kate said. "Nathan Ramsey did say that's often a side effect of the kind of bite you have."

"The spider didn't bite my stomach, Ms. Kate."

"Side effects are other things that happen as a result of the bite. In your case it can be headache, swelling, a blister or an upset stomach."

"You're so smart. I wanna be just like you when I grow up."

Ben returned in time to hear his daughter praise Kate. "See," he murmured, "we both want you around. So don't be thinking about leaving us in May."

"Leaving teaching here, you mean?"

"Did I say anything about teaching? Here's something to think about while I'm gone to fetch Bobbalou. Remember what Clover said about Vida being the only woman I've invited to sleep over? Vida's sixtyish.

If I've been slow to let a woman into my private life, Kate, it's because I never met anyone I wanted there… until now." Letting his words hang between them, Ben gathered up Clover and backed out of the truck.

Kate swung open her door to follow, but he stayed her. "I'll return for you. Let me get Clover in first."

Danny and Goldie intercepted Ben. Kate saw them all go inside.

"Ben, I don't need carrying," she called, sliding out before he reached her. "Nate Ramsey said to exercise."

Ben rushed to assist Kate anyway. He steadied her with an arm around her waist. "What else did Nate say?"

"That my recovery was profound. I promised I'd have Dr. Pearsall send my health records to the clinic, since he said my paralysis would eventually go away." Her last word got sucked in on a sharp breath as the wind drove snow past them into the carport.

Ben ushered her into the kitchen where both kids huddled and Goldie dripped on the tile floor. He chafed Kate's arms a few seconds, then said, "I'll help Danny dry Goldie if you feel up to settling Clover in the living room. There's wood in the fireplace and long matches in a metal container on the mantel."

When Kate had a fire blazing and tucked an extra quilt around Clover, she studied her surroundings. She hadn't known what to expect of Ben's home. Perhaps that it would be more masculine? The room had a decidedly Western flare, with leather and wood furniture. But the warm colors of the window coverings and throw pillows kept it from looking like a hunting lodge. Watercolors of sunsets brought life to the off-white walls.

But she was not here to judge Ben's decor. Pitch crackled and popped in the fire so vigorously that Kate yanked the screen closed to avoid being showered with sparks.

"Last night I slept out here," Clover said from her cocoon on the sofa. "Daddy Ben slept in that chair."

"That works for me." Kate opened the screen a few inches and turned the wood with the poker. She returned it to its stand and dusted soot off her hands. It struck her how much she'd missed standing in front of a crackling fire. She realized that until Clover was well again, the impact of being able to walk again wouldn't fully sink in.

"I directed Danny to the guest room," Ben said, walking up behind her. "He wanted to check out the bed where he'll sleep tonight. He'll be right out because he's starved. I stopped to let you know I'll saddle up and take off. Kate…uh…thanks. It hardly seems enough to say."

She turned to face Ben. "If Danny's starved, you must be, too. Let me heat some soup before you go. It'll be fast and you'll start out warm inside. Do you have any soup on hand?"

"I do. Come, I'll show you. You wouldn't be stalling my departure out of worry for this ol' rack of bones, would you?"

Her gait was unsteady as she followed him. "I am worried. About Clover. And you. It's horrible weather. Anything could happen to you out there."

Ben opened the pantry and pointed to a stack of cans. He curved his hands over her shoulders as she reached for one. "I'm not used to having anyone waste their worry on me. I hope that means you care more than a little, Katie."

"Only my mother ever called me Katie," she said slowly. "Ben, I've tried hard not to care. It's a battle I'm losing." Turning, she raised her hands to rest on his jacket. Her eyes spoke of her ambivalence, but rather than step back, she traced her fingers up past his collar and lightly stroked the cool flesh of his neck.

He caught her hand. Carrying it to his lips, he nibbled soft kisses over her knuckles.

"Please…" she said helplessly.

"I'd be happier if I didn't feel you wanted to add *don't* after that *please*." Sighing, he tugged her inside his unzipped coat and felt both of their hearts accelerate. The close contact stirred other parts of his anatomy to life. Ben would have kissed her on the mouth so he could take her taste with him on his journey, but she ducked her head under his chin. Oddly, he discovered it was as comforting just to hold her.

"We both feel…a pull, don't we?" she asked softly, turning her face up to look at him as she tentatively traced his lightly stubbled chin. She liked that Ben didn't have much facial hair. "How much is circumstance?" she murmured. "By that I mean, Clover's condition, the storm, coupled with all you've done for me at the cabin. You realize a lot has happened lately to throw us together. Is any part of what we think we're feeling real, Ben?"

He released her with reluctance. "If it's not real, Kate, it will surely die a natural death." He stepped back. "You know, soup will hit the spot." Removing a Thermos from the cupboard, he said, "Put mine in this, please. I'll pick it up after I saddle up. And Kate, our talk about the two of us will wait until I know Clover is on the mend."

It would only take a word on her part to bring him back, Kate knew. She felt bereft watching him walk away, but said nothing as he opened the door and went out. Then it was too late for second thoughts.

Operating blindly, she took down three cans of tomato soup and dumped them in a pan she found hanging on a copper rack over a freestanding chopping block. The fridge held more milk than she needed. After the soup began to steam, she started to regret how they'd left things up in the air.

Hearing the squeak of leather and the jingle of his horse's tack, she hurried out to the carport with the Thermos so Ben wouldn't have to dismount.

"Thanks," he said, bending to take the jug. "Tell Clover I'll be back with Bobbalou before she wakes up." He slid the Thermos into a black saddlebag. A flat-brimmed black hat kept his face in shadows. For moments after he wheeled the gelding, Ben and his horse became a black slash against the white background. Then the slanting snow swallowed horse and rider.

Kate shivered. "Ben, take care," she called. Unsure if he'd heard her, she kissed her fingertips and held them out in the direction he'd disappeared, breathing a prayer for his safety. It was almost as if he'd been a mirage.

Briskly rubbing her arms, Kate went back inside to the welcoming warmth. With directions from Clover, she located saltine crackers to go with their soup. Danny filled his bowl twice, and Kate was able to coax Clover to eat a little, as well.

Goldie had to make do with the beef Kate picked out of a can of beef stew she'd found behind the cans of soup. She drained off most of the rich gravy and let the dog eat some of the vegetables. After eating, they sat around the fire, restless. Outside the wind slapped the windows with stinging snow.

"Clover, where did your dad put the books I sent home? I'll read a story aloud and it will help time pass."

Kate easily located the books and Danny flopped down on the sofa at Clover's feet. "*Harry the Dirty Dog* is the book you had in your lunch box the other day," he said. "I read it to you at recess, remember, Clover?"

"Ah, so that's how you were able to give me such a good report." Kate frowned and picked up another of the books. "Clover, getting someone else to read and then memorizing the information seems to have worked for your dad. But it's a scary way to go through life. He admitted he was terrified someone would find out he couldn't read. The minute you feel yourself again, hon, I'm going to start helping you read better."

"And Ben?"

"Him, too."

Later, once the kids had both fallen asleep, Kate

located a pad and a pencil stuffed in a kitchen drawer. She curled up in Ben's leather recliner and outlined a rigorous reading plan.

When Clover began to fidget and moan, Kate set aside her work. She scooted the recliner nearer the sofa so she could stroke the restless girl's hair.

Kate tried not to think of Ben out alone in the storm, riding through rugged canyons in total darkness. She sensed, though, that he'd spent much of his life alone, which saddened her. Was she becoming too attached to the Truebloods? Clover opened her eyes, blinked, then took Kate's hand and smiled before snuggling back into her quilt. How could she help it? Kate thought.

Kate hadn't intended to sleep, but something had her bolting awake, feeling panicked and disoriented. She heard the clink of Goldie's dog tags and her snuffle as she padded around an almost dark house. Goldie would bark if there was an intruder. Just then a shadow cut off the dim glow from the fireplace. "Ben?" Kate thought she must still be caught in the throes of a dream, until his icy hands gently framed her face.

"Shh." He bent closer, placing a finger over his lips. "Sorry to wake you," he whispered. "You and Clover looked so peaceful. How is she? How are you getting along?" Sliding his hands around and under her, Ben lifted Kate up and carried her over to the now smoldering fire. Not waiting for her answers, he nibbled her lips, then fit his mouth more fully over hers in a hungry greeting.

Dizzy from his kiss, Kate breathed in the damp smell

of the wintry outdoors clinging to Ben's clothing. She felt droplets from melting snowflakes in his hair and on his broad shoulders. "Couldn't you get through to Mr. Bobolink?" she asked jerkily, when he finally let her breathe. "Clover's fever goes down with ibuprofen and up as it wears off. She was thrashing in her sleep, but calmed if I laid a hand on her."

"I made it there and back, Kate." He let her stand, then guided her into the kitchen, where he indicated they could talk less quietly. "Bobbalou's gathering what he needs to make a poultice and a salve from herbs and things he has at his cabin. He'll be along shortly. He lives a quarter mile from here."

"I must've slept," Kate said, shaking her head, still leaning heavily on Ben. "What time is it?"

"It's a bit after four. Almost dawn."

"I really did drop off. Last I remember is looking at my watch by the light of the fireplace—it was one. I read to the kids. I had to wake Danny up to send him to bed. You're freezing, Ben! I can feel the chill through your jeans. I'm sorry I let the fire burn so low."

"Hot coffee would sure taste good. I'll go stoke the fire, if you fix a pot."

"Sure. I hope the fire isn't too far gone to stoke."

"There are embers. It won't take much dry kindling to boost it. Katie…" Ben said and took her hands, "while I can, I have something to say. Do you have any idea how I felt when I walked in, was greeted by Goldie and then saw you curled up asleep in my easy chair, your hand holding Clover's?"

"Like your home's been invaded by strangers?" Kate joked.

Ben's dark eyes burned into hers. He made a fist and tapped the vicinity of his heart. "More like I'd walked into one of my dreams, Katie."

"I...wasn't trying to make light of your feelings." Kate felt bad. She could see the admission hadn't come easily. All at once she ached to hold him and be held by him. Reaching out, she let her breath escape in a happy sigh as Ben enfolded her again in a close embrace.

Her kisses drove the chill from Ben's bones. Want battled need. If circumstances were different, he would carry Kate back to his solitary bed and make love with her.

A car door slammed outside.

Ben slipped Kate's arms from around his neck. "Bobbalou's about three steps from walking in on us, Katie, love. Damn, it seems I'm always saying to be continued," he said with wry regret.

Kate agreed. She had barely managed to straighten her sweatshirt before the door opened and a man with gray braids and a heavily lined face staggered in, his arms full of plastic containers. Eyes like chips of coal missed nothing, Kate thought guiltily. The newcomer took everything in at a glance.

Kate didn't wait for Ben to introduce her. "I'm Clover's teacher, Kate Steele," she said, and smiled. "Ben promises you can make medicine to reduce the pain and swelling in Clover's arm. I'm afraid I'm a bit of a skeptic, but Clover believes in you—and Ben. So," she added, "if I can do anything to help other than make coffee, keep quiet and stay out of your way while you get down to business, just yell."

Lou gave her a gap-toothed grin, and from the millions of laugh lines, Kate saw he laughed often. "The power to heal is a sacred gift," he said, helping himself to the largest pan hanging from the rack. He filled the copper-bottomed saucepan half full of water from a jug he'd carried in. The label said it was distilled water.

Before he turned on the stove burner, Lou dumped bark, dried roots and what looked like weeds into the cold water.

Fascinated, Kate started to make coffee, all the while watching Lou out of the corner of one eye.

Ben leaned a shoulder against the door casing. It brought him joy to see the two people he cared most about in the world, outside of Clover, working side by side in his kitchen.

Letting his mixture heat to a boil, Lou reached around Kate and helped himself to the smallest crockery bowl from a set of three in a cupboard. Using a spatula, he scraped a gooey substance that smelled strongly of pitch into the bowl, followed by a capful of vinegar. Into that he stirred molasses and shredded black tobacco straight from a Prince Albert can. He took a mortar and pestle from his bag, washed and dried them well, then crushed black currants and stirred them into the thick, now-reeking mixture.

By then the coffee was done. Kate filled a mug and slid it across the counter toward him. "Do you take cream or sugar?"

"Black," he snapped, plainly not wanting to be distracted.

Kate poured her own coffee and Ben's and carried their mugs to the table, where he was sitting. "You can't mean to let him put that horrid, primitive potion on Clover, Ben," she murmured. "It's putrid."

He sipped his coffee, lightly applying pressure to Kate's arm until she sat, too. "Relax, Kate. Bobbalou said that if his father had been allowed to treat Toby, my friend would not have lost his leg, and I believe that's true. If you were me, I know you'd try this before subjecting your child to doctors who already admit they don't have a known cure for a brown recluse bite."

"But...tobacco, Ben. And...he started with pitch."

"I'm not deaf," Bobbalou said, though Kate would've sworn he was too far away to hear her. "I used pure white-pine pitch. It's hard to gather. Now I know why I was led to bleed trees on the ranch this past spring. Ben, maybe while my poultice finishes simmering, you should take the teacher home."

Kate stiffened immediately and glared past Ben, who anchored her with a strong hand. "Come on, you two," he said, "get along. Bobbalou, it's still dark out and I'm just warming up. Kate's son, Danny, and the dog are fast asleep. Or I assume that's where Goldie got off to."

Kate shrugged. "I guess my skepticism is pumping negative ions into the air," she said peevishly.

"You did tell him you'd stay out of his way," Ben reminded.

"You're absolutely right." Clasping her mug in both

hands, Kate limped toward the living room. At the doorway, she was seized by a cramp in her right thigh that almost sent her to her knees. She might have fallen, if Ben hadn't bounded up and caught her about the waist. He held her tight, but half of her coffee sloshed from her mug. Shaking loose from Ben, she grabbed a cloth from the counter and tried to swab up the spill.

Bobbalou observed the entire mishap from his spot at the stove. "I didn't bring the right ingredients, but I have herbs that'll ease the semitendinosus muscles in your legs, Ms. Steele."

She tensed at the way he easily used the same medical term Nate Ramsey had earlier.

As Ben's fingers flexed several times and rubbed her troublesome thigh, Kate asked herself what she was doing getting huffy at an old man who might be able to help her more than her doctors in Texas. Of the dozen she'd consulted during her confinement, only Dr. Pearsall offered her the hope she would walk again. What harm would a poultice do, no matter how stinky? "I appreciate the offer," Kate said, "but get Clover better first, then we'll discuss me. Although I probably should ask how much you charge for a consultation."

"I'll barter. My herbs in return for you tutoring Clover…and teaching Ben to read."

"You didn't tell him I've already offered to do both of those things?"

Ben aimed a dirty look at his old friend. "He's afraid I'll weasel out."

The older man smiled warmly at Kate this time and in a sweeping gesture touched two fingers to his heart.

Clearly he was too emotional to speak further, but in his mind he was sealing their bargain.

"All right, you two." Ben closed a hand around Kate's upper arm. He'd have said plenty more, but glanced down and saw her unsuccessfully stifling a huge yawn.

"I interrupted your snooze, Kate. I want you to go to my room, it's the last door on the left down the hall. Grab a few more hours sleep."

"Me? You've been up far longer, Ben. Clover said you were up with her a lot last night. Add two days of moving wood and driving back and forth to town. If anyone needs rest, it's you."

"I'll catnap until Bobbalou is ready to wake Clover."

Kate yawned again. All at once she did feel drained. It had been an eventful day for her, as well. "All right," she agreed, setting her mug on the counter. "Wake me in an hour. Danny and I should go home as soon as you're free to take us. When do you think this storm will end and we'll get back to normal?"

"Bobbalou claims it'll blow out and start melting by the afternoon. Don't ask me how he knows these things, but he's never wrong."

"You mean a lot to him, Ben," she said as he steadied her down the hall. "He must really be troubled by your inability to read. He said his healing power is sacred, yet he offered it to me in exchange for teaching you and he doesn't even like me."

"What do you mean, he doesn't like you?"

She shrugged. "Ask him. He wants badly for you to read, but I sense he has an underlying worry that I'll somehow turn your life upside down."

Ben grinned lazily, stopping outside his bedroom door to kiss her. The kiss went on and on, and Kate had wrap her arms around his waist to keep her balance.

"Bad idea," he muttered. "To bed. Just you. ASAP."

"ASAP is good," she said raggedly, then slid her arms around his neck to kiss him again.

"I know I started this, but you're killing me, here."

"I'm going, I'm going." She limped off with a smile, but glanced back to see the depth of longing in his dark eyes before he spun away and strode down the hall.

She hesitated to follow him, but didn't. She did look in on Danny, who slept in the guest room across the hall. From the night-light in the room, she saw he lay on his back in the middle of a double bed; the big dog stretched beside him. Both snored. At home Kate didn't allow Goldie to sleep on Danny's bed. She backed from the room and shut the door softly.

The master suite had an unlit fireplace covering much of one wall. Ben's bed was huge, but he was a big man. The colors in his private quarters were dark—browns, blues and rich reds. A large dream catcher hung above his bed. Kate found that endearing but at odds with the person Ben presented to the world. Her sense was that other than clinging to an old style of ranching and this faith in his friend's healing powers, he'd mostly shed his native roots. Kate found him to be a man of contradictions.

As she stripped back his spread, still gazing around the room, she realized what was missing. Books and magazines. There were none here and none in the living room, although a large bookcase there held knick-knacks. Did none of his friends think to question that?

Yawning again, Kate pulled off her boots and crawled between Ben's dark blue sheets. Snuggling down, she was determined to stop analyzing Ben's life. But surrounded by his scent, she drifted to sleep picturing ways she'd open his life up to the world of books.

KATE SLOWLY CRACKED ONE EYE open. Natural light poured through a bank of windows, revealing a strange room. *A new hospital,* her fuzzy brain concluded as her heart tripped frantically.

Little by little she recalled memories of the previous night. *Ben's house. She was in Ben's house. They'd left his friend Lou Bobolink brewing up medicine in the kitchen for Clover.*

Sitting up, she threw back quilts and a comforter. Sounds penetrated her sleepy brain. Across from her, a fire sizzled and spit. Water dripped off the eaves outside and muffled voices filtered past the door, which was left ajar. *What time was it?* A bedside clock said five-thirty. Had she only slept an hour?

She still had on the jeans she'd worn yesterday. Her boots lay helter skelter on a burgundy wool rug. *Yesterday she'd walked.* The realization came back to her, leaving her apprehensive. *Could she repeat the miracle today?* She had feeling in her legs. In the past they'd felt wooden after a night's sleep.

Carefully, she slid out of bed. Blood tingled reassuringly in her toes. Kate took a couple of test steps, and when she didn't fall, was elated. She sat down again, pulled on her boots, then got up and slowly made her way down the hall.

"Ah, sleeping beauty awakens." Ben sat in the recliner and held a steaming coffee mug.

Goldie lay on a braid rug by the fire. Clover reclined against pillows at one end of a long leather couch, and Danny sat at the opposite end, his stocking feet tucked beside her. His hair and Goldie's fur looked wet.

"But it's not even six."

"You slept for eleven hours." He rose. "You probably want breakfast, but it's almost suppertime. I did just make fresh coffee."

"*Suppertime?* But…but…we have to get home to look after Flame. And what about Clover's arm?" Kate couldn't believe so much time had passed.

"See for yourself." Ben, who'd started for the kitchen, returned to stand beside his daughter. "Bobbalou said not to remove the gauze pack he has covering the spot starting to crater. Not until I change the bandage and put new medicine on later tonight."

Kate leaned over the back of the couch. "The swelling is practically gone! I see only a few patches of red around the gauze. How does your arm feel?" she asked the little girl.

"Lots better. E-12, Danny. Is that a hit or a miss?"

Kate looked confused. It was Danny who cleared things up. "I drew out squares for the game of Battleship, and taught Clover how to play. It took me a lotta time. Remember how she said she learns stuff fast? She does, she's beating me all to pieces."

Clover grinned cheekily. "It's a fun game. Danny says he has one with plastic ships, but this is how you taught him."

"I did." Kate ruffled Danny's hair. "We wiled away a lot of rainy days in our trailer playing this and cat and mouse."

"I'll show you that next," Danny told Clover. "This is funner."

"More fun," Kate corrected. "When you finish this game, kids, we need to have Ben drive Danny and me home. I heard water dripping off the roof. So, I gather Lou was right about the snow melting?"

"A Chinook wind blew up around two o'clock. He was right about it and a lot of other things. Oh, he left two herb packs to heat in water and wrap around your legs."

"Where is he? I need to thank him and apologize for doubting he could help Clover. The difference in her arm is unbelievable."

"He's back cooking for the buckaroos. He volunteered to swing past your cabin and feed your horse and check on the state of things there. So, see, he does like you, Kate."

"I still need to get home, Ben. I have lesson plans to do, especially if the snow melts enough for school to be in session tomorrow. Will it?"

"Probably." He looked unhappy to admit it. "It's been great having you here. The cabin will be cold inside. Can't I talk you into eating supper with us and maybe spending another night?"

Kate blinked, not completely sure all that he was

asking. She'd only counted three bedrooms down the hall. He didn't clarify, and she didn't ask. But she did relent and say, "Staying for supper is okay. Shall I cook?"

"Let me. After we eat…I thought maybe you could read with Clover."

"And you? Oh, Ben, I would, except I have the proper materials at home. Last night I drew up a schedule. The three of us can meet Monday, Wednesday and Friday after school. To start, I'll assign you both work to do on your own between sessions. Clover's at a higher level, of course, but you can still help each other."

Ben rocked back and forth on his heels. Without agreeing or disagreeing, he ducked into the kitchen.

Hearing the way he slammed pots and pans around in the kitchen, Kate wondered if Ben was going to need a little more convincing.

CHAPTER TWELVE

AT SUPPER THEY DISCUSSED the weather mostly and, after clearing the table, Ben drove them to the cabin through slush.

Danny sat on the edge of his seat. He worried that Ben might slide into a ravine.

"Danny, I promise I'm taking it really slow and easy. We'll be okay, son."

Kate liked the way Ben took the time to reassure Danny. She thought again how well the four of them got along. Lengthy shadows cast by the pines strafed the clearing as Ben stopped beside the cabin. Great clumps of snow fell from tree branches, thudding against the ground.

Danny snapped on Goldie's leash. "Bye, Clover. Get well so you can come back to school."

"Hang on to Goldie and don't walk under the pines," Kate cautioned. "I don't want either of you bonked on the head." She had her door open, but hadn't gotten out.

"I'll unload your wheelchair," Ben said. "Where would you like me to put it?"

"On the porch? I still have a hard time believing I

no longer need it." She noticed Ben's gaze was drawn to her pickup and the lift.

"For the time being I'll make do with the hand controls," she said, reading his thoughts. "If and when I stop having leg cramps, perhaps I'll take my pickup to one of the big dealerships in Boise and trade it in. I imagine they have some call for handicap controls, wouldn't you think?"

They headed toward the house. "I'll take you to Boise—just the two of us," he said. "I'll be burning up the highway between here and the city on business for a few weeks while we present the ranchers' next appeal. I'll be done by Thanksgiving. That'll give Bobbalou's herb packs plenty of time to get rid of your cramps."

"This is the first you've mentioned trips to Boise. I hope they won't interfere with our lessons. Ben, it's important to establish a routine and stick with it. Three afternoons a week is minimum. I thought if Clover rode home with Danny and me, you could meet us here."

"Not this week. Bobbalou made salve to last Clover through Sunday. He says to keep her out of school until new skin forms over the crater." Ben set the wheelchair under the eaves and stopped to wind a lock of hair blowing across Kate's face around his index finger. "About Boise...I'd be taking my tutor. We'll leave the kids at my house with Vida. Danny can read with Clover. What do you say?"

Not usually so slow on the uptake, Kate finally realized that Ben was proposing an overnighter for the two

of them. Heat streaked through her, along with excitement, but also more than a few reservations.

"I see questions in your eyes. Ask away, Kate."

"I'm wondering if we're rushing things."

"We're not going tomorrow," he said matter-of-
factly. "I figure we'll see each other a lot between now
and then." He cleared his throat. "Ah, you probably
think I'm planning to spend every waking minute in bed
with you. I can't deny that's appealing, but I've learned
restraint." He smiled crookedly. "Boise's a good place
to Christmas shop. And I want to show you around.
You've never been there, have you?"

"No. And it's nice of you, Ben." She brushed his lips
with two fingers, rose on her toes and exchanged her
fingers for her lips. Easing down on her heels, she said,
"I can't explain, but I'm relieved and disappointed we
aren't making that trip next week."

Because Danny and Goldie were galloping toward
them, Kate hurriedly unlocked the cabin. Ben passed
her a bag with the herb packs Bobbalou had made. "See
ya, buddy," he called to Danny. Ben whistled a tune as
he made his way back to the truck and Clover.

Knowing she should go straight in to shower and
change, Kate couldn't help but linger at the door and
watch Ben drive off. Already she missed him.

"Is it okay if I phone Mimi and Pawpaw?" Danny
called.

Earlier, when Kate had first felt an interest in Ben,
thoughts about her in-laws had brought feelings of guilt.
Since then, she had come to realize she had a right to
happiness. She'd stayed with Royce and Melanie's son

and had done her best to make the marriage work for Danny. She and Colton hadn't had a real relationship for some years prior to the accident.

"Are you sure we have cell service? It was out yesterday."

"We do, Mom. Is it okay if I tell them about Clover's spider bite?"

"I suppose. Be sure to tell them those spiders are rare. Nate Ramsey said it's the first brown recluse bite he's seen in the ten years he's lived here."

She lit a fire but had to opt for a quick cold shower since her power remained out and she had no generator. In the middle of buttoning a flannel shirt over jeans, Danny ran in and handed her the cell. "Mimi wants to talk to you."

Kate took the phone. "Hello." She waved Danny out and was glad she had after hearing what Melanie wanted.

"Royce and I want Danny to come to Fort Worth for Thanksgiving. He can stay on to compete in the Little Britches Rodeo. It's a week past the holiday. We'll buy his ticket, of course."

"That's impossible. I'm not letting him miss a week of school."

"Really?" Melanie sounded skeptical. "Hearing him tell how fast you've gotten cozy with a local rancher, I'd think you'd jump at the chance to be unencumbered for a week. As a matter of fact, Danny told me you up and walked. Convenient, if you ask me. You let us think for two years that you were crippled."

That burned Kate. "You were in the room when Dr.

Pearsall told my medical team he was sure I'd walk again. I'm sure you hoped that would never happen. It would give you less chance of turning Danny into a clone of your spoiled son."

"How dare you!"

"Melanie, I'm sorry." Kate dropped down on the end of the bed and massaged her calves. Danny had come back and was hovering in the doorway. "I've done my best not to color Danny's view of Colton. But you and Royce were always blind to his faults. I won't restrict your calls to Danny…yet. But let's be clear, he'll end up chasing rodeos over my dead body." The line hummed in Kate's ear, signaling that her mother-in-law had hung up. Kate sighed and closed the phone.

"Mom," Danny said anxiously. "Did your legs quit working again? Why were you and Mimi arguing about Dad?"

"Honey, that's between your grandmother and me. As for my legs, they ache. I wish our electricity wasn't out or I'd try one of the packs Lou Bobolink fixed. He swears they'll ease my cramps."

"That's what I came to tell you. The heater in my bedroom is making noises."

"The lines must be repaired. I'll warm one of these packs. Hmm. Smell this. Isn't it heavenly? Lavender. With rosemary and a hint of mint," she added, taking a second whiff. She offered it to Danny, but he plugged his nose.

"Oh, you," Kate scoffed. "You've ruined your sense of smell shoveling horse poop." They both laughed and Kate felt harmony had been restored.

AT SCHOOL THE NEXT DAY it seemed the students couldn't settle down. They were excited and full of stories about their experiences during the big snow. As well, they had endless questions about why their teacher was now able to walk. Kate had to shrug off the questions she couldn't answer and finally gave up on schoolwork, letting them decorate the classroom for Halloween. Most of the children lived too far from neighbors to go trick-or-treating, so the real holiday next Wednesday was just an ordinary day.

Sarah Keevler hung around Kate at lunch. "My dad heard Clover got bitten by a spider at your cabin. Is she okay? I hope so. She was nice to me when I got sick."

"Her father says she'll be better soon. I thought it'd be nice if we make her get-well cards."

After school, as they drove toward the Rising Sun, Kate asked Danny if he'd like a party for his birthday, which was coming up in a few weeks.

"Naw, I'm too old for a party," he said. "You can bake a chocolate cake, though. For when Clover and her dad come for a reading lesson."

"All right. You haven't given me any ideas for a present."

"Mimi and Pawpaw are sending me money for a new saddle. The check will be in the same box as the cell phone she's gonna buy for me. It will be here next week."

"A cell phone? Why on earth…" Kate's grip tightened on the steering wheel.

"She said I'm old enough. And that way I can call

them without always asking your permission. She's paying the monthly bill."

Kate clamped down on her anger. She'd take the matter up with Melanie. No need to involve Danny.

She parked in front of Ben's and considered asking Ben what he'd do in her place.

He wasn't home. Kate worked to hide her disappointment.

"Ben's gone out to help the buckaroos count how many cows died in the storm," Clover told them. "Vida's here. She's sewing buttons on a skirt and blouse Ben asked her to make me."

Clover sounded less than enthusiastic, and it only took Kate a glimpse of the gingham ruffled outfit Vida Smith had in her lap to realize the problem.

The clothes were straight out of *Little House on the Prairie.*

Vida Smith was a big, raw-boned woman, who wore a lived-in housedress and a stained bibbed apron. Kate introduced herself and Danny.

"Coffee's hot," Vida said. "Care to join me for a cup?"

"I can't stay," Kate said. "I brought Clover school assignments and the kids all made get-well cards. Maybe you'd like Danny to help you read them?" she said, passing the folder to Clover.

The girl looked eager, so Kate said, "I guess I will have coffee. No, please don't get up again. I spent Monday night here and know my way around the kitchen." It wasn't until she was pouring the coffee that it dawned on Kate why Vida had given her a strange look. Rushing back to the living room, she stammered, "Uh, Danny and I stayed here with Clover while Ben went to fetch Mr. Bobolink."

Vida continued to sew brown buttons down the back of the beige flowered top.

"I brought Clover a packet of word flash cards. If you have time, Mrs. Smith, you could go over them with her."

"The girl's not into books. I was shocked Ben asked me to sew her skirts. She's always on a horse. Of course, it's no secret he's grooming her to take over the Rising Sun one day. Slow as the courts are in deciding the fate of our ranches, and fast as they're folding, she's liable to be the last buckaroo left."

Could that be true? Might Ben lose his ranch?

Kate finished her coffee and called to Danny.

Clover came running into the room with Danny.

"Remember to practice your flash cards tomorrow, Clover," Kate said.

"I can't," Clover told her. "Tomorrow I'm riding out to the winter lease with Ben so Bobbalou can make sure his medicine's working. Danny can come, too. Justin and Zach will teach him to make a clear-horn catch or an around-the-neck catch so his team will win."

Kate felt uneasy. "What team?"

Clover frowned. "In Fort Worth at the kids' rodeo— after Thanksgiving. Danny says he needs more practice."

"Danny?" Kate asked.

Her son cocked his head to one side. "Mimi said she'd fix it with you so I can fly home for Thanksgiving and enter the Little Britches competition. She said

Pawpaw paid my fees. I'm set to single calf rope and then team rope with Brett Gardner."

Kate shook her head. "There's no way you can miss a week of school. Not for a rodeo."

Danny glared at her, then ran outside. Kate caught Vida Smith eyeing her pityingly. Picking up Danny's jacket, Kate said, "He's disappointed, but we'll talk this out. Nice meeting you, Mrs. Smith. Clover, I hope we'll see you at school, Monday. Tell your dad I'm still planning on your first reading lesson right after school at the cabin. If anything's changed, ask him to please phone me."

The girl bobbed her head, and Kate left.

Danny slumped in the backseat and sulked all the way home. But when he jumped out of the pickup, his anger seemed to have dissipated. "I'm going out to ride Flame," he called in his usual cheery voice.

"Okay. But take Goldie and don't go near the river. The snow melted fast. I noticed when we crossed the bridge that the river is over its banks in places. Be back by supper. I'm baking a chicken and fixing the curried rice you like."

He was gone until almost dark, but Kate was glad he seemed like his old self and decided not to bring up his earlier rude behavior just this once.

"Ms. KATE, I'M SO GLAD you found a bunch of horse books. I can't wait to learn how to read every word by myself."

Clover had come home from school with Kate and Danny. It was two weeks later than Kate had planned, but finally the reading lessons were to begin.

When Ben arrived, he wasn't nearly as enthusiastic as his daughter.

Kate got right down to work.

"Ben, you have to concentrate," she said at the end of a frustrating hour. "It's like your mind is a million miles away."

"Not a million, but with my crew. I lost quite a bit of stock in the storm. It hit early and hard. I thought we'd fare better. But the snow melted fast, too, and that's the problem now. Cattle get mired in mud. I'm here instead of helping pull them out."

"We could delay until next week if you feel it's necessary."

He crossed his arms. "I'd like a permanent delay. Thing is, Kate, I feel stupid. I listen to Clover reading to Danny. She stumbles, but she gets some words."

"Kids' minds are sponges. Give yourself time, Ben. Relax." She smiled and he pulled her around the corner out of sight of the kids and kissed her.

"I've been dying to do that since I walked in." He kissed her again.

"So, the story about your cattle was an attempt to distract me?"

"It's true. But you're my biggest distraction."

"I could put a sack over my head, but that would make teaching difficult," she teased.

"Before I forget, next Wednesday is Danny's birthday. We'd like you and Clover to stay for supper. I'm making a sinful, four-layer chocolate cake for dessert."

Ben fit his hands around Kate's waist and brushed

noses with her. "I never turn down a meal I don't have to cook." He half closed his eyes. "I'm imagining how sinful chocolate frosting will taste on your mouth."

"Ah, I've found the incentive to insure you do your homework."

"Now there's a thought. The better I get, the better the prize?"

That statement had Kate blushing.

Lessons that week and the Monday of the following week progressed well. On Wednesday, Clover bounced excitedly all the way to the cabin. "Wait till you see what we got for your birthday, Danny. Can he open presents before supper, Kate?" Clover had taken to dropping the *Ms.* when they were alone. "It's something he can use and…" She clapped her hands over her mouth. "I don't wanna spill the secret."

Kate turned her head and smiled indulgently. "Secrets are hard to keep. I'm fine with Danny opening gifts before we eat, but after your lessons. I told your dad not to buy Danny anything. Gifts aren't why I invited you for supper and cake."

Ben was already waiting on the porch of the cabin. Kate liked that he was prompt. She'd been worried that he might give up learning to read, but he recognized a number of words now.

Knowing it was Danny's birthday, everyone was a little distracted. The minute Kate closed her textbook, the kids leaped up. Danny retrieved the gift from his mother and one from the Truebloods. He started to unwrap Clover's present first, but Ben said, "Open your mom's gift. She's sitting on pins and needles."

Almost reluctantly, Danny switched and tore paper off a second box. "Mom always gets me stuff to wear." This time, though, her gift wasn't clothing. She'd made him a photo album. The cover had a small frame and in it she'd put his baby picture.

"Jeez, Mom, how embarrassing. I had no hair and big ears." At first it seemed he might not open the book in front of guests. But Clover wanted to see and sank down beside him on the couch.

"Who are all of these people?" he asked.

"This is a keepsake album, Danny. That's my mother as a baby, as a teen and up to when she had me. After the first divider I've done the same with your dad's family. Next are a couple of pictures from my wedding, followed by you from birth to age ten. There are blank pages to take you through high-school graduation."

"Is that your dad?" Clover asked. "I don't see any of him with his trophies."

"Mimi has lots of pictures. Did you ask her for some, Mom?"

"No. I made this spur of the moment. Your dad wore a suit to our wedding. I wanted you to see him as more than a bronc rider, Danny. I put in pictures of me at my proms and graduation. Your dad missed those things because he was off at rodeos."

Danny shut the album and reached for the next gift.

Ben reached over and took Kate's hand in one of his. He could tell she was disappointed by Danny's lack of enthusiasm for her gift.

"Wow, oh, wow!" Danny jumped to his feet and

pulled a lariat out of a square box. "This is like the horsehair rope you showed me at school, Ben."

"It'll be the best rope in the competition," Clover said, rising on her knees to clap her hands. "Let's go out and see if you can rope better with this than your old one."

Kate jumped up. "Danny, I wasn't kidding. You're not going to Fort Worth for that competition."

The kids had already shrugged into their jackets. "Clover meant it's the best rope any kid my age owns," Danny said. "I can still rope posts." They ran outside and down the steps.

Kate didn't budge until Ben rubbed her back, causing her to glance up. "He's a good little roper, Kate."

"How would you know that?"

Ben frowned. "Justin told me. Kate, what's the harm in roping calves?"

"We don't own any. Oh, Ben, if Danny thinks he's good, he'll want to be better, then the very best. To find that out, he has to compete."

"Or become a rancher. If you have something against that, we need to thrash this out now. I liked how you looked sleeping in my bed. I've started thinking along those lines, if you get my drift. And well, Danny and Clover get along better than a lot of brothers and sisters."

Her jaw dropped. "Ben, are you…proposing…to me?"

"Too soon? Bobbalou said so, but I told him same as I told you the other day. This is the first time I've ever wanted to share my life with any woman. Kate, I didn't plan to bring this up today, it being Danny's birthday and all. To tell you the truth, I figured you wouldn't consider marrying me until I could read. But, hell, that'll take too long. I'm thirty-seven, Kate."

She stilled his tirade with her lips. When she pulled back, her eyes were teary. "Ben, my marriage to Colton has left me wary. We disagreed on so many issues that matter. I didn't see that until after we were married. I care deeply for you, Ben, but do we know what's important to each other?"

"I like seeing you happy. The health and welfare of our kids matter. Family's important to me. I had a lousy one." He toyed with her fingers. "What's your favorite stone?" he asked, his eyes probing.

"Now I'm the one saying to be continued. I hear the kids on the porch. And that was the stove buzzer. It means our pot roast is done."

Ben hadn't wanted to turn her loose and was still holding both her hands when the kids and Goldie burst in on them. They all skidded to a halt. Danny said, "Are you guys holding hands?"

Kate pulled away. She clasped her elbows, then gestured toward the kitchen.

"We were holding hands," Ben said. "I'm trying to convince your mom that she and I can be good together, that we'd all be better as a family. How does that sound to you two?"

"Cool," the kids said in unison.

Clover sounded most smug. "I told you I saw them kissing the night you slept at our house, Danny."

The boy gripped Goldie's fur, then he said, "Ben, will you make the honda in this rope?" He meant the slip knot that calf ropers kept in one end of their coiled rope so that it was always ready to swing a loop.

Scowling, Kate left the room. She was annoyed that Ben had brought up marriage with the kids, but what bothered her even more, she realized with a start, was that Ben had never mentioned love. Maybe she was too much of a romantic, but Kate had promised herself that next time she would have it all, the flowery words, love, good sex and vows that meant something.

BEN HADN'T BROACHED THE SUBJECT of marriage again and he missed his reading lesson the following Monday, the week of Thanksgiving.

He called Kate the next day. "Sorry I missed yesterday. I've also gotta miss tomorrow. I tracked down a guy involved in the BLM wild-horse roundup. He's always supplied us with unbroken horses for our spring Rope and Ride, but he quit the business and sold his stock. I've had to quickly locate a new supplier. We just don't use horses that are pretrained to buck."

"How long will it take, Ben? You're making such good progress."

"That's…uh…another reason I'm calling. I've turned up a rancher near Lucky Peak on the way to Boise who claims he has a canyon full of wild mustangs. He's invited me to see them Friday after the holiday. I took the liberty of speaking to Vida about…well, about keeping the kids at my house. Since there's no school, I hoped you'd go with me.

You can cover what I've missed on the drive. I'll check out Tim Cortez's horses, then we can spend the remainder of Friday and Saturday in the city, shopping or doing whatever you'd like, and return home Sunday."

Kate waffled. Part of her brain argued that sleeping with Ben was foolish. Another part spiked her heart rate and left her fanning herself at the thought. "Let me talk to Danny first."

"Okay, but it was the kids' suggestion that I invite you."

She wasn't sure she'd heard right. "When did you see the kids…well, Danny?"

"Thursday afternoon when he rode over. Wait, I thought you changed your mind and said he could take Justin's roping clinic with Clover."

"What clinic? Is it free? Never mind, his grand-mother sent him money for his birthday. Ben, you know my feelings on the subject of roping. Danny has deliberately defied me to do this."

"I'm sorry. I've been swamped getting ready for the appeal hearing and tracking down horses for the Rope and Ride. Justin led me to believe both kids said you'd given your okay. Does this mean you won't let him spend the weekend? The clinic is over, by the way."

"I should make that his punishment. But that would also punish me. I've been dying to see Boise."

"Don't expect another Dallas. Some call the city woodsy."

"At the risk of sounding like a woman, Ben, what should I take to wear?"

"That's a loaded question. I'm tempted to say a short red nightgown, or nothing." He laughed, and Kate felt a tingle run up her spine.

"Dream on, big guy. I'll pack what I think is appropriate. Not to change the subject, but if Danny acts surly over turkey on Thursday, it's because he'll know you told me about the clinic."

"He and Clover may be in for a talking-to from me, as well. They need to know right up front that you and I talk things over and we stick together. And we won't tolerate them lying."

"Your saying that means so much to me, Ben."

They exchanged soft goodbyes. Hanging up, Kate went in search of her son. She found him out roping a stuffed animal he'd nailed to a sawhorse.

"How was roping clinic?" she asked, casually leaning on the corral. His color drained, but then his chin rose sharply. "I'm most angry about the fact you went behind my back," she added.

"You wouldn't have let me go. I like roping and I'm good at it. Everyone says so. Pawpaw, Clover, Justin— they all think I can win calf roping in my age level."

Frustrated, Kate tried a new tack. "What do you get from winning, Danny? A certificate. A little trophy that sits around and collects dust?"

"It's not about what I win, it's how I feel when I do better than everybody, Mom. People whistle and clap and I know I did something good. Mimi says Dad did, too."

"You're capable of doing a lot of things well, Danny. In order to continue being the best at one thing, like roping, you have to spend hours practicing. It means you'll miss out on a lot of other fun things."

"Yeah, so?" He swung the rope over his head and let it fly. It neatly circled his floppy toy bear. Flipping the rope loose, Danny repeated the process, rarely missing.

After the sixth throw, Kate grew exasperated and left. At dark Danny clomped inside. She heard him on the phone bragging to someone, maybe Clover, or his grandmother, about how many times he'd hit his target compared to the number of throws.

It was the bragging that made her stomach drop. But, he was young. Maybe this was a phase boys went through. Was she being too hard on him as Ben intimated? Ben said calf roping was harmless. And Danny wasn't Colton.

Midway through supper, Danny surprised her by asking, "Mom, are you going to marry Ben?"

She tread carefully. "Does the thought bother you?"

"Does it mean Mimi and Pawpaw won't be my grandparents anymore?"

"They will always be your grandparents." She did her best to explain.

"Do you think they'll like Clover?"

"Who?"

"Mimi and Pawpaw."

"Honey, I doubt they'll ever meet Clover. You know Pawpaw won't leave the ranch to travel. When you get older, you'll go visit them on your own in the summer, but Clover will probably stay here."

"Why do I hafta be old to go visit them?"

"I don't want you traveling alone yet. I wouldn't want you changing planes. I doubt there are direct flights from Boise to Fort Worth. But getting back to your original question, Danny. Ben and I haven't decided about marriage."

"You're going to Boise with him this weekend, aren't you?"

"We've discussed it." She felt herself blush.

"You'd better go, Mom. Justin said that's the best way to find out if you want to marry somebody. Go off and sleep together."

"Danny Steele! Justin shouldn't discuss something so grown-up with a kid. I intend to tell Ben. He needs to have a talk with Mr Padilla."

"Aw, Mom. Jeez, I'm no baby."

"All the same…"

"Sheesh! It's no fun being a kid." He got up from the table and carried his dishes to the sink.

After he went off to his room, Kate made holiday pies. She wasn't sure how she felt about Ben's buckaroos knowing she and Ben were planning to share a room.

But for all that she'd been unsure before about going with Ben, Kate knew she was definitely ready to move forward with this part of her life.

CHAPTER THIRTEEN

THE FOUR OF THEM HAD ENJOYED a fun Thanksgiving. Kate had asked Ben to extend an invitation to Bobbalou, but he'd declined, and rightly so. He was the camp cook and the buckaroos counted on him to cook a holiday bird that allowed each lonesome man a small taste of home.

Kate thought she'd be embarrassed taking Danny, Goldie and Flame to the Rising Sun Friday morning, where she'd transfer her weekender suitcase to Ben's pickup. But there was no time for awkwardness. Flame had to be turned into the corral with Ben's stock, and Ben was busy showing Vida how to flush the crater in Clover's arm with a Waterpik. The hole in her arm was healing, but Ben was fanatical about keeping the area clean and covered in sterile gauze until fresh skin grew over.

"If it was your idea to use a Waterpik, Ben, it's very clever."

"I wish I could claim I was that smart," he said as they were driving off the property. "Zach Robles said a friend of his went to a Web site after his son was bitten by a brown recluse. Victims exchanged info on what they did that worked. Several said they tried the Waterpik flushing and it healed the lesions faster. I guess because it forces water in deeper to wash out the poison."

"Between that and Lou's salve, Clover is one lucky girl. The prognosis listed in those papers you got from the hospital in Boise painted quite a different picture."

"Did Bobbalou's herbs help you?"

She nodded. "I'm getting stronger every day. Worried that I won't keep up with you this weekend?"

Ben leaned his left arm on the Ford's window ledge. He looked more carefree today than he had in weeks and very handsome in polished brown boots, chinos and a black long-sleeved knit shirt. Kate scooted closer and flashed him a smile.

"Those pages that the hospital faxed me scared the bejesus out of me, Kate. The words may as well have been Chinese. It made me realize that because I can't read I've been living one step ahead of disaster."

"I know you're far from alone, but what amuzes me is how you compensated so well, especially when Clover was a baby. I recall my pediatrician's nurse giving me stacks of instructions on caring for a newborn."

"I figured it couldn't be any harder than raising a calf, and I'd kept plenty of those alive after they'd lost a mother."

"Well, she's a happy, healthy girl. Except for..." Kate hesitated. "She's not happy with the skirts and tops Vida sewed, Ben. I admit they're pretty old-fashioned. Yesterday Clover told me if she wears either outfit to school, girls like Meg Wheeler will make fun of her. I wish I could control them, but stuff happens on the playground. I may be out of line, but I made up my mind to ask you if we can shop for a few new things for her in Boise this weekend."

Ben smiled over at her. "I wish you didn't think you had to ask, Katie."

She hiked up a knee on the seat and faced him. "I have something else I want to ask, Ben. I had the impression Lou wasn't happy you never learned to read, yet I recall you saying that at fourteen you worked for him. Why didn't he make you stay in school?"

"My mother was probably too stoned when I was little to get up every day and send me to school. Percy and I skipped a lot. Lou knew I'd run away if he made me go to school. We were on the verge of getting into real trouble when Bobbalou gave us jobs." Ben wasn't angling for sympathy from Kate. "My mother did her best. She got in with a bad crowd. Not all Paiutes. Bobbalou called them instigators, white trash from the mining camp. One of them was my dad."

"There are good and not-so-good people in every walk of life. I used to think values were taught by example, but I'm not so sure that's always true."

Slowing his pickup, Ben squinted out Kate's side window. "We're looking to turn at a road near a bent pine that has an old wagon wheel propped against its trunk."

"Is there a street sign?"

He shrugged.

"Of course, you couldn't have read a street sign.

Ben, aren't you glad you're finally learning to read? There…" She pointed. "Is that the bent tree and the wagon wheel?"

He made the hard right turn down a bumpy road before answering her. "It's a relief to have it out, Kate. Not so much for myself as for Clover. I knew I was failing to help her and I did all the wrong things by ignoring my problem. Pride, see?"

"She's bright and so are you. Clover's also talented at art. We need to nurture that."

"We? I like the sound of you being involved. Clover needs you."

Kate looked down at her hands. "I had a lot of time after the accident to think about what went wrong in my marriage. I realize now that I wanted a partner, and Colton wanted a replacement for his mother. I'm trying to figure out what you want."

"Don't confuse me with any other man." Ben jammed on his brakes outside a redwood ranch house. A man and a dog appeared at the door and stepped outside. Ben ripped off his shades and hung them in the open neck of his shirt. His dark eyes drilled Kate. "I plan to spend this weekend convincing you of what I want. I guess this break will give you time to decide if you want to be convinced."

He climbed out of the pickup and retrieved a worn, handmade rope. Opening Kate's door, he pulled leather gloves out of the glove compartment. "Come on, poky. Let's go get this done. I want to have plenty of time to show you Boise and save time for…other things." He waggled his dark eyebrows.

Kate scrambled out, her heart pattering. "I can wait here," she offered. "That trail looks steep and I don't want to hold you back. Or fall," she said under her breath.

"I won't let you fall, Katie. Come on. Tim wants me to buck out one of the mustangs to prove our committee is getting what we want. Breaking green horses is part of what I do at my ranch and as head of the yearly Rope and Ride committee. It's a small part," he added, taking her by the hand.

He seemed to be asking for her understanding. And no wonder. She'd made no bones of disliking all things to do with rodeos.

"So, Ben, I guess what you're saying is this is who I am, take it or leave it."

"No, I'm asking you to watch something that's in a day's work for me, is all." Settling a hand on her waist, he shortened his stride, guiding her to a spot that opened out on a series of corrals. Tim waited at the gate of the pen with the highest fence. Kate could see horses circling in it. She heard them snorting and blowing.

"I'm going to cut out a promising mustang. Tim said I can use that small corral. Are your legs strong enough to let you crawl atop a fence?"

"I haven't had a cramp in days. I talked to Dr. Pearsall. He said he couldn't prove it, but he believes my paralysis is a result of guilt I assumed for the accident. He said my worry that Danny might get bitten by the spider was greater than the guilt."

"I think you're too strong a woman to be held back, Kate."

"I don't know about that. In fact, Ben, if these horses are wild, isn't what you're doing more dangerous than using rodeo stock?"

"I don't know about dangerous, but it's a lot more humane. I've never liked how rodeo stockmen cinch a horse to make the animal go crazy with pain so they'll buck at event after event. Our contest is about showing off the skill of the buckaroo." *wrong – there's no pain.*

"What happens to your horses afterward?"

"They're divided among our rancher sponsors. Our crews finish breaking them to halter and saddle. Eventually they wind up in a cavvy. Cavvy horses have a lot of freedom out on our cattle leases."

"I'll watch how you go about this," she said, and headed for the smaller corral. Stepping up on the first rung brought back memories of earlier times when she'd loved attending rodeos. When she was young, loved horses and went mushy over cowboys. That had all changed after she'd married one who'd had no life beyond the circuit.

From the minute Ben roped a long-legged, dun-colored filly with a shaggy coat, a regal arch to her neck and fire in her eyes, the breathless wonder Kate once experienced came hurtling back. The horse reared high. Ben played out the rope he'd softly circled over the snorting animal's head. Kate moved up a rung.

Sidling into the small corral, Tim attempted to pass Ben a slick fork saddle with a bucking roll. Kate surprised herself by how knowledgeable she was about the equipment. And the horse. She guessed the animal to be around three years old. Declining the saddle, Ben slung a second rope around the filly's belly and, with the grace of a high jumper, vaulted onto the animal.

The trim horse spun right, then left, then twirled on her hind legs like a ballet dancer. Kate's heart lodged in her throat. Her skin went hot then cold. But not for anything could she have torn her eyes from the pair in the ring. The horse pawed air three times, each time landing stiff-legged in an all-out effort to dislodge her rider. Ben stuck like a leech. Kate knew the mark of a champion bronc rider was to show no space between the horse's back and a rider's crotch. Ben's execution was perfect. Then, as the filly's acrobatics intensified and her bucking grew more fierce, Kate found herself enthralled. She held her breath, crossing her fingers for Ben to ride out the storm.

In time the piston motion got to Kate. Her hands grew sweaty; her mouth felt dry. It was too easy to imagine her and Ben locked in a similar wild ride. All friction and bare skin to bare skin. Then suddenly it ended, with Ben and the mare lathered.

Except it wasn't really over. The cagey little filly bunched her muscles and tore off in a wild ride around and around the corral. Just when Kate's heart quit socking her breastbone, the graceful animal sailed over the fence and bucked up the bank, trying desperately to scrape Ben off on the low-hanging branches of a pine tree.

He ducked and flattened his torso along the dun's thick mane. For a while the two blended—the filly's long sooty mane almost burying the man in black. They made an arresting picture tearing up the trail.

Kate's mood shifted, this time stoking a frenzy of sexual need she hadn't wanted to finally acknowledge. *What had she told Ben about her legs being strong? All bunk.* She was hot and damp and weak all over. Finally Ben appeared on the rim overlooking the box canyon— every inch the conqueror. His back and hips formed a perfect *L* along the spent filly's back. His long muscular legs curved around the quietly subdued female.

Kate felt for the once-fiery horse when Ben trotted right up to her wearing one of his devilishly self-satisfied grins. She let him ride near enough that she was fanned by the filly's hot breath—close enough for Ben to read her thoughts before her lungs slowly hitched out air.

They were both aware that next time Ben wore that smug smile, Kate would be the reason. She would be the conqueror and Ben made no attempt to hide the fact he wouldn't mind one tiny bit.

He rode over to Tim Cortez and swung down from the mare.

Kate sagged against the split rail. She was impatient to have it over, this edginess stretching between them.

Ben, darn him, didn't seem in any rush. Cortez produced a sheaf of papers, a contract, Kate supposed. She hesitated and wondered if she should join them. What if Ben needed help reading the terms of the contract?

As she dusted wood chips from her hands, Kate realized he wouldn't thank her for interfering. He'd managed his business affairs on his own for a long time. He didn't need her barging in and taking over.

Kate decided to phone and check on how Vida was getting along with the kids. The phone rang three times before the housekeeper picked up.

"Vida, it's Kate. How are you getting along with the kids?"

"They're fine, Ms. Kate. A good match, those two. They've been out in the corral all morning chasing half-grown calves Zach brought in right after you and Ben left. Zach came for supplies, but he said let them have fun playing rodeo."

Kate tensed. Then she forced herself to relax. Pretending to rodeo with Clover might get Danny past his disappointment at having to tell his grandfather to scratch him from next week's junior contest.

"Zach said they can't hurt anything," Vida continued. "Roping calves is a standard pastime for ranch kids."

"All right, then. Well, I won't keep you. Tell the children I phoned. Remind them we'll see them Sunday. I'm guessing by lunchtime or shortly after."

Ben saw her tucking the phone away. "All well at the Rising Sun?"

"How did you know I called there?"

He just smiled and slid his arm around her waist, tugging on her until their hips brushed. "After that wild ride I need to shower before we go sightseeing. Let's check into the inn where I reserved our room."

A low flutter clutched at Kate's belly. "Well," she drawled. "Since you're finished here, we could go home tonight, Ben."

The little shake he delivered was the same thing as

saying *like hell.* Even at that, Ben didn't rush to reach the inn. "I could drop you at the outlet mall and you could shop to your heart's content while I shower off horse smell. Or, if outlets aren't your preference, there's plenty more shops in Boise Towne Square."

Kate blinked at him in disbelief. She'd had other activities in mind for before, during and after Ben's shower.

He knew exactly what she was thinking and tipped back his head and laughed.

She punched his arm, which eased the tension she'd felt building between them. By the time he pulled in and parked at the rambling bed-and-breakfast, Kate had regained her cool.

Ben walked around the Ford and assisted her out. He retrieved their overnight bags from behind her seat. "We're in what's called the Warm Springs District. I thought you'd like being within walking distance of restaurants and the marketplace."

"It's perfect," Kate murmured. "So Victorian. Is this where you always stay?"

He shifted both bags to one hand and guided her up the steps to the veranda. "No, but Percy brought Winnie here on their tenth anniversary. She hasn't stopped talking about it. I hope you like it."

Kate was touched by the fact he'd picked this place to please her. "I'll love it," she said.

She read the history of the inn and examined the antique lobby while Ben signed his name and picked up the key. Kate had never asked how he'd taught himself to write his name.

The room caused her to exclaim in delight, "Oh, Ben. If I'd gotten to pick any room in the house, I'm positive this would be it." She walked around, touching the oak bed, the Victorian wallpaper, the frilly curtains. Ben set down their bags and took her in his arms for a long heated kiss.

"I apologize." Stepping back, he began unsnapping the pearl buttons studding his black Western shirt. "That filly smelled strong. I hope I didn't ruin what you're wearing," he said, dragging his shirttails out from his belt.

Kate brushed his hands aside. "I want to do this." The last two buttons popped free and she slid her hands inside his open shirt, running all ten fingers up and down the warm flesh that covered his flat belly.

Controlling a shiver, Ben shrugged out of his shirt. It fell at their feet and very soon her blouse joined it. He might have hurried through preliminaries, as Kate urged, but Ben refused to be rushed by her husky murmurs, or her urgent nipping kisses, even though she was driving him crazy. He fingered her hair and murmured over and over how pretty it was. Her answer was a moan and her own fingers struggling to divest them both of snug jeans.

Eventually Ben took pity on her and helped. His lips were doing such delicious things to her weighty breasts, Kate hated to pull away for even the little time it took to ask one important question. "I'm going to assume you came prepared," she whispered jerkily, trailing a hand downward from his belly button.

"Good thing one of us still has an operating brain."

Ben left her just long enough to unzip the outer pocket on his suitcase and toss a dozen plastic packets on the bed.

Her eyes widened, but no sound crossed her lips. A fully aroused Ben Trueblood left Kate thinking just maybe he hadn't planned generously enough for this weekend.

They made frenzied love under a cascade of water until it grew so cold it puckered their heated skin. Then they reverently dried one another with thick bath towels and made their way to the bed, where their lovemaking was less frantic.

Drowsy, Kate settled her cheek into the hollow of Ben's shoulder. "I like cuddling." Her fingertips circled one of his flat nipples. "It was first to go after Danny was born."

Ben tugged her on top of him and looked her in the face. "Was Colton your only lover?"

"Does that matter?" She knew she sounded defensive.

"Of course it doesn't." He soothed both palms along the curve of her back.

Crossing her arms on his chest, she rested her chin on her fists. "What about you, Ben? It's easy to see you have experience. Is the reason you've never married because you prefer variety in your love life?"

"I'm not all *that* experienced." He actually sounded miffed by her charge. "I've dated enough women to know what I don't want in a wife. And it goes without saying I'd never settle for anyone who claimed to love me, but not Clover. That's not an issue with you."

Kate shook her head. "No. That's not an issue."

"Come to think of it," Ben said, a teasing glint in his eye, "wouldn't it be a whole lot easier to teach me how to read if we lived under the same roof?"

She flashed a surprised glance at him. "Are we about to finish the conversation we had the other day?"

"There's nothing stopping us now, Kate. We have the time to clear the air. I know something that bugs you—our difference of opinion when it comes to Danny tossing a rope around. I make my living ranching. Tell me straight out, do you respect what I do?"

She rolled off him, sat up and tucked the pale yellow sheet under her arms. "Back at the Cortez ranch when I watched you tame that horse, I had an epiphany. But because I waited to tell you, now you might not believe what I have to say."

"Try me." He scooted up and draped an arm loosely over her bare shoulders.

"I grew up in mid-America. Mom taught. I read. Tons of Western romances. Like a lot of girls, I fell in love with cowboys, horses and rodeos. Dodge City was our closest real town. Rodeos were entertainment for me and my friends. That's where I met Colton. He was flash and dash and full of himself."

She partially turned and picked up Ben's hand. "You need to know I fell in love with the man I thought Colton was. A man like the gentle, loyal cowboys I'd read about. Turns out he wasn't at all like that. But you are, Ben. When I was hanging over that fence today, watching you ride, it hit me. I blamed Colton's weaknesses on the rodeo life. I also think his mother indulged him. I've been so afraid Danny will turn out the same, that he'll be full of himself and bent on winning. I know I've come down too hard on him. Away from his grandmother's influence, Danny won't stay obsessed with buckles and trophies. But I'd be happy if he followed in your footsteps, Ben," she said almost shyly.

Gathering her in his arms, Ben slid down in the bed to show her how much her words had pleased him. "We should be exhausted, Ben," Kate said an hour or so later. "I don't know about you, but I'm not. I feel alive for the first time in years. But…I'm starved. For food," she said, playfully poking him in the ribs.

"Then let's go feed you." He swung his legs over the edge of the bed, stood up and pulled clean jeans out of his suitcase. Kate watched with admiration as he tugged them on, making it plain he planned to go commando on their outing.

Ben winked at Kate. "I want to be ready to carry on where we left off as soon as we get back." He tossed her bag on her lap. Then, while she dug around inside her case, he knelt down beside the bed on one knee and casually extended a small white satin box. Inside glistened a two-carat sapphire, ringed by sparkling diamonds. "Will you accept this now and for all time as my wife, Katie?"

Tears trickled through her lower lashes. She dropped the bra she held. With hands shaking and lips trembling, she slowly lifted her glistening eyes to meet Ben's. Very slowly she held out her left hand. Salt from her tears stung her kiss-swollen lips as she patiently waited for him to push the ring over her knuckle. When it felt snug on her finger, she flung her arms around his neck. "Yes, yes, oh, yes, I'll be your wife forever, Ben Trueblood," she breathed against his mouth.

It was dark before they made their way along Eighth Street and into town. Strolling hand in hand, they discussed how they would tell the kids. Ben would have liked the ceremony to be in a day or two.

"I'd rather wait until spring break," Kate said. "Not because I want to delay, but to give the kids longer to get used to the idea. And Ben, I'd love to make my wedding dress. Nothing elaborate, but I want to do every single thing right this time."

Ben raised their joined hands to his lips. "Don't leave anything out, Katie. This is going to last us a lifetime."

She abruptly stopped in front of a children's shop. "Ben, can't you see Clover in that dress? It was red taffeta with a white velvet bolero jacket.

"I'll bet you're glad I stopped short of buying out the store," she said when they emerged carrying several bags.

"I'd gladly have shelled out more. It's a wonder girls like Meg Wheeler haven't hurt Clover's feelings long ago. I never set out to make her a tomboy, but I've sure been in the dark about what little girls are wearing these days."

"One of the outfits I bought is for her to wear at our wedding. If you agree, I'd like Clover and Danny to be our only attendants. Oh, but do you think Lou would consider walking me down the aisle? A church," she said suddenly as they passed a church with a softly lit spire. "I want us to be married in a church."

"Your choice," he said quickly. Talk stopped as he gently guided her into a rustic steak house.

She looked around once they'd been seated. "Could there be a more perfect place to celebrate our engagement? I predict lots of beef in our future," she teased, swirling her hand over a wineglass, pretending it was a crystal ball. Candlelight glinted off her sapphire ring.

Ben waited until they had wine in their glasses to make his toast. "To us, Kate. I promise I'll spend the rest of my life making you happy."

Kate raised her glass. "I couldn't be happier than I am right now," she said, and it was the truth.

THE THREADY GOLDEN-GRAY LIGHT of dawn woke Kate. She leaned up on one elbow, watching Ben sleep, when his cell phone chimed somewhere out of her reach.

Half-asleep, he had trouble fishing it out of his jeans pocket.

"It's the ranch," Ben said, once he had the phone firmly in hand.

Kate panicked. "Answer it, Ben! What if Clover took a turn for the worse?" Worry darkened her eyes.

"Her bite was healing." Frowning, Ben pressed the button and put the phone to his ear. "It's Vida," he mouthed. "What do you mean the kids are gone?" he said into the phone. Covering his free ear, he strained to hear the woman on the other end, although his eyes cut to Kate, who had leaped from bed and started throwing on clothes.

"Slow down, Vida. You're saying neither kid slept in their bed last night? When did you last see them? Six? You ate early, but then never looked in on them afterward? You know Clover argues over a nine o'clock bedtime. Six is ridiculous. Okay, okay, that's neither here nor there. The question is where did they go?"

Kate yanked on Ben's bare arm. "Get up and dress. We've got to head home right now. Hashing this over with Vida on the phone solves nothing. Call the sheriff. Something bad's happened, and it's my fault for going away with you, Ben."

"That's just wrong thinking." He scowled. "No, I didn't mean you, Vida. Kate would like you to get hold of the sheriff. Yes, we're here together. Vida, calm down, no one is blaming you. Let me see if I can get hold of Bobbalou. Those crazy kids probably got it in their heads to go spend the night in the tepees with my crew, or in Bobbalou's wagon. Vida, we'll be rolling in within hours. Call my cell or Kate's if they turn up."

CHAPTER FOURTEEN

THEY CHECKED OUT AND RACED over to Ben's pickup. While backing out, Ben flipped on his radio unit and spun the dials to contact a matching base unit in Bobbalou's wagon. The effort netted nothing but static, so he phoned Vida again. "I can't reach Bobbalou. Will you try Percy? Explain our situation. Have him ride out to my winter lease, just to ease my mind. The kids are probably there and the whole crew is out on the range."

"Why would they sneak off anywhere after dark?" Kate asked. Her hands were as unsteady as her voice.

Ben just shook his head.

"All of these traffic lights are slowing us down," she complained. "Isn't there a route you can take so we'll get there faster?"

Ben removed his hand from the gearshift and captured her fluttering hands. "We'll get there as fast as we can. Vida's putting feelers out."

"You said she was reliable. How could she not hear them leave your house?"

"Honey, Vida's plenty upset, herself. We all are."

Kate cast a worried glance his way. "I'm sorry. I can

see you're as alarmed as I am. Ben, what troubles you most?"

He hesitated, but she pressed him.

"The Owyhee River is running high from our snow runoff," he said. "If either of them fell in…" That statement went unfinished.

"There's more, isn't there? Oh, I'm already half-sick."

"Me, too. If they did get it into their heads to go out to the camp, but got turned around in the dark, the hills around the Rising Sun are pockmarked with abandoned mine shafts… And this rain makes for slick rocks."

"Did Vida say they rode their horses? Or Goldie? Did they take her? With or without rain, I'd feel better if Goldie's with them."

"Good questions. Vida never said, and I didn't ask." He dug for his cell and passed it to Kate. "Just hit number one and Vida should pick up."

"Vida? It's Kate. Ben and I are wondering how the kids left. On horseback… I'll hang on while you check the barn, Vida. Scour it. Maybe they thought it'd be fun to sleep there instead of in bed. I almost forgot to ask about Goldie. Oh, she's with you?" Kate bit her lower lip. "Yes, do see about the horses. But…wait, I should let you call us back. What if I tie up your phone while the sheriff or Percy tries to reach you?"

It was agreed Vida would phone after checking the barn.

Ben had reached the interstate. Luckily, early morning traffic was light for a Saturday. He reached over and took Kate's hand. "Hang on, sweetheart. We know they're smart kids. They'll be okay."

Kate's spirits plummeted when Vida called again to say Glory and Flame were in their stalls and nothing else seemed out of place in the barn.

"Just so you know," Vida said, "their backpacks aren't in their bedrooms. The one Danny brought and the orange one Clover takes to school are missing. Tell Ben it looks as if she dumped her school stuff out. I 'spect he'll be able to tell if anything else is missing from her room."

Ben stroked his chin grimly. "My money's on finding them with Bobbalou," he said again, glancing at the dashboard clock. "We should hear from Percy before we reach the ranch."

A little over four hours after leaving the inn, Ben brought the Ford to a stop outside his house, right behind Sheriff Chandler Keats's aging Crown Victoria.

The sheriff, Ben and Kate all made it to the broad veranda just as Vida flung open the front door.

The sheriff tossed away a toothpick he'd been chewing. "Well," he began, shaking rain off his Stetson. "I've half been expectin' you to drive in with the kids, Ben."

"Us? Chandler, we've come from Boise."

"Yep." The sheriff nodded, re-creasing his hat before he settled it back on his balding head. "I made the rounds asking questions in town. Lucille McDaniel said she was locking up the café around nine last night, like she's done every Friday for nigh on twenty years, when she saw Clover and the teacher's boy climb aboard the Greyhound bus."

"A bus? That's impossible," Kate exclaimed. "How would they have gotten from here to town?"

"It would be a long walk," Ben agreed.

Kate wasn't buying it. "I don't believe it, Ben. Where would they go on a bus? Where would they get the money to buy tickets?"

"They went to Boise," the sheriff said. "We only got two buses that pass through town. One's the 6:00 a.m. run to Bend, Oregon. Other is the night coach to Boise. Schedule says it arrives there 'bout midnight. All along I've been thinking they'd call you and you'd have 'em in tow."

"They didn't, and we don't," Kate snapped. "Someone tell me why they'd even dream up attempting a trip to Boise. And Ben, who is Lucille?"

"Lucille's a good woman, Kate. She knows Clover. It's the money that disturbs me. I don't leave money lying around the house."

Fear crept into Kate's voice. "Oh, Ben, Boise's a big place for two kids." She clutched his arm. "And bus depots are notorious hangouts for all kinds of degenerates. Ben, we have to do something. Drive back to Boise. Maybe they got a harebrained notion to find us."

"Kate, let's not get hysterical. I really doubt their intention was to hook up with us."

"Then what?"

"I don't know," he said, tramping up and down the porch, rubbing the back of his neck. Goldie nudged her way out the screen door.

Kate dropped to her knees and hugged the dog's shaggy neck, weeping openly.

"Phone the Boise Greyhound depot," the sheriff said. "And we'll get in touch with the Boise police. If they've gone on a lark, they should be easy to spot."

Ben hooked Kate's arm and gently tugged her upright.

"Vida," he called once they were inside the house, "if you don't have coffee on, will you brew a pot?"

Kate perched on the edge of a living-room chair, moodily twisting her engagement ring around her slender finger.

"That a new bauble you picked up in the city?" Vida asked when she handed Kate a mug of coffee.

Stiffening, Kate cast a wary glance toward Ben, who'd been put on hold by Greyhound while the sheriff was on his cell to police.

Hearing Vida's comment, Ben smiled. "Vida, that bauble means Kate agreed to make me the happiest man in ten counties by saying she'd be my wife. Once we find the kids... What?" He spoke into the phone. "Great, you've had eastbound buses go out this morning to Portland, Oregon. And one en route to Salt Lake City. Okay, so the two kids I'm calling about could only have connected with the bus headed for Salt Lake? The bus terminates there? Ah, but you have several buses that left for other parts of the country." He swore roundly then asked in a weary voice, "Is it possible you could connect me with a real live person in the Salt Lake depot? Say a ticket agent who may have seen my daughter and her friend? They're not runaways. They're eight and eleven." Ben rolled his eyes. "Yes, ma'am. I suppose technically the term fits since we don't know where to find them."

Kate jumped up, almost spilling her coffee. "Salt Lake City? It's even bigger than Boise. Does Clover know anyone there? I'm sure Danny doesn't."

Sheriff Keats drained his mug and rose. "I'd better mosey back to town, Ben. You're way out of my jurisdiction, and Boise cops have put out an APB. By my calculations the kids have been gone from here fifteen, sixteen hours. You two better put your heads together and think of people they know well enough to visit." He looked at Kate. "None of my affair, mind you. But has your boy got a dad he'd be hightailing it off to see? Now maybe it don't make sense he'd drag Ben's girl along. On the other hand, with you sportin' that rock on your left hand, this could be how a couple of kids show their displeasure. You know," he added, "you two may have had your heads in the clouds. But Clover and the boy…maybe they're not so thrilled at the prospect of acquiring a stepmama and papa. Get my drift?"

"They didn't know," Ben said as he stood waiting to have his call transferred. "Anyway, the kids would be happy."

"But, Ben," Kate said. "You did say something in front of them. On Danny's birthday. They came into the cabin and saw us holding hands. Clover admitted seeing us kiss another time. You said you were trying to convince me we'd make a good family."

"You're right. I'd forgotten. But they were happy. You were the one with reservations."

Kate nodded.

"Good luck," the sheriff said. "Ben, maybe you'd like me to call Salt Lake and ask what it takes to get out one of them Amber Alerts. If so, I'll need pictures of the kids to fax."

Vida uttered a cry and sank down on the couch. "Amber Alerts are for kidnapped kids. Lord love us, what have I done? My daughter said I'm getting too old to ride herd on a pistol like Clover. You've gotta believe me, Ben, they were both sweet as cotton candy all day. Like I told Kate when she phoned, those two were having themselves a high old time roping the calves Zach drove in."

Ben set a hand on his housekeeper's shoulder. "We still haven't heard from Percy. Hell, Lucille's eyesight could be going. She's pushing eighty. Could be she should've retired and quit flipping burgers," he joked lamely.

Vida buried her face in her stained apron. "Don't mention burgers. At supper I fixed cheeseburgers like the kids wanted. All they could talk about was Danny's good roping. Clover praised my burgers, then goes and makes off with the leftovers. Leastways they're gone from the fridge."

Signaling the sheriff, Ben said, "Chandler, ask Lucille if she remembers what the kids were wearing. If this ticket-agent supervisor in Salt Lake can't help us, I'll be in touch and we'll talk about notifying the Utah cops."

The door banged behind the departing sheriff. Goldie barked so long they almost missed hearing Ben's cell phone ring.

Kate grabbed it. "Hello," she said. "Percy, this *is* Ben's cell phone. It's Kate Steele. He's on another line." Her shoulders sagged and she dropped down next to Vida. "The kids aren't at camp? No one's seen them since Zach dropped off the calves. I see. Thanks for riding out there." She looked up at Ben. "No, Percy, I don't think he wants a search party yet. We have reason to suspect Clover and Danny left town on a bus." She said goodbye and shut the phone.

Vida sat up. "Have you tried calling your boy's phone?"

Ben and Kate both jerked.

"What?" Kate reacted first, almost vaulting off the couch. "Of course! Danny's grandmother sent him a cell phone for his birthday. What kind of mother forgets her son has a phone?"

"One that's shaken up and scared," Ben said. "His birthday wasn't that long ago. Quit beating up on yourself."

"Lord, help me remember the number. Melanie pays the bill."

"Call your in-laws." Ben handed her back his phone.

"Let me think. I'll call them as a last resort, Ben. I hate worrying them. Since Colton died, Melanie and Royce have doted on Danny."

Finally Kate thought she remembered Danny's number and punched it into Ben's cell with shaking fingers. "It's busy," she said, diving for her purse. "Maybe he's calling me." But her phone was silent.

"If Danny's not calling me," Kate said, "he must be talking to his grandmother. Who else?"

Ben covered the mouthpiece on the phone. "I'm on hold again. Kate, I know you'd rather not upset your in-laws, but we've about exhausted all other leads."

"You're right." Kate punched in a longer series of numbers. The phone was answered almost instantly.

"Hello, Melanie? I...ah...don't quite know where to begin. By asking, I guess, if you've heard from Danny recently. If so, please, Melanie...did he give any clue as to where he might be phoning from... Dallas?" Kate's voice squeaked as air fled her lungs. "Dallas, as in Texas?"

Ben slammed his phone back in its cradle. "The ticket agent says she sold tickets to Dallas to a couple of kids matching Danny and Clover's descriptions. She said Danny acted so mature and he counted out cash for the tickets without blinking an eye."

"What are you saying..." Kate looked angry as she spoke into the phone. "You wired Danny money to come there and compete in the Little Britches Rodeo? I don't give a damn if your intent was for him to take a plane by himself. He's my son, Melanie. I already said no to your request. Not only that, Danny didn't fly. He boarded a Greyhound bus with a friend's child. Ah, you know? You had better believe I'm outraged. I'm furious. Have you any idea of the anxious moments you've caused me and Clover's dad?"

Ben's chest expanded and contracted a couple of times as he pressed his head against Kate's so that he could listen to both sides of the conversation.

Melanie Steele didn't sound very remorseful. Ben heard her say defensively, "Danny never let on until he phoned to have me pick him up that he planned to bring another child. You know he wanted to come home, Kate. He's unhappy living in Idaho. You're to blame. Danny said you went off for a weekend with a man. It's appalling to him, and me, to think you'd forget Colton so fast. Danny said that he and his little friend think you're planning to marry the girl's father. Obviously Danny objects. Who knows what kind of man…" She didn't complete her sentence.

Ben tried to wrest the phone from Kate, but she wouldn't release it.

"Melanie," she said, "you've been had. Danny likes Ben fine. This is all about Danny competing in that rodeo. I hope you're happy. Danny is his father's son. The saddest part is you've allowed and encouraged Danny to manipulate everyone the way Colton did." Kate hauled in a ragged breath. "If I can book a flight out of Boise, I'll be there by morning to collect the kids. I suggest you use the little time you have with Danny to reflect on the thirty-plus years you and Royce overindulged Colton and turned him into a spoiled, selfish man. He wasn't a good husband, or father. I should've taken Danny and left Colton long before the accident. He lived to please himself, Melanie. He indulged in numerous affairs during our marriage. That's not how I want Danny to end up. Mark my words, if you and Royce expect to continue a relationship with him, going behind my back has to stop. And before you hang up on me, think about this, I could charge you with reckless endangerment of minors. Or if not me, Clover's dad. He's standing right here. We thought our kids were in serious danger, Melanie."

Ben's arm circled Kate's waist. He squeezed lightly, but pride gleamed in his eyes.

At first the woman on the phone sputtered indignantly. That stopped and there was muffled chatter as if she'd covered the receiver. Like flipping a switch, Melanie's tone changed. "Kate, Danny verified most of what you said. Please, we must make time to talk if...when you come after him. I accept partial blame. I may have let Colton get out of hand. But, Danny is all we have left of our son."

Turning to Ben, Kate said, "Is it possible to drive back to Boise, fly round-trip to Dallas and be back by tomorrow night? I have to teach on Monday."

"Tell her we'll look into flights and call her with an arrival time. I'm going with you," he said firmly.

THEIR FLIGHT WAS TWO HOURS late arriving in Dallas due to a breaking storm, and they had less than two hours before their return flight boarded. Royce, Melanie and two contrite children met them when Kate and Ben emerged in the main terminal.

Clover launched herself at Ben. "Daddy, don't let Kate be mad at Danny. It was my idea. Danny wanted to be in the roping contest. I didn't know Texas was so far away."

"You frightened us, Clover." He hugged her fiercely. "We had no idea where to start hunting for you. I still can't believe you kids could walk to town without anyone seeing you and calling me."

"We walked to Mr. Torkelson's and hid in the back of his truck. He delivers milk, butter and eggs to Ms. Lucille at the café every night. She likes it fresh for the morning breakfast crowd. I'm real, real sorry." Her dark eyes grew teary. "Can I still be Danny's sister?"

"That's entirely up to Kate," Ben said sternly. He

looked over at the Steeles, who hovered off to one side. "You couldn't have succeeded without outside help. Without money."

"Kate, it's good seeing you out of that damned chair." Royce Steele, a big man with a full head of salt-and-pepper hair, stepped up and extended a hand to Ben. After introductions, he said, "I realize you don't have the time for a run to the ranch, but there's a decent restaurant upstairs. Let me buy you all a meal. We'll sit and try and iron out a few details."

Again Ben deferred to Kate. "Why not," she said. "We need to lay down rules to be certain this never happens again. Right, Danny…"

The boy dragged his backpack over. "I'm probably grounded for a long time, huh? Hey, that's a cool ring you've got, Mom." His eyes flew wide-open. "Wow, is that like a wedding… Did you and Ben get married in Boise?" He ran over to Clover and they both pumped fists in the air.

"Hold on," Kate said. "We wouldn't get married without talking it over with you kids. But that's a separate issue from why we're here, so don't try to change the subject."

Royce took his wife's arm, beckoning the others to follow him on the escalator. So far Melanie had remained silent.

A hostess seated their group at a round table that happened to place Kate directly across from her former mother-in-law. Things were awkward until drinks came. Royce Steele nudged his wife, who sat turning her coffee cup around and around.

"Royce wants me to tell you where I went wrong. It started when we got married. The Steele family didn't welcome me into the fold. I grew up impoverished. You probably didn't know that, Kate. The Steeles were powerful in Fort Worth. Royce's sisters, Brynna and Ava, put me down at every opportunity."

"I was in the dark about any of this until Melanie phoned all upset about this crisis," Royce said. "I thought she'd had a wreck and I raced here to meet her. I wish she'd told me a long time ago. I know my sisters, but I was busy keeping the ranch afloat. Melanie never said a word before, nor did she complain." He patted her hand.

"Why would I? I wanted to fit into your family. I wanted to be like your sisters. We all were married about the same time, then got pregnant one after the other. Of all things, we each had a boy. Doug and Rod were rough and tumble from the get-go. Colton was smaller. He was built like my family. Well, starting in first grade, Brynna and Ava decided their boys were going to grow up to be football stars." Melanie looked at the children hesitantly, as if she wasn't sure whether she should go on.

Ben suggested Danny take Clover over to the window to watch the planes take off until their food arrived.

Melanie shot Ben a grateful glance. "It was plain Colton could never match his cousins. I know you've all heard about Texas cheerleader moms. Women who become obsessed with seeing their girls chosen for the squad at any expense. That was me," she admitted.

"Only I dedicated myself to finding a sport where my son could excel. I was determined he'd bring home as many trophies as his cousins." Her eyes grew teary.

"Bronc riding and calf roping," Kate said.

Royce wrapped his hands around his bottle of Coors. "I unknowingly opened the door when the school asked me to set up a program of roping lessons for ranch kids who might not be interested in other intramural sports. I can't deny I was happy when my own son got involved. Up to a point."

"After Colton got married, Royce started saying enough was enough," Melanie injected softly. "He expected Colton to leave the rodeo circuit and help around the Bar R-S," she said, gesturing with a bejeweled hand. "But, that's about the time Cousin Doug hit his stride. He won the Heismann trophy. Rod, bless his heart, was named two years in a row as most valuable player for the Dallas Cowboys. I pressured Colton to enter bigger events. What I didn't see and didn't want to see was that it was a losing proposition. The money he won didn't compare to the salaries his cousins earned. I subsidized Colton and cajoled Royce to let him be. I dedicated my life into making him a superstar. Then you had the accident and things started to crumble. I tried not to resent you, Kate, but I did, because all I had were Colton's buckles and trophies, and you didn't seem to value them at all."

Kate wasn't sure where this was leading.

"My sister-in-laws dropped by and started bragging about their grandkids. Personally I happen to think they're rude, insufferable children who can't hold a candle to Danny. So, I started to brag about him. Ava saw how good he could rope and, well, it started all over again."

Their food came and the kids ran back.

Kate shoved her salad around on her plate. "I wish I'd known all of this years ago, Melanie. I might've been better able to explain to Danny the importance of having a balanced life."

"I know, Mom," Danny piped up. "I figured it out. I like roping and seeing if I can beat other guys my age. But I never want to live out of a dinky trailer like we did so Dad could go to a different rodeo every week. I like living in Ben's cabin. Or his house would be okay. I just don't see what's so bad about me entering roping contests while I'm still a kid. Contests around home in Idaho or at Pawpaw's ranch."

All eyes converged on Kate, but it was Ben's dark gaze that made the biggest impact.

"Seems reasonable, Kate," he said. "Does it make sense to you to say you'll think about it for the future? Danny and Clover, there are consequences for pulling this stunt. You scared us to death and cost us, the police and the bus company a lot of time and money. Add in last-minute airfare for four..."

"What about six months doing household chores?" Kate suggested.

Ben shrugged. "If our ranchers win our case over the ATVers, Danny could conceivably be out of the doghouse in time for next summer's Jordan Valley Big Loop."

The tight knot in Kate's chest loosened a bit. Enough to allow her to relent. "I'll consider it," she said, leaning her head briefly on Ben's solid arm.

"Really, Mom?" Danny elbowed Clover. "Ben, will you explain to Pawpaw the difference between cowboys and buckaroos? The other day when Zach brought in the calves, he said ranching the buckaroo way is almost a thing of the past. I hope not. Clover and me, we want the Rising Sun to be the way it is forever."

"Yeah," Clover agreed.

"Well, Danny, not all change is bad," Ben said. He squeezed Kate's hand under the table and a look passed between them, a reminder of the strides they'd all taken since she'd arrived in the valley. "For one, we may get a bigger family out of all this." His glance took in everyone at the table.

The talk moved on to discussing plans for Christmas and even possible arrangements for Ben and Kate's wedding.

Melanie surprised Kate by saying, "Would you consider inviting us to the wedding? After you and Danny moved to Idaho, I talked to Royce about us finding a way to leave the ranch occasionally. He's hired a nice, capable manager."

Kate deferred to Ben for that decision.

"That's probably a good start," he said, finding her hand under the table. "A way for you and Royce to see Danny while he's grounded and all."

Kate watched the interaction between Ben and Danny's grandparents. Pleasure replaced the knot that had resided in her stomach for far too long. "It will take work, understanding and compromise," she murmured, squeezing Ben's hand, "but everyone here needs an extended family—and a fresh start."

Set in darkness beyond the ordinary world.
Passionate tales of life and death.
With characters' lives ruled by laws the everyday
world can't begin to imagine.

n●cturne

It's time to discover the Raintree trilogy....

New York Times *bestselling author*
LINDA HOWARD
brings you the dramatic first book
RAINTREE: INFERNO

The Ansara Wizards are rising and the Raintree clan
must rejoin the battle against their foes,
testing their powers, relationships and forcing
upon them lives they never could have imagined
before....

Turn the page for a sneak preview of the captivating
first book in the Raintree trilogy,
RAINTREE: INFERNO
by LINDA HOWARD
On sale April 25.

Dante Raintree stood with his arms crossed as he watched the woman on the monitor. The image was in black and white to better show details; color distracted the brain. He focused on her hands, watching every move she made, but what struck him most was how uncommonly still she was. She didn't fidget or play with her chips, or look around at the other players. She peeked once at her down card, then didn't touch it again, signaling for another hit by tapping a fingernail on the table. Just because she didn't seem to be paying attention to the other players, though, didn't mean she was as unaware as she seemed.

"What's her name?" Dante asked.

"Lorna Clay," replied his chief of security, Al Rayburn.

"At first I thought she was counting, but she doesn't pay enough attention."

"She's paying attention, all right," Dante murmured. "You just don't see her doing it." A card counter had to remember every card played. Supposedly counting cards was impossible with the number of decks used by the casinos, but there were those rare individuals who could calculate the odds even with multiple decks.

"I thought that, too," said Al. "But look at this piece of tape coming up. Someone she knows comes up to her and speaks, she looks around and starts chatting, completely misses the play of the people to her left—and doesn't look around even when the deal comes back to her, just taps that finger. And damn if she didn't win. Again."

Dante watched the tape, rewound it, watched it again. Then he watched it a third time. There had to be something he was missing, because he couldn't pick out a single giveaway.

"If she's cheating," Al said with something like respect, "she's the best I've ever seen."

"What does your gut say?"

Al scratched the side of his jaw, considering. Finally, he said, "If she isn't cheating, she's the luckiest person walking. She wins. Week in, week out, she wins. Never a huge amount, but I ran the numbers and she's into us for about five grand a week. Hell, boss, on her way out of the casino she'll stop by a slot machine, feed a dollar in and walk away with at least fifty. It's never the same machine, either. I've had her watched, I've had her followed, I've even looked for the same faces in the casino every time she's in here and I can't find a common denominator."

"Is she here now?"

"She came in about a half hour ago. She's playing blackjack, as usual."

"Bring her to my office," Dante said, making a swift decision. "Don't make a scene."

"Got it," said Al, turning on his heel and leaving the security center.

Dante left, too, going up to his office. His face was calm. Normally he would leave it to Al to deal with a cheater, but he was curious. How was she doing it? There were a lot of bad cheaters, a few good ones, and every so often one would come along who was the stuff of which legends were made: the cheater who didn't get caught, even when people were alert and the camera was on him—or, in this case, her.

It was possible to simply be lucky, as most people understood luck. Chance could turn a habitual loser into a big-time winner. Casinos, in fact, thrived on that hope. But luck itself wasn't habitual, and he knew that what passed for luck was often something else: cheating. And there was the other kind of luck, the kind he himself possessed, but it depended not on chance but on who and what he was. He knew it was an innate power and not Dame Fortune's erratic smile. Since power like his was rare, the odds made it likely the woman he'd been watching was merely a very clever cheat.

Her skill could provide her with a very good living, he thought, doing some swift calculations in his head. Five grand a week equaled $260,000 a year, and that was just from his casino. She probably hit them all, careful to keep the numbers relatively low so she stayed under the radar.

He wondered how long she'd been taking him, how long she'd been winning a little here, a little there, before Al noticed.

The curtains were open on the wall-to-wall window in his office, giving the impression, when one first opened the door, of stepping out onto a covered balcony. The glazed window faced west, so he could catch the sunsets. The sun was low now, the sky painted in purple and gold. At his home in the mountains, most of the windows faced east, affording him views of the sunrise. Something in him needed both the greeting and the goodbye of the sun. He'd always been drawn to sunlight, maybe because fire was his element to call, to control.

He checked his internal time: four minutes until sundown. Without checking the sunrise tables every day, he knew exactly when the sun would slide behind the mountains. He didn't own an alarm clock. He didn't need one. He was so acutely attuned to the sun's position that he had only to check within himself to know the time. As for waking at a particular time, he was one of those people who could tell himself to wake at a certain time, and he did. That talent had nothing to do with being Raintree, so he didn't have to hide it; a lot of perfectly ordinary people had the same ability.

He had other talents and abilities, however, that did require careful shielding. The long days of summer instilled in him an almost sexual high, when he could feel contained power buzzing just beneath his skin. He had to be doubly careful not to cause candles to leap into flame just by his presence or to start wildfires with a glance in the dry-as-tinder brush. He loved Reno; he didn't want to burn it down. He just felt so damn *alive* with all the sunshine pouring down that he wanted to let the energy pour through him instead of holding it inside.

This must be how his brother Gideon felt while pulling lightning, all that hot power searing through his muscles, his veins. They had this in common, the connection with raw power. All the members of the far-flung Raintree clan had some power, some heightened ability, but only members of the royal family could channel and control the earth's natural energies.

Dante wasn't just of the royal family, he was the dranir, the leader of the entire clan. "Dranir" was synonymous with king, but the position he held wasn't ceremonial, it was one of sheer power. He was the oldest son of the previous dranir, but he would have been passed over for the position if he hadn't also inherited the power to hold it.

Behind him came Al's distinctive knock on the door. The outer office was empty, Dante's secretary having gone home hours before. "Come in," he called, not turning from his view of the sunset.

The door opened, and Al said, "Mr. Raintree, this is Lorna Clay."

Dante turned and looked at the woman, all his senses on alert. The first thing he noticed was the vibrant color of her hair, a rich, dark red that encompassed a multitude of shades from copper to burgundy. The warm amber light danced along the iridescent strands, and he felt a hard tug of sheer lust in his gut. Looking at her hair was almost like looking at fire, and he had the same reaction.

The second thing he noticed was that she was spitting mad.

nocturne™

IT'S TIME TO DISCOVER THE RAINTREE TRILOGY...

There have always been those among us who are more than human...

Don't miss the dramatic first book by *New York Times* bestselling author

LINDA HOWARD

RAINTREE:
Inferno

On sale May.

Raintree: Haunted by Linda Winstead Jones
Available June.

Raintree: Sanctuary by Beverly Barton
Available July.

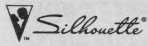

REQUEST YOUR FREE BOOKS!
2 FREE NOVELS PLUS 2 FREE GIFTS!

HARLEQUIN®

Super Romance®

Exciting, emotional, unexpected!

YES! Please send me 2 FREE Harlequin Superromance® novels and my 2 FREE gifts. After receiving them, if I don't wish to receive any more books, I can return the shipping statement marked "cancel." If I don't cancel, I will receive 6 brand-new novels every month and be billed just $4.69 per book in the U.S., or $5.24 per book in Canada, plus 25¢ shipping and handling per book and applicable taxes, if any*. That's a savings of close to 15% off the cover price! I understand that accepting the 2 free books and gifts places me under no obligation to buy anything. I can always return a shipment and cancel at any time. Even if I never buy another book from Harlequin, the two free books and gifts are mine to keep forever.   135 HDN EEX7 336 HDN EEYK

Name _____ (PLEASE PRINT) _____

Address _____ Apt. _____

City _____ State/Prov. _____ Zip/Postal Code _____

Signature (if under 18, a parent or guardian must sign) _____

Mail to the **Harlequin Reader Service®**:
IN U.S.A.: P.O. Box 1867, Buffalo, NY 14240-1867
IN CANADA: P.O. Box 609, Fort Erie, Ontario L2A 5X3

Not valid to current Harlequin Superromance subscribers.

Want to try two free books from another line?
Call 1-800-873-8635 or visit www.morefreebooks.com.

* Terms and prices subject to change without notice. NY residents add applicable sales tax. Canadian residents will be charged applicable provincial taxes and GST. This offer is limited to one order per household. All orders subject to approval. Credit or debit balances in a customer's account(s) may be offset by any other outstanding balance owed by or to the customer. Please allow 4 to 6 weeks for delivery.

Your Privacy: Harlequin is committed to protecting your privacy. Our Privacy Policy is available online at www.eHarlequin.com or upon request from the Reader Service. From time to time we make our lists of customers available to reputable firms who may have a product or service of interest to you. If you would prefer we not share your name and address, please check here. ☐

HSR07

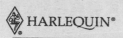

HARLEQUIN®

American **ROMANCE**®

A THREE-BOOK SERIES BY BELOVED AUTHOR

Judy Christenberry

Dallas Duets

What's behind the doors of
the Yellow Rose Lane apartments?
Love, Texas-style!

THE MARRYING KIND
May 2007

Jonathan Davis was many things—a millionaire,
a player, a catch. But he'd never be a husband.
For him, "marriage" equaled "mistake." Diane Black
was a forever kind of woman, a babies-and-minivan
kind of woman. But John was confident he could
date her and still avoid that trap.
Until he kissed her...

Also watch for:
DADDY NEXT DOOR
January 2007

MOMMY FOR A MINUTE
August 2007

Available wherever Harlequin books are sold.

HARM07JC

COMING NEXT MONTH

#1416 THE BEST-KEPT SECRET • Melinda Curtis
Singles…with Kids
What if your son's grandmother calls, wanting your help? The problem? The woman doesn't know she's a grandmother. Rosie DeWitt is given the career opportunity of a lifetime—campaign manager for Hudson McCloud. But Hudson and his mother have no idea Rosie had a child with Hudson's brother. And she wants to keep it that way.

#1417 SAFE IN HIS ARMS • Kay David
Count on a Cop
Daniel Bishop is a cop. And a good one. Which is why he never expects to fall in love with a suspect in his latest case.

#1418 THE WRONG MAN FOR HER • Kathryn Shay
Going Back
She still loves him desperately, even though he once broke her heart. But Nick hasn't changed at all, which means that now he's back, Madelyn has to stay as far away from him as she can. The problem is she's his new boss, so how far can she actually get?

#1419 HER SISTER'S CHILD • Cynthia Thomason
A Little Secret
When you want something badly enough, seems you'll do just about anything to get it. And Julia Sommerville wants custody of her sister's daughter about as much as she's ever wanted anything…even if it might mean losing the man she's fallen in love with—for the second time.

#1420 SMALL-TOWN FAMILY • Margaret Watson
It seemed to Charlotte that Dylan's quest to find his real father would destroy the only family she'd ever known. And so she did what she thought she had to do to protect herself. Would the man she loved ever be able to forgive her?

#1421 IT TAKES TWO • Joanne Michael
Single Father
It's hard enough being a single dad, but when your bright young daughter is struggling after losing her mom, it can also be heartbreaking. So when Marc Doucette encounters Abby Miller and she offers to help, he thinks she's a gift from above. It's the heated glances and stolen kisses between Marc and Abby he's not sure he's ready for.

HSRCNM0407